"A WRITER OF UNUSUAL TALENT"
RICHARD CHRISTIAN MATHESON

S. P. SOMTOW

RIVERRUN

The face of Katastrofa Darkling smiled up at me from the water in the goblet. I drank and drank but the goblet stayed full. I drank death and oblivion, and with each gulp I thought less and less of the other world. I let myself be taken.

Suddenly I was flying on the back of the dragon woman, through clouds of fire, following the course of a sulfurous river. Fire filled the sky. The vortex swirled. I was dreaming, but with my eyes wide open. I knew I was going through a kind of death.

RIVERRUN

S. P. SOMTOW

AVON BOOKS ◆ NEW YORK

riverrun is an original publication of Avon Books. This work has never before appeared in book form. This work is a novel. Any similarity to actual persons or events is purely coincidental.

AVON BOOKS
A division of
The Hearst Corporation
1350 Avenue of the Americas
New York, New York 10019

Copyright © 1991 by Somtow Sucharitkul
Cover illustration by Tim White
Published by arrangement with the author
Library of Congress Catalog Card Number: 91-91801
ISBN: 0-380-75925-X

First Avon Books Printing: September 1991

AVON TRADEMARK REG. U.S. PAT. OFF. AND IN OTHER COUNTRIES, MARCA REGISTRADA, HECHO EN U.S.A.

Printed in the U.S.A.

RA   10 9 8 7 6 5 4 3 2 1

for
my friends in Baud Town,
whose private universes intersect with mine
by way of
an electronic metaphor:
I wonder sometimes if you are real.

Row, row, row your boat
Gently down the stream;
Merrily, merrily, merrily, merrily,
Life is but a dream.

Contents

book one

alph, the sacred river

". . . sad and weary I go back to you, my cold father,
my cold mad father, my cold mad
feary father . . ."

—*Finnegans Wake*

To My Sons

They are standing at the river's edge; sometimes
I watch them, sometimes
I cannot bear to watch, sometimes
I wish for the river to run upstream, back to the mountains,
Blue as the sky, as grief, as delusion.

They are playing by the river's edge; sometimes
Long past sunset, I hear them in the wind that shakes
The cottonwoods. I cannot bear to listen.
In my heart I know sometimes
That the river has reversed its course; I know sometimes
That the river will not turn back till its watery end,
Black as the sky, as grief, as disillusion.

They have walked away from the river's edge; I have named
   them
After the gods. Sometimes
I do not think they are coming home. Sometimes, not daring
   to look,
I say when I open my eyes they will be long gone, not gone;
That the river will run upstream, downstream.
Better not to look at all; for in the momentary closure,
The blink's breadth between two truths, two truths can both
   be true.
The tension between two truths is what I feel for them; some-
   times
I know it to be love.
Red as the sky, as grief, as joy.

chapter one

The Dream Book of Theo Etchison

Theo Etchison

It was the nineties, the time before the mad millennium. I was young and puffed up with shiny new epiphanies. A dollar could still buy a Coke and a candy bar and telephones were disembodied voices that left everything to the imagination. And some people still chose to die at home.

Oh God, I really want to remember it all. I want to see, taste, feel my family's journey across the Arizona desert then down the dark river that leads every place. So much of it seems dreamlike now, fabricless, fantastical. It's so easy to think I made it up. I have too much imagination anyway. They always used to tell me that. Too much imagination. Especially when I would tell the truth. Too much, too much.

How much is a universe? A thousand universes?

I was young.

When I try to recall that time, it's not the airconditioner spluttering dust into the old stationwagon that I remember

first. Not the shimmering sand. Not my father's eyes, hypnotized by the road, not my brother Joshua cussing out
that eighteen wheeler zipping past us in the right lane.
No. It's a smell I remember first, a smell hanging in the
air like stale orange juice, the smell of my mother dying.

I'm young. Bursting with hormones and ideas, on the
brink of simply everything, and here I am sucking in death
with every breath as we drive across the desert on our
way to Mexico and the laetrile clinic.

It's suffocating. I climb over the back seat so I can lie
in the back, propping my head with a Stephen King novel.
My mother stirs. I hear the rustle of her blankets but I
don't look back at her. I'm afraid to look.

A country and western song is blaring. We haven't been
able to get any other station since we left Buckeye. Dad
and Joshua are fighting.

"Dude, Dad, it was a stupid idea for you to leave the
10. At least we could have found ourselves a truck stop
by now."

Dad sighs.

"I'm hungrier'n shit," Josh says.

My mother stirs. I do not look back because I know
how her eyes will be—sad and sunken, the color of pea
soup. She'll be sitting with her head squashed against the
window and the blanket wrapped tight round and round
her like a winding-sheet. And she'll be shivering. Even
though the air is stifling and the sweat is pouring down
onto my teeshirt. I want it to end, I'm thinking. I want
her to die.

"Hungrier'n shit," Josh says. I hate him.

Phil, my dad, says, "Look, Mary. Dust storm up there.
Whirling against the blue mountain."

"It's beautiful, dear." Her voice is tiny and feelingless.
"I'm cold."

"Look at that sucker, kids," Phil says.

"Dude," says Josh.

I want her to die. I don't look. I don't turn around,

don't even acknowledge with a grunt. After a while the Stephen King book starts bruising my neck as I lie back. I root around for my knapsack and try to scrunch my head up against that instead. My own book is inside, a three ring binder where I've written down all the brightly-colored dreams I've been having since we left Virginia. The dreams have been much more vivid than this journey. Outside my dreams, the smell seeps into everything and fogs up the whole world.

I want it to be over.

I close my eyes for a while, hoping somehow to shut out the smell. The perspiration penetrates my closed lids and I wonder if I'm crying. My father says, "Is Theo asleep?"

Josh says, "Wake up, shitface. You won't see anything that lies ahead."

"Perhaps he prefers looking back," my father says.

"Sometimes the past is all we have," says my mother, almost inaudibly. Sullenly I look at the highway we've been traveling. The road shimmers. On either side are mountains, blue-gray and twisted. The road climbs and the car groans even though we're nowhere near sixty-five miles per hour. My head slams against the back seat and I grimace from the pain as we lurch toward the crest of the mountain.

"Hungrier'n shit," says Joshua.

That's when we see the billboard for the Chinese restaurant.

It's framed in the dip between two jags of sandstone, Day-Glo pink letters against a green background. It's twenty-five miles down the road and it features Charlie Chan's World-Famous Peking Pizza.

"Talk about nouvelle cuisine," my dad says.

"Feed me already," says Joshua.

"Feed your fucking zits, you mean," I say. I'm craning to see the billboard, cradling the side of my head in my crooked elbow so I won't have to look at her.

"I have no zits, little brother," says Joshua, "not since I started eating—"

"Organic," I say, sneering.

"Lay off each other," Dad says. I can tell he's not paying any attention to the road, I keep thinking he's going to have an accident any minute. Veer off the embankment. Like Wile E. Coyote. We might as well all die, I think. "We've got more important things to think about than—"

"I'm cold," says Mary. The heat is intolerable.

"I'll eat Chinese," Josh says. "I'll eat anything as long as the place is airconditioned."

The road is level now. Another billboard tells us that we can also expect Szechuan burgers topped with sizzling spicy shrimp.

"You find culture in the strangest places," says Dad.

I want us all to die. That's the first feeling that comes back to me when I force myself to think about those times.

I've seen those movies where some pretty pasty-faced girl is riddled with cancer and she lies there dying for the whole movie while the others recite strings of platitudes and the girl stays pretty until the very end when they close her eyes and the credits start to roll over the sappy love theme. There's just been a slew of those movies, last summer back in Virginia, before we knew the truth about our own family. Joshua and his girl friend Serena used to go to the drive-in a lot, and sometimes they would take me. Sluglike Serena would always bring three handkerchiefs (because she'd seen one of those TV critics refer to them as three-hanky movies) and she'd lay them out on the dashboard. Then she and Joshua would retire to the back seat so I was always the only one who got to endure the movie. I would sit, arms folded, with my head jammed between the two bucket seats, and sometimes my back would get clawed up some, especially in the drawn-out death scenes which seemed to get them pretty worked up. Serena had this morbid sex thing with death (she talked about the sick-dying scenes in the soaps a lot) but when she learned about Mom she never set foot in our house again. She could tell reality from fantasy all right.

Movies can show you everything about death except the smell. Death isn't beautiful. It's humiliating and gross and embarrassing and when you know it's about to happen it tears you apart in ways you never dreamed of.

The third billboard shows Dr. Fu Manchu waggishly waving a chopstick. Even the country and western song has turned to crackling. I slump back down against the knapsack. The three-ring binder protrudes and I feel hot plastic on my ear. I take out the book. There's a purple felt tip in it and I start hunting for the last page I was working on.

"What's the boy doing?" my father says.

"Scrawling in that notebook of his," says Josh. "The one he won't let any of us look at."

It's the book I've been writing down all my nightmares in. All those bad dreams that have been coming at me since our journey began.

The car rattles and my felt tip does a spider dance along the faint blue lines. I close my eyes. I try to remember my last dream, the dream about the burning world.

This is how it goes:

It's pitch-black. All I can hear is the sound of a battle, something like one of the battle scenes in Ivan the Terrible *which Dad makes us watch on PBS a lot when he gets into his really down-on-sitcoms mood. A lot of screaming and rifle reports and weird flashes and people crying out in a language I can't understand. Now and then there's lightning and there's someone's face . . . a skull . . . a man with slate-colored eyes who stares at the carnage.*

He has a thin smile on his lips and a droplet of blood at the corner of his mouth. He's staring straight at me out of the darkness. He knows my name. The lightning flash fades and the battle rages on in the dark.

I hear the sound of water.

I hear the man with slate-colored eyes say, "Truth-sayer . . . truthsayer . . . truthsayer." I do not know who he is speaking to.

Somehow I know he's on another world. I know that the world is burning and he has to reach the water.

The water roars.

I see a woman riding in a chariot drawn by animals with antlers. Smoke streams all around her and her cloak flaps over her face and her face is covered with serpent scales. She looks at me across the void between the worlds. There's water running between us. A creek maybe, a lake, a river.

Suddenly I know her name: Katastrofa Darkling.

I feel Joshua breathing down my neck. I try to wrestle the book away from him. "This is private, Josh."

He climbs over the back seat. He sits down next to me. He won't let go of the book. He's trembling. Suddenly I realize that he's scared.

"Where did you get that name from?"

He looks at me. For the first time in several days I feel the bond between us and I know that I love him. It hurts me and it makes me angry.

"You shouldn't read my book of dreams," I say. "It's private. I'm entitled."

He wipes the cold sweat from his forehead, sweeps back his long dark hair. "I dreamed that dream," he says. "I heard that name." Something in his eyes . . . something to do with sex, I think.

"She's an ugly bitch. A scaly woman, an evil woman. Her eyes are red and empty."

"She's beautiful," he says softly.

"Then you didn't dream my dream, bro," I say, furious because I desperately need to have a place inside my brain that doesn't belong to anyone else in my family.

"I dream about Katastrofa Darkling a lot," my brother

says. "You plucked her out of my mind somehow. You always do things like that. You're one of those ESP freaks . . . you fucking ought to be on talk shows."

I realize that he fears me.

Arrogantly, Katastrofa Darkling gestures. . . . The soldiers' tusks glimmer in the light of many moons.

"No magic about the kid," my father says, almost missing the turnoff to the Chinese restaurant. "Too much imagination is all." I have been hearing this all my life.

"Give me back my book," I say. My brother is about to turn the page. He is engrossed. I can tell he is aroused somehow. His cheeks are flushed and he won't look at me.

None of us are looking at each other.

"Get to the river! Before the whole world blows!"
The man with the slate-colored eyes is listening to the voice of a dying man. I can't see the dying man's face at all. But now I see that the man with the slate-colored eyes is wounded. He's crawling toward the river and—

I feel betrayed when my brother says, "I never saw any of it this clearly, Theo. But I saw something."

The dying man is a magician, I think. He cries out: "Get to the river! Find a new truthsayer!"
The man with the slate-colored eyes sees the water. I see the water through his eyes. The water is a gateway. The water gushes as the earth rumbles. Behind us, the whinnying of alien beasts of burden over the death-rattles of men.
He can't see clearly. Tears sting his eyes and fumes choke him. The water rushes down a precipice toward a vague mist fringed with rainbow steam.

"Sometimes when I dream of Katastrofa she is like a dragon and she sucks me into herself and folds her wings around me—"

"Like Serena," I say. We're carrying on this conversation in a whisper because we sense that it has something to do with sex. Our parents are pretty liberal, I mean they really don't mind when we say *fuck* and like that, but we both get pretty selfconscious when it comes to discussing . . . well, if we didn't have ourselves as evidence, we'd wonder if Phil and Mary knew anything at all about the birds and bees.

"Serena was a slug," I say.

"You asshole," says my brother, but he's not angry about it. I can tell that he's thinking about the other woman, the woman in my dream. Somehow the same name has cropped up in both our dreams. It's happened before. We are close, Joshua and I, although I do hate him most of the time. He is more handsome than me, when he's relatively zitless as he is right now, and he knows how to talk to people, and he's good at bullshitting, which has always been totally difficult for me. And he drives, which I can't yet for another two years at least.

In the dream I am swallowed up in the water, dark and warm and full of promises.

There's a game my Dad and I once used to play. It goes like this:

Sit on my lap and I will close my eyes. Sit on my lap and steer and say, "Trust me." We'll be like a single person, father and son, a team, each one of us holding the life of the other in his hand.

We have not played this game for seven years.

The stationwagon stops. The airconditioning stops. The air stops moving and the dust settles on me and my brother.

"I suppose we should get out of the car now," my father says.

"I'll help Mom," Joshua says, and bounds over the seat to open the door and to let me slither out of the back into the sunlight, still clutching my binder under my arm, trying to soothe my rumpled Redskins teeshirt.

"Jesus! What kind of a place is this?" I hear Joshua say.

"In the middle of nowhere . . ." my Dad says, "as if we've somehow stumbled into another country."

There are no cars in the parking lot. There's nothing all around us, no gas stations, no Circle K convenience stores . . . nothing but this thing that looks like a palace out of a 1950s spectacle. It's got fifteen-foot-tall portals with gold-colored plastic bas-reliefs. It's got a roof with pointed eaves and murals with long bearded men in faded robes. Everything's caked with dust, and the lettering over the cracked façade reads:

IN XAN D D KUBL KH
A ST   PLEASURE D   DE

There's a smile in my Dad's voice as he says, very softly, behind me, "Where Alph, the sacred river, ran . . ."

And Joshua says, "Through caverns measureless to man . . ."

And my mother says, "Down to a sunless sea." And begins to cry. Bitterly, so bitterly.

My Dad has resigned from the poetry chair of a small university in Northern Virginia so we can make this trip together. Before all this happened we lived in Alexandria in a small house by the Potomac and I went to GW Junior High, and on Sundays, when other families went to church, we read poetry together. "Poetry *is* religion," my Dad used to tell us. I know a lot of weird words (and even now some line comes clanging in my head like a cracked church bell) but I am young so the lines all jangle inside me and I don't know what they mean but I don't care because they sound awesome.

The sun burns us. But there's a gritty wind that bears away some of the fragrance of death.

"Shall we go in?" It's my mother talking.

At last I turn to look at her. The Navajo blanket she's been draping herself with slips down to her shoulders. She is almost bald from the chemotherapy. Her hollow cheeks are soaked. She draws the blanket tight around herself and wipes at her tears with a frayed corner.

"Maybe it's closed . . . maybe it's . . ." Joshua starts to hum the *Twilight Zone* theme in an ominous falsetto.

A tiny placard is taped to the door. It says WELCOME. Funny how we haven't noticed it till now.

I hear the roar of water . . . as if we were standing by the sea. But it's the middle of the desert, I tell myself, the middle of nowhere.

chapter two

In a Chinese Restaurant

Joshua Etchison

I had always known that my brother did not live in quite
the same universe as other people. You and I and everyone
we know, we go from *A* to *B*, from morning to night,
from six in the morning to six oh one. But to Theo everything always seemed to be eternally in the present. We
see the world as a series of discrete entities, but to Theo
they were always connected. Sometimes I swear he could
see the future. And he was bad at lying. That's what drove
me crazy the most.

Before we got to the Chinese restaurant, we'd been on
the road for weeks. My mother had been sick for almost
two years, and this journey was supposed to bring us all
together, as well as maybe cure her, if we made it as far
as Mexico and the macrobiotic laetrile clinic of the notori-
ous Dr. Isabella de la Verdád. I don't know if anyone
really believed that part of it would work, although reading

the brochures had set me off on an organic food kick that
I've been trying to stay on even now.

My brother stood apart from the three of us, hearing
something we didn't hear, an alien music. He was a
malnourished-looking boy, and my Redskins teeshirt hung
all the way down to his knees on him, past his shorts.
He had big eyes, the color of the creek in back of our
grandmother's house in Spotsylvania County, and he was
looking shiftily around, like there was someone watching
him. It was a make-believe cloak-and-dagger game I'd
often seen him play when he thought he wasn't being
watched.

My stomach was growling and so I pushed open the
door into the gaudy restaurant. In the hall there were three
funhouse mirrors. Beyond the inner door, a ceiling fan
turned, squeaking, and there were some dilapidated tables
set with candles. Tourist posters of the Great Wall and the
Forbidden City hung on the walls. No airconditioning, I
thought bitterly.

I led my Mom inside by the hand and helped her into
a chair. It was one of her good days today. Dad sat down
next to her and helped her with her medication. Theo was
off by himself, peering into every booth.

"Some place, huh, Josh," said Dad.

"Yeah."

"I wonder why they built a place like this in the middle
of nowhere. . . . I wonder how they can make a
living. . . ."

"Maybe some people just too rich to think of being
practical, sir." A sort of Chinese Peter Cushing loomed
above us. His shadow crossed my mother's face. She
looked down at the table. "Twenty years ago, a man mis-
read a map, thought the freeway would pass through here,
buy up all the land . . . make Xanadu at the center of the
wilderness."

"A poet," Dad said, smiling a little . . . only the second time that day. I knew my Dad was only forty but for a year now he had seemed as old as King Lear.

"It take one to know one," Peter Cushing said, arching one eyebrow. "My name is Cornelius Huang."

"And I am Philip Etchison."

"Ah, but I know your work. I thought *The Embrasure of Parched Lips* particular fine. Bittersweet, autumnal, almost like death-drinking songs of Li Po."

"Mr. Huang—"

"Please do me singular honor of calling me Corny. All my friends to."

I could tell that my Dad couldn't quite believe his ears. It's the kind of coincidence that only happens in a Victorian novel or a Woody Allen movie. He blushed all the way up to his receding hairline. When Mr. Huang told us he was going to make us his ten-course Peking banquet—no charge—and began shouting orders at the kitchen—and his whole staff started lining up at our table, tallest to smallest, bowing to us smartly one by one—my Dad just started laughing and laughing. He didn't look like King Lear anymore . . . more like Old King Cole.

I was happy for him, and even Mom managed a wan laugh.

Then we started eating.

Around the third course, Theo came and sat down next to me. We were never a family for all sitting down together and making small talk through a meal, and Theo was always too hyper to sit through dinner, so no one much minded.

"Had any more weird dreams, little brother?" I said. The incident in the car still disturbed me, wouldn't let go of me.

"Shh," he says to me over the sweet-and-sour fish. "Shh. Don't you hear it? Don't you hear anything?"

"Hear what?"

"The water roaring."

I listened. Somewhere in the distance I could hear something that sounded like Chinese heavy metal. But behind that noise was there something . . . something like the trickle of water? Chinese water torture? I dismissed it. "Don't hear it. It's just your—"

"Imagination," my brother said, and sulked for a few moments over the beef in oyster sauce, which I only picked at for fear of MSG.

We ate in silence. The waiters—members of Corny Huang's family—slithered about, noiselessly replacing our dishes. The Chinese heavy metal music segued into lush strings. I ate a lot, not because I was hungry, but so that I wouldn't have to think.

"Enjoying the meal?" It was Cornelius Huang, towering over my mother and scrutinizing me and Theo.

Theo looked up, saw him clearly for the first time. I'd never seen him look so panicstricken.

"Corny Huang," said my Dad. "You missed it when he introduced himself to us, Theo. He's . . . a fan of mine."

Theo's eyes widened. He got up.

"The next course is conch," said Mr. Huang.

"I know you." Theo began backing away. His chair thudded on the linoleum tiles.

Suddenly an image burst over me—

He's standing beside the river. His plumage is the colors of alien suns. He lifts the conch to his lips. The river parts and the dragon comes forth—

"I know you. You're the gatekeeper. The herald. The servant of—"

My Dad was laughing. "So much imagination," he said. "He'll be twice the poet I was when he's older, when he starts bombarding the *New Yorker* with—"

I know Theo when he's like this. He's dead serious. This was one of the times when he was seeing all those interconnections that go right over us normal people's heads.

"Dad"—I said it even though I knew it would be futile—"listen to Theo. . . . When he feels that something's wrong, it always is." I got up too. There was something going on between my brother and the Chinese dude. They were gazing into each other's eyes and Theo was still backing away, right into the window against the view of endless desert.

"Truthsayer," said Mr. Huang. He began muttering to himself in Chinese, and his relations looked at each other in consternation.

Truthsayer? I thought. That's a word from Theo's notebook . . . a word out of one of his dreams. For a few seconds I thought I could hear the rushing of a mighty flood. And the screams of a dying world.

Can't be, I thought, shrugging. Probably just someone flushing a toilet back there.

Our family had a game we play with fortune cookies. This is how it went:

No one reads their fortunes. The first player picks someone at the dinner table and asks him a question—*any* question—and the person he picks has to open the cookie and read whatever it says. Then the *second* person picks another person, and so on, all the way back to the original person. It always works. You always get a viable answer. Doesn't matter what the questions are.

Mr. Huang knew about our game. "Ah, Mr. Etchison," he said, "you explain about it at length in your immortal *Sonnets about Chinese Cooking*, a nineteen seventy-nine chapbook I believe—"

My father beamed.

"For this, you must get special cookies. I have these printed specially in San Francisco." He clapped his hands and one of his daughters brought in a silver tray with four oversize cookies. "These are very special fortune cookies, you like, I know."

"Theo, come back to the table," my Dad said, as Mr. Huang discreetly withdrew. When Theo saw that only the four of us were left he sat down sullenly.

I whispered in his ear, "Theo, your dreams're leaking into your real world again. . . . Get a grip on yourself, dude."

"You heard what he called me," Theo said softly, intensely.

"Mary, ask the first question," my Dad said, and he pointed his finger at her. She looked at me. I tried to meet her gaze.

She asked me: "Will Joshua Etchison get into an Ivy League college next fall?" And they smiled at each other a little, to show us that they were still in love, despite everything.

I opened my fortune cookie, and read, " 'You will receive an unexpected award.' "

Dad laughed. "The question is, Josh, whether you're *expecting* to get into an Ivy League school or not." He took a bite of the green tea ice cream and he squeezed my mother's hand. I knew he was on the verge of cracking but he was trying so hard to be strong.

It was my turn, and I said to my dad, "Is Phil Etchison's poetry going to be quoted a hundred years from now? Like Keats, Byron, all that crowd?"

He chuckled and opened his cookie. "Poetry! How appropriate!" And he read these words to us in stentorian tones:

" 'The sky will be blue forever, and forever
The earth will stand, and every spring will blossom
Till the end of time. But you, O Man,
How long do you live?'

                                                    —Li Po

"I wonder what this fortune cookie is trying to tell us. Perhaps," he mused, "I should desist from the hubris of seeking immortality. Perhaps I should sell out, pursue the vulgar taste . . . perhaps . . ."

"Oh, Dad," I said, "I don't see you turning into a Rod McKuen type—not with all those $64 words."

"I guess not." He waved a chopstick at Theo and said, "Tell me, son, that book of yours that you've been writing in all the way from Alexandria . . . the one you're so secretive about . . ."

Theo looked nervously around. For some reason he seemed to be afraid of Mr. Huang, who was nowhere to be seen.

"Will I ever get to read it?"

"That's your question?" I said. I didn't want to get Theo all worked up, because he was liable to blurt out things that people didn't want to hear.

"Sure," Dad said. "I'm allowed to ask anything I want, aren't I?"

"There are things you just shouldn't ask, Dad," Theo said. He feigned a laugh, but I could tell he was much more unnerved than he looked. He opened his cookie and read: " 'It is often a mistake to pry into the mysteries of nature, as witness the predicament of Dr. Frankenstein. And yet, there is little one can do to prevent it.' "

"These are the weirdest fortune cookies I've ever encountered," Dad said.

There was a long silence.

I watched my brother. I could see that he was falling into that inner world of his. "Go on, Theo," I said, "ask Mom a question."

He looked straight at my mother and said, "When are you going to die?"

His words died away in the wheezing of the overhead fan.

My Dad was absolutely white. He was clenching and unclenching his fists. My Mom seemed strangely calm.

"Let him say it, Phil," she said. "We have to come to terms with it; we've never really talked it over as a family before. . . ."

It was appalling. I could feel my rage uncoiling inside me.

Trying to control himself, Dad said, "Theo, learn some tact."

Theo turned to me. He had this blank possessed look and he made me so mad that I just couldn't stand him, I really hated him for always putting his foot in his mouth like that and I grabbed him by the neck and I just started punching him again and again.

"You tell the fucking truth too fucking often," I said and I shoved him hard against the next table and I could see blood pouring from his nose.

"You're hurting me," he said.

I stood there breathing heavily, sweating. I had all this fury and I didn't know what to do. I heard my mother weeping quietly to herself. I couldn't hit him anymore.

He looked at me with that same blank look. What was wrong with him? I heard the roaring of distant water. I knew he could hear it too, more clearly than I, and I knew that my parents heard nothing.

Slowly he turned from me and began walking toward a door marked RESTROOMS.

"Don't go after him," Dad said. "He didn't mean to—"

"I'm sorry," I said.

"We're all upset," my mother said. Then, "Do you have any more of those painkillers?"

Only then did I notice the fortune from her cookie, lying half-crumpled on top of a half-eaten piece of shrimp.

It said:

"Dark is life, dark is death."

—*Li Po*

chapter three

The Sunless Sea

Theo Etchison

I always ask the one question everyone wants answered and doesn't dare ask. I don't know why I said that. I feel like I'm about to cry but the tears don't come. I'm not surprised Joshua punched me out. I hate myself. Why am I like this, why do I always blurt out things that are true that no one wants to hear?

I can taste blood. I have to find the bathroom and wash it off my face. I have to get away from all of them.

I go down the corridor. An arrow points toward the men's. The corridor slopes down and the walls are damp. Where's the moisture coming from? I think. We're in the middle of the desert, aren't we?

I hear someone call my name. It's my brother. He's coming after me. The corridor slopes downward, downward. There are mirrors against the walls, funhouse mirrors and normal mirrors and mirrors I don't dare look at because I think they show my nightmares. What kind of

a place is this? I'm in a tunnel. I come to a neon arrow
that points further ahead and it still says RESTROOMS. I
guess I'm getting too imaginative again. Like in school
sometimes during finals when I drift away for what seems
like a ninety-minute action-adventure-comedy-drama but
when I drift back again only a minute has passed and I'm
still trying to answer the same true or false question.

I can hear someone breathing. Footsteps behind me.
The sound carries along the walls of the chamber. I feel
like I'm in a cave. I can hear water lapping against stone.
I stop. Behind me, the footsteps stop too. A metallic echo.
I feel cold suddenly. Scared.

I turn a corner.

Truthsayer.

I think about the bad dreams I've been having. I've
been standing on the edges of other times, other worlds.
They've been consumed by fire. One by one. The universe
is like my mother's body, slowly being eaten away by
something dark and malevolent. Maybe that's all the
dreams mean . . . they're all about her, about how scared
I am she's going to die.

Suddenly there's the bathroom. I'm not quite sure how
I got there. It's a big clean place, with flower tiles, smelling faintly of lemon. I take a leak, then go to the sink
and start to swab at the blood with a hand towel. It doesn't
hurt anymore but I feel pretty fucking humiliated.

I hear a voice. My name. Startled, I turn around. It's
only Joshua, leaning against the door. I think he's trying
to make peace.

"Look, I didn't mean—"

"It's okay."

"I'll make it up to you."

"All right." The blood and water are draining down
the sink. "So make it up to me."

"What do you want me to do?"

"Well," I say, "you're bigger and stronger than me.

Give me something to hold over you. Something that'll even up the odds.''

"You want me to tell you one of my secrets."

"Yeah."

"I'll kill you for this."

"You offered."

"All right." He thinks about it for a long time. I tap my fingers on the sink. At last he says, "You remember Serena Somers?"

God, do I. "Sluglike Serena," I say, "how could I ever forget her. I guess you're going to tell me how you made it with her in the back seat . . . but you forget that I was there. What kind of a secret is that?"

"I never fucked her," he says, kind of shy.

"What?"

"I told you! We were just making a lot of noise to give you . . . ideas."

"Gross me out!" I was looking at him with a newfound admiration. I mean, Sluglike Serena had been had by half of GW, let alone the high school. "Well," I say, "no need to stoop to Serena when you had the buxom Beatrice Pfeffer."

"Didn't fuck her either," my brother says, which is a truly astounding revelation, because I can't think of anyone else he's even claimed to, and that leads me to the inescapable conclusion that he must be a . . .

"You guessed it, dude," he says. "I'm a v-v—"

This is a totally heavy secret. He must really feel bad about hitting me. "C'mon, bro," I say, "you didn't hurt me *that* bad. Like, you didn't have to tell me that big of a secret."

"Fuckin' Jesus, Theo," my brother says, "when *is* she going to die?" And he starts to cry. I mean really cry, like a kid. And I feel terrible because I don't remember ever seeing him cry even though he is the closest person in the whole world to me. I don't know what to do.

Just then, I hear a toilet flush and the door to one of

the stalls opens. Shit! I think. Someone's been in here all this time, and me and Josh've been spilling our guts.

Now I hear water. A lot of water. Water cascading down cataracts, racing toward the sea. The roaring numbs me. I know that Joshua can hear at least a faint echo of what I'm hearing, because he looks where I'm looking . . . the toilet stall.

"Something wrong with the plumbing around here?" he asks.

"Nothing wrong with plumbing." It's Peter Cushing Cornelius Huang himself, standing by the swinging door, peering at me from beady eyes set in a cadaver's face . . . except that he's wearing these weird robes, an iron collar studded with diamonds, and he has sort of a mohawk and a cape that billows all about in the wind that has suddenly sprung up, and he has a jeweled conch shell in his hand that he's about to lift to his lips . . . and there's smoke all over the restroom, and dust, and there's the smell of my mother dying that I've known so well these past weeks. . . .

"I know you," says my brother. "I saw you. For a moment. I think Theo put the image in my head."

"The herald," I said.

"Truthsayer," says Cornelius Huang. "I've been sent to fetch you . . . by the man with the slate-colored eyes."

And suddenly the wall behind him bursts asunder and I see a river so wide I can barely make out the far shore, where a castle perches on a crystal mountain girt with rainbow fire. . . . I know this place so well, it's the place I go to every time I close my eyes at night in motel room after sleazy motel room, the place I've been going to to get away from the nightmare of reality. . . . The water is pouring into the room now, pounding savagely at me, but I don't feel any wetness. . . . One world is melding into the next.

"What's going on?" Josh says. "Let him go!"

Tongues of blue flame spew from the herald's eyes. I'm

rooted to the cold white tiles as the water that I can't feel swirls and churns and crashes around me. The lines of fire wrap themselves around me and I can't move. My brother reaches for me. He grabs the sleeve of my teeshirt. My shirt tears. "Theo!" he screams. The fire burns me with its searing cold.

"The man with the slate-colored eyes," says Mr. Huang, "he been waiting for you for long long time. He been waiting for his own personal truthsayer." He never speaks above a whisper but his voice cuts through the thunder of the river.

"Where are you taking me?" I scream.

"To the Land of Nod," he says, "the Desert of Dreaming . . . beyond the Sunless Sea."

"But those are just dreams," I say.

I flail against the ropes of icy flame. I try to grab my brother's arm, but the herald turns his head and Joshua is thrown against the sink by an invisible force. The mirror shatters against his face and I see splinters in his cheeks and see his forehead speckled with crimson. Behind him, the water rises. It is dark and warm.

"Dark is life," says Mr. Huang. "Dark is death. You should have read that fortune cookie, Theo Etchison."

In the dream I cannot help being drawn toward the water, dark and warm and full of promises. . . .

But it's not like the dream! I fight the water. I can't leave my family like this, my mother dying, my last words to her full of bitterness and frustration. The water wells up. The restroom is engulfed in Spielbergian mist. Lights flash. Water in my eyes, water in my nose, pouring into my lungs, and Mr. Huang still standing there with the conch to his lips, blaring out an irresistible summoning. . . . His hair is the color of seaweed.

There's a ghostly outline of a boat. The prow is carved into a gargoyle gushing blood that trails into the water. . . .

A man stands with his hand resting over the gargoyle's eyes. He wears a cloak and all I can see are his eyes . . . slate-colored, lifeless. He looks at me and suddenly I am in the grip of the summoning and I am so far away from my old anger and from my strife-torn family and I feel the tug of distant universe and I want to give myself to the rhythmic swell of the dark dark waters.

I hear Joshua's voice: "Theo, Theo . . ." but it is dying away. . . . My brother is fading like an old pair of jeans. . . . The wind is rising over the waters. . . . Another voice calls my name, "Theo, Theo, Theo." A rich voice, murmurous and echoing like the voice of the very river. I feel more than myself, I remember all the weird words from family poetry evenings by the fireplace; I feel them jangling inside my mind and I feel like all at once I know what they all mean.

I know that my brother is watching me fade away like some hokey special effect. Deep inside I am still calling out to him but I do not think he can hear me. I wonder whether he will ever hear me again. I can often see true things about other people that they don't want me to see, but I can't see anything about myself, I just see blank when I try. . . . I have no reassuring words for Josh, I can't tell him that I will ever return.

chapter four

Lethe-wards

Joshua Etchison

What was happening to us? One moment Theo and I were just carrying on a regular convo in the men's room, the next a kind of a Viking ship was bursting through the toilet stall and Mr. Huang had turned into some kind of space ninja with superpowers and he was sucking my brother into a watery vortex. . . .

I couldn't see what Theo was seeing. The boat, the man with the slate-colored eyes, the swirling water . . . all these things were blurry, dreamlike. I could hear him cry out to me and I tried to grab him but the first time I tore off a piece of his shirt and the next time my hand went right through him and then he wasn't there at all, none of it was there, it was just a squeaky-clean restroom in a Chinese restaurant in the middle of the Arizona desert.

Maybe I was dreaming, I thought. Maybe Theo's just taking a shit in one of these stalls. I knocked on the only one that was closed. A hollow echo. Wildly I looked around. I started to panic.

Then I pushed open the door of the stall and saw—

Churning water! And Theo being pulled up into that Viking ship, spectral now, fading from view, and—

Nothing.

I turned and ran.

The restaurant. My parents sitting where I'd left them. My mother staring off into space, my father shaking his head, Theo's knapsack leaning against the upturned chair.

"Something terrible's just happened," I said. "Theo— Theo's—"

It seemed almost too absurd to tell them.

"What is it, dear?" my mother said faintly.

"He's gone . . . something happened in the bathroom."

"Did he trip?" my father said.

"No, goddamn it, he's . . . gone, vanished. I saw something. . . . I don't believe what I saw." How could I explain ships from other universes, old Chinese guys shooting blue sparks from their eyes? "I think Mr. Huang knows . . . but I don't think he'll tell us."

"If this is one of you guys' pranks—" said Dad.

"No, Dad."

Something in my manner must've convinced him I wasn't totally bullshitting, because he whispered a few words in my mother's ear and got up to follow me.

"In the bathroom, Dad. Look, I know this sounds ridiculous, but I think Mr. Huang kind of . . . kidnaped him."

My mother started at this. Maybe she had felt something when it was all happening. Dying people are psychic, I've heard.

"Where is that man anyway?" Dad said. "We haven't even paid him anything." He wasn't quite grasping the gravity of all this. "Oh, Mr. Huang!" He stood straightening his glasses for a moment. None of the employees were in sight—no Mr. Huang and not one of his sisters, cousins and aunts. "C'mon, Josh, we'd better get Theo out of wherever he's hiding."

We followed the sign to the restroom. I could have sworn the corridor wasn't the same. It sloped gently downward and the walls were almost like the walls of a cave, and they were covered with picture writing . . . not hieroglyphics exactly, because the letters seemed squatter and there were more colors and some of the characters looked like aliens from a space opera. I remembered the funhouse mirrors, but this time there were more of them and they seemed to distort more.

"It's taking a long time to get there," I said. "And it feels different somehow."

"To paraphrase Lewis Carroll," my Dad said, "sometimes it takes all the running you can do to stay in the same place."

We kept walking. I don't think we were getting anywhere.

"Theo!" I kept shouting. My voice echoed and I could swear I heard water rippling.

Then the corridor turned sharply and we were in a kind of grotto. There was an underground stream that gushed down from a hole in the rock, ran for about twenty feet, and disappeared down a shallow tunnel to our right. A shaft of blue light played over the water. Dust motes danced.

"We must have taken a wrong turn," said Dad.

"Look!" I said, pointing to a little shrine in a niche in the rock. A jade figurine sat on a gilded throne. There was so much incense that I couldn't see its face. Beneath it was a bronze plaque with the legend:

Where Alph, the sacred river, ran
Through caverns measureless to man
Down to a Sunless Sea.

CORNELIUS HUANG, A LOVER OF FINE POEMS, EXPLORER OF SUBTERRANEAN CAVERNS, FOUND THIS STREAM BENEATH

THE EARTH AND ERECTED THIS MODEST LITTLE XANADU
ABOVE IT . . . ANNO DOMINI MDCCCLXXXVI

"Well, that's a hoax for sure," Dad said. "Get a load
of that date—eighteen eighty-six! Corny's not that old—I
don't care how many ancient Chinese secrets he knows."

I was nervous. This place wasn't here the last time.
Something was terribly wrong. The incense smoke cleared
from the figurine's face and my heart started beating even
faster. I knew that face . . . I'd seen that face in my
dreams and in my sleepless nights, I'd been so turned on
by that face that I hadn't been able to get it on with Serena
Somers or any other girl . . . that face, part woman, part
serpent, so sexual that even now I could feel my penis
stiffening. . . .

I felt hot all over. I know I was blushing.

*She says to me: "My name is Katastrofa Darkling. I
am the woman in the dragon, the woman in the dragon's
breath, the breath of the dragon . . . I am Katastrofa
Darkling." She bares her breasts to me and—*

"Joshua," my father said.

I must have been staring at the statuette like an idiot.

"Looking for the bathroom?" No mistaking that voice.
I whirled around. Mr. Huang was standing at the only exit
from the grotto. I started to shake.

"What have you done to my brother?" I screamed.

"Josh, your manners," said Dad.

"There is no bathroom down here," said Cornelius
Huang. "I am sorry, but the signs are misleading. But I
see you have discovered my little secret . . . my elfin grot.
The water comes from a spring far beneath the earth.
Allow me to . . . show you the way."

"You were standing there when Theo disappeared," I
said. I was angry now, I didn't care if my Dad thought I
had gone crazy. "You were standing there with weird

lights in your eyes and wearing some kind of wizard robes.''

Mr. Huang laughed, very softly. Even my Dad seemed unnerved. "Don't you stand there looking all innocent," I said. "I saw you . . . I *saw* you! Maybe you've got some kind of child-sacrificing cult or maybe you're one of those psycho sex killers. . . . Maybe you've got a big battery of machines with sound effects and images and smoke and lightning. . . . I don't know, I don't care. You've done something to Theo."

"Wizard robes? Child sacrifice?" said my father. "Really, Joshua . . . some of Theo's flights of fancy must be rubbing off on you. . . . Mr. Huang, you'll excuse—"

"Call me Corny." And he gazed at me, all snake-eyed, and chilled me. I didn't want to admit how much he scared me, especially since Dad was acting like it was somehow all my fault.

The three of us walked back. There were no cavernous corridors, no stalactites. Only the funhouse mirrors were the same. We climbed some steps covered with thick shag. There had been no steps coming down. And then we were suddenly walking into the main hall, and my mother was where we left her, propped against her pillow and wrapped in her Indian blanket, looking out of the window at the setting sun.

I half expected to see Theo sitting beside her. But he wasn't there. She looked up at us. "Where's Theo?" she said.

Dad shrugged. "I expect he's just fooling around somewhere—you know how he gets," he said.

We waited for one hour. It grew dark.

"He knows better than to go out in the desert," Dad said.

"It's fucking freezing," I said. There was dust in our eyes, and the temperature had dropped to 29°, and the wind was howling. Three beams of light from our three flashlights crisscrossed over a desolate vista: stones, sand, many-armed cactuses.

We had gone outside with Mr. Huang. My mother had been put to bed on a couch in the restaurant's lobby, and one of the innumerable relatives was tending her. I felt queasy leaving her with them. My mind was fogging up. I wasn't sure I could remember what happened anymore. Something watery. There had been a ship . . . a man with gray eyes . . . another man in robes whose eyes sparked laser lightning. I couldn't have seen those things. My Dad had to be right.

The heat of the day . . . the oppressive closeness of the car . . . stepping outside had made me light headed, prone to suggestion . . . that's all it was. Maybe the MSG did something too. MSG always fucked with my brain cells. Yes. Theo had gone outside to play by himself, the way he always did. He'd wandered off somewhere.

It was easy to believe that.

We stumbled about in the darkness, shrieking out Theo's name. We looked for footsteps but soon we were treading in our own. And always Mr. Huang talked, calming us, regaling us with arcane fragments of poetry. And I could see that my father was bewitched by him, and that even I was beginning to feel the strange seduction of his soft-spoken words, and there was a kind of despair in me too, because under his spell I was rapidly forgetting the things I knew to be true.

Inside, past midnight, we sipped tea in dainty cloisonné cups and my father brought up the police for the first time.

"There are no police here," said Mr. Huang. "Tucson, perhaps . . . a hundred miles, no freeway. Your son is not that far away. They will not come."

"Telephone?" Dad said.

He chuckled. "I have, of course, no telephone," said Mr. Huang.

Of course not, I thought.

On the sofa, my mother moaned.

"I have to wake her up and give her her medication," said my Dad.

"A beautiful woman, even in death," said Mr. Huang.

"She's not dead yet," I said.

"Ah, but I was merely speaking in a metaphysical sense. She is, as Wagner put it in *Tristan and Isolde,* already '*todgeweihte*' . . . consecrated to death."

"And Theo? I suppose you consider him dead already."

"If he is out there," said Mr. Huang, "the desert is harsh."

"There's got to be someone you can contact."

"Ask your father."

I looked at my father. He had my mother cradled in his arms. Her gaze darted fearfully from side to side and he was whispering to her. He waited.

Another hour passed. I could see that my parents were both drifting off. I was struggling to fight off this unnatural weariness. . . . My eyelids were fighting me; my limbs were leaden. I kept seeing Katastrofa Darkling whenever I closed my eyes.

I could almost hear her voice. She was saying something like: *"There are some things you were never meant to remember, Joshua. . . . It were best if you forgot them."* I tried to open my eyes. It was dark. A single candle flickered from the nearest dining table. There was some kind of incense, too, drenching my lungs in a suffocating odor. I looked around. My mother was fast asleep . . . my father stirred a little. Mr. Huang was hovering over him, moving his hands back and forth over his scalp like a conjuror about to pull a rabbit from a hat. Dad's eyes were open but glazed. The incense burner was right next to the couch on an ornate marble end table.

Then Mr. Huang took out a silver bowl of water, dipped a handful of twigs in it, and started to sprinkle my Dad with it.

I said, "Dad? What's happening? What are we going to do about Theo?"

"Theo?" my father said, in utmost bewilderment.

"Theo . . . your son . . . remember?" I said. "A kid who tells the truth too much . . . a dirty blond kid with eyes like—" I blinked. I couldn't remember Theo's eyes. Had I said blond?

I couldn't remember his face.

My father looked at me blankly.

I felt cold water droplets on my face. Mr. Huang smiled.

Jesus! I thought. They're fucking with my mind. . . . Suddenly I knew we couldn't allow ourselves to fall asleep here. Maybe it was the incense. Maybe it was Mr. Huang's mystic passes in the air or his weird water. But they—whoever *they* were—were stealing memories from our heads, and I knew that when we woke up we would be a family of three, with no recollection of poor crazy Theo at all. . . .

I forced myself to get up, tried to hold my breath . . . I went over to my Dad. Angrily I elbowed Mr. Huang aside. "We've got to leave!" I said.

He just looked at me. Then he began reciting in a high-pitched singsong:

" 'As though of hemlock I had drunk,
Or emptied some dull opiate to the drains . . .
And Lethe-wards had sunk . . .' "

A dim memory from a mythology lesson. Lethe . . . the river of forgetfulness . . .

"Very fine poet, Keats," said Mr. Huang, and sprinkled more water on my father.

I looked around. There was Theo's knapsack, still leaning against the chair! I seized it. The dream book tumbled out. I took the book and shoved it under his nose, turning the pages. "Look, Dad . . . these dreams . . . Theo's dreams . . ."

In her sleep, my mother mumbled, "Theo? Theo?"

"*She* hasn't forgotten!" I shouted.

"She's delirious," my father said, but I thought I saw uncertainty in his eyes.

"Let's go. . . ." I said.

"We're tired. Your mother needs to rest. Mr. Huang has kindly offered to let us stay here as long as we want. . . . He's so lonely without human company," he said.

In the candlelight Mr. Huang's face, etched with shadows, looked like a bird of prey.

"The laetrile clinic!" I said. "They can only hold her reservation until next week. . . ."

"Mexico's less than a day away," my father said.

The voice of reason. I knew I had to trick them somehow. I saw the bottle of Mom's medication beside the couch. I leaned down, knocked it to the floor. "I didn't mean to—" I said. The bottle shattered.

"You clumsy—" said Dad. He started to go after the pills.

"It was an accident!" I felt like a little kid saying that, but I was desperate. I spun around as if to avoid a blow, karate-chopped the incense burner so that it flew across the floor and—

Clang! Ashes and pills strewn across the floor . . . the little capsules charring, giving off a foul vapor . . . "Goddamn it, Joshua, where are we going to get more pills. . . . She'll be writhing in agony if she doesn't get her next painkiller in four hours. . . ."

"Tucson," I said. "We're getting out of this place, Dad."

I turned to Mr. Huang. He glared at me. There was defeat in his eyes. I gathered up my brother's secret notebook, slung the knapsack over my shoulder, started resolutely for the door, pausing only to grind the crushed painkillers into the ashes with my foot.

I could hear my father lifting Mom to her feet. I could hear him shuffling behind me. I opened the door and breathed in the sweet frigid desert air.

"I'll drive," I said quickly, before he changed his mind.

Half an hour later we switched off. My Dad seemed energized again and I was getting drowsier and drowsier. I climbed into the back of the stationwagon.

This is what I read by flashlight in my brother's dream book as the car strained up curvy mountain roads toward Route 10.

I remember the first dream really well and that's why I'm going to write them all down. The first dream is more than a year ago so it really isn't supposed to be in this book which is a book of what I am dreaming about on this journey. But I think it is important because it is the first time I see the man with the slate-colored eyes and it is only a day after Dad has told us that her cancer is fatal. That was also the day our family went to see King Lear *at the Wolf Trap Festival so some of it is probably mixed up into the dream.*

I see a desolate landscape with ice and snow everywhere and mists tendriling out of caverns and frozen lakes and waterfalls.

I see a castle.

I see a King. He is about to divide his kingdom up between three children . . . not daughters like in the play but a man and a woman and I'm not sure about the third one. The throne is surrounded by a river that leads everywhere. I am walking toward the throne. They're all talking softly in kind of Shakespearean English and I can only make out a few words.

The king has a scepter in his hand and there is a jewel that contains men's souls.

I'm standing at the river's edge now. The smell is so familiar . . . I know that it's the smell of my grandma's house in Spotsylvania County.

I know that the king is dividing his kingdom and that something bad is going to happen. A blood-tinged mist rises out of the river.

The king's son turns to me. He smiles. He is cruel. He has slate-colored eyes. He loves to destroy. He has smashed whole planets just to see sparks spiral in the starstream. There is a void in his heart and yet I feel . . . drawn to him.

A man stands next to him . . . a tall Chinese-looking man with a mohawk. . . . He raises a conch to his lips and blows an ear-splitting note and the king looks up. . . . I see the king's hands, palsied as he feebly tries to grip the scepter.

The jewel in the scepter: lights dancing. Men's souls.

I'm afraid. The man with the slate-colored eyes is coming to me and I want to run but I can't, I'm rooted to the riverbank like the trees by my grandma's house, I'm powerless, and there's a part of me that wants me to like him, empty eyed, soulless.

Now I wake up.

I remember this dream for the first time today, the day after Easter, 1990. It's the day we're packing to go to Mexico. That's when I decide to go down to the 7-11 and buy this three-ring binder to record my dreams. It's got to mean something.

I think the sun was rising when I finally dozed off. I was trying to remember little things about Theo, those details that make someone a real person to you. Theo and I were close, I knew that . . . but where were the things I should have remembered vividly?

. . . a baseball flying past the sun . . . stubby fingers

clutching a stolen beer can . . . trying to beat the high score in Gauntlet . . . what else, what else? . . . I still couldn't remember his eyes.

I concentrated. The sun was in my eyes. I tried to picture him. The sandy hair . . . a slender body, almost shadowlike . . . a mole on the back of his left hand that he was too sensitive about . . . the eyes! I could see his face in my mind, but it had someone else's eyes. Slate-colored eyes.

As I finally drifted into fitful sleep, I wondered if I would be the same person when I woke up . . . whether all of us were somehow being transformed into other people, people from a world not quite our own.

book two

the river lethe

"—Et le rêve fraîchit."
"—And the dream grew cold."

—Illuminations

TO MY SON

He is standing at the river's edge; sometimes
I watch him, sometimes
I cannot bear to watch, sometimes
I wish for the river to run upstream, back to the mountains,
Blue as the sky, as grief, as desolation.

He is playing by the river's edge; sometimes
I feel he is not alone, I hear a second laugh in the wind that
    shakes
The cottonwoods. I cannot bear to listen,
Knowing as I know the one unborn, the one I have named
God, because he is my son's dark elder self.
If the river had run backward my other son would not
Cry out to me from the depths. In my heart I know sometimes
That the river has reversed its course; I know sometimes
That the river will not turn back till its watery end,
Black as the sky, as grief, as disillusion.

He is walking away from the river's edge;
I think he will never come home.
Better I do not look at all; for in the momentary closure,
The blink's breadth between two truths, two truths can both
    be true.
When I close my eyes I have two sons, and each
Is the other's shadow. Surely he would not play alone,
Or stand alone at the river's edge, or walk away
And leave behind his shadow,
Gray as the sky, as loneliness, as love.

chapter five

Thornstone Slaught

Theo Etchison

He has thrown his cloak over me and I can taste blood and darkness. We're rocking and I hear planks creaking and rope squeaking and a howling wind but I can't smell the salt sea . . . it's another odor, a stench of something putrefying. I want to puke into the cloak but I'm so choked my vomit can't make it up my throat. "Jesus Christ, get me out of here!" I try to scream but all that comes out is a strangled whisper.

I try to tear at the cloak but the fabric is too tightly woven . . . it's almost like polythene . . . and I'm sweating. At last I manage to claw my way through its folds and I poke my head out at the ship.

The deck of the ship is slick with thick red fluid. Blood is soaking into my teeshirt and seeping up my shorts. Where I am is close to the ship's edge and I see the water. It's black and it smells of stale meat. It's flecked with bloody foam. The wind is howling.

The man with the slate-colored eyes stands at the prow, one hand on the head of the gargoyle, looking out over the water. He doesn't seem to notice that I've crawled out of his cloak. The only light on the ship comes from lanterns that dangle on wooden posts and give off a sulphurous smoke as well as light. I can't tell how the ship moves. There are others on board, but they shy away from me. I see someone at the stern, pulling on something— maybe a rudder, maybe a punting pole. Maybe he'll tell me what's going on.

I make my way across to him. He leans into his pole, away from me. "Where am I?" I say.

He laughs. I touch him on the shoulder. He's made of bone. He turns around and his face is a skull.

He says, "The River Styx." And laughs again. "Surely, truthsayer," he says, "you knew that already."

I've heard of that place. It's the river in the underworld, the river that the dead have to cross to get to the kingdom of Hades. It's just a myth, I tell myself, and this is one of those dreams, only it's more real than ever before. I start to shiver. My breath hangs in the air, but the skeleton has no breath at all.

"So," says a new voice, "he has regained consciousness."

I can smell his breath. It's like meat that's been left out overnight. I can't let him scare me, I think. It's a dream. A dream. I'm really back in that old Chinese restaurant with that Mr. Huang dude hovering over me waiting for my brother to finish taking his leak.

"Come to me, my child," he says.

I am suspicious. "You shouldn't have grabbed me out of where I was."

"Why not? You were not happy in your world."

"People are dying. Not just Mom, I mean . . . my whole family's dying, one way or another. They—"

"Need you . . . yes, yes, yes." He looks into my eyes. I feel what he's feeling . . . the hatred, yes, but beneath it a kind of sorrow, a kind of bereavement. "My kingdom needs you . . . needs a truthsayer."

The wind springs up and his cloak spreads out like the wings of a pterodactyl. I can't look away. I'm fascinated by him. There is a kind of longing in the way he looks at me. There's something I have that he can never have. I don't know what it is. "You don't need me," I say. "I don't even know who you are; I don't understand what I'm doing here except dreaming up a storm." Usually when I start dreaming like this there's a surefire way I can force myself to wake up. I start thinking about how badly I have to pee . . . I think over and over, I'm going to wet the bed, I'm going to wet the bed. I used to do that a lot all the way into puberty.

I try that now . . . over and over—*wake up you're going to wet the bed wake up wake up*. . . . His gaze never leaves me. It's not working, I realize. In fact, I've just pissed all over my shorts. Oh God, I'm terrified. I'm so fucking terrified I could—

He reaches out and squeezes my shoulder. "We're going to be friends, Theo Etchison."

"Jesus Chirst! What gives you the right to know my name? Who the fuck are you, anyway?" I scream. My voice dies away in the wind's howling. The skeleton man has let go of his pole and he's chuckling . . . his teeth chattering like one of those windup skulls you buy in joke shops.

"Oh, didn't I introduce myself?" says the man with the slate-colored eyes. "I am Thorn. Prince," he adds, "Thorn. And you are Theo Truthsayer."

I twist free of his grasp. My shoulder aches. "No I'm not," I say.

"Don't fight it, my child. Being a truthsayer isn't easy, but you can't help what you are. None of us can. For example . . ."

He looks out toward the water. I see a woman with seaweed hair, floating on the water. She's naked. Her skin is pale, iridescent like a seal's. The skeleton man beckons to her and helps her on board. She walks toward Thorn, mesmerized.

He grabs her by the shoulder just like he grabbed me. Then he snaps her neck like a dry twig. Blood comes spurting out of her mouth. He kisses her. Slurping up the blood. Hungrily. It's the first time I've seen him show any kind of passion. He covers her neck with kisses and blood oozes from each kiss and he laps it up and I can hear his heavy breathing above the squall.

At last he seems satiated. He casually drops the woman onto the deck. The corpse slides back and forth on the blood-slick wood in an eerie counterpoint to the pitch and yaw of the ship. Casually, Thorn finishes his sentence. "For example, I am a vampire." He kicks the body out the way and it sort of rolls all the way up to the prow. I hear dogs howling. They've come loping out of the hold and they're tearing her apart. No, there's only one dog, and it has three heads. We pass through a cloud of mist. "Want to make something of it?" says Thorn.

"But . . . that girl . . . did she just let you suck her . . ."

"Why shouldn't they? They're my subjects. . . . I own them. Duty to the empire and all that."

"You killed her!" I scream, forgetting to be scared for a moment because he makes me so angry.

Thorn begins pacing the deck. It's very misty and I can only hear the creaking of the planks and glimpse his cloak now and then flapping through gusts of fog.

I'm scared of him but I still think I've got to be dreaming. So even though I'm standing there with piss on my underpants I tell myself to get it together, force myself to wake up. If you concentrate hard enough you can wrench control of your dreams into your own hands and you can turn dark things to light. So I just stand there hollering for him to take me home and telling him to get the fuck out of my dream, and finally he just says, very softly,

"You have nowhere to return to, my friend. Just make the best of it."

"My family."

"They're dead by now. My herald was under orders to leave no traces. . . . They will have been erased from your world completely. . . ."

"Killed!"

"No . . . erased. No one will remember them. . . . They will never have existed . . . excised from the fabric of your universe like a malignant cancer." Water laps against the side of the boat and I feel sick to my stomach from the pitch and yaw and the wind that smells of dead people. "Oh," and he laughs a little, "perhaps I should not have used the cancer simile; how thoughtless of me."

"They're not dead." And as I say it I know it is true. And I look him right in the eye with all the rage I've carried with me on this trip.

For the first time I think he seems uneasy, shaken.

"Why wouldn't they be dead?" he says.

I close my eyes. I see an image of our stationwagon straining to climb a mountain road. I'm looking down at it, like from an airplane, and it's blurry. . . . The road is shimmering in the sun.

"They're alive," I tell him, "so that means you don't know everything."

He looks away. He is angry. I think he's going to strike me, but instead he stalks away. "Truthsayers," he mutters as he strides into the mist that masks the prow. There is something about me he doesn't like, that much is certain, but he needs me. I can feel that.

"Truthsayers," he says again. I am just standing there and now he won't look into my eyes again and I think he is afraid.

No one has ever been afraid of me before, not like that.

I close my eyes. This isn't the real world. The real world is that mountain threaded by the thin gray road and the groaning stationwagon. I'm far from it, so far away . . .

but there's a way there, a way through the stream that
tunnels through the basement of the Chinese restaurant.
The stream is part of a river that twines around everything
and holds the universe together, and when I concentrate I
can almost see the pattern, link by link; I can trace the
convolutions as the streams fork and unfork.

Mom! Dad! Joshua! I'm crying out with my mind. The
car has reached the top of the mountain and now it's
careening downhill. Dad's absentmindedly riding the brakes
and I hear Josh saying my name and suddenly it occurs
to me that Dad doesn't know who he's talking about.

He doesn't know who I am.

Abruptly I snap out of the vision and now all I can see
is the swirling dark water and the ship and the bloodless
corpse and my host, striding back and forth, and the fer-
ryman whose face is a skull. I stare past the gargoyle prow
and see the mist parting. There's land, I think; a dark rock
jutting from the water like a leaping whale. I can't tell
how far it is, but closer to us there are drowned obelisks
thrusting out of the water, their hieroglyphs caked with
algae, half-submerged sphinxes with insectoid eyes. We
are moving toward the whale-rock. Navigating between
the heads of sunken statues. Thorn summons me. I go and
stand beside him. There is a bond between us because
of my nightmares. Sometimes I feel this way about my
father.

"Thornstone Slaught," he says, and points to something that looks like a barnacle on the top of the whale-
rock. I squint. That's when I realize the scale of this thing.
The barnacle is a castle. I can make out eaves, towers,
crenellated walls, a statue of a woman with a flaming torch
and the face of a demon, a Statue of Liberty gone wrong.
The castle is perched on a mountain and the mountain is
wreathed in mist and around me the wind howls ceaselessly.

"Thornstone Slaught?" I say. "What are you talking
about?"

"It's the name of my castle, stupid," says Thorn. "It's

the largest, darkest, most terrifying castle in the universe. It's where you're going to be living.''

"Look, we're not communicating or something," I say, knowing that there's a little part of him that is afraid of me. "You kidnapped me. I intend to go home. You need me for something, but I have a hunch it's nothing that's gonna benefit the human race or any other race. I won't do it.''

"Saving the universe, Theo Etchison, is hardly what I'd consider detrimental to the human race. Or—" he looks away, his eyes gray, distant "—any other race, for that matter.''

"Saving the universe! Easy on the high fantasy, dude.''

He looks out over the water. He's calling out—with his eyes, I think—calling to someone. Soon another of those people with seaweed hair is rising out of the water; a boy this time. Casually Thorn pulls him up onto the deck, draws him into his arms, punctures his jugular with a quick bite, slurps down the spurting blood.

"Yes, boy, there is a universe out there to be saved all right," he says softly. "And soon it will be too late. Unless you help me. But people like you have no conception of these things. You cannot imagine anything outside that tiny circle of family, friends, country, planet. . . . What if I told you you could save your mother?''

"Why should I believe you?" I say. "You told me five minutes ago that you'd ordered her killed. You were pissed when I said she was still alive.''

"I can show you how to reach the source of the river that flows between the worlds," he said, "the place where times and spaces merge . . . where you can catch a moment in your past, like a fish, before it can wriggle downstream toward reality. . . .''

I don't trust him. But I see hope. I think. That's why I decide to stay on for a while, watch, learn. Not that there's anything I can do right now anyways. We're pulling in toward Thornstone Slaught now and the sea is strewn with sunken monuments.

I try to see my parents and my brother in that station-wagon. They're very faint. They're on the 10 now, heading toward Tucson. Dad has already forgotten me. Maybe Mom remembers, but she is too delirious to speak. Even her pain seems faint to me.

Joshua is thumbing through my dream book and Dad is driving with his eyes fixed on nowhere, on nothing.

chapter six

First and Oracle

Phil Etchison

There we were at a cheap motel on First and Oracle, me, a middleaged academic whom some called a poet, my wife, sick in body, my son, sick in the head.

I left them in the room. I sat at the bar beside the pool, watching bloated women with crimson faces bobbing up and down in the Jacuzzi under the blazing sun. I sat nursing an exotic drink, looking past the pool, past the desert palms, to the corner of First and Oracle, trying to sort out the patterns in my disordered existence—for was that not what poets were supposed to do?—and finding only more and more bewilderment.

Mary's illness was chemical, easy to understand in a way. We both knew she was going to die. We always knew that. We are not stupid. We know that laetrile does not work. That was not what the journey was about.

The journey was a symbol. The journey was to bring our fractured family together before it came apart forever.

The journey was to end in death for Mary; we were resigned to that. But perhaps there would be life for Joshua, life free from delusion.

A neatly gift-wrapped ontological metaphor—that was what the journey meant to me. My wife would give up her life and Joshua would finally stop imagining he had a younger brother named Theo.

Theo!

He always wanted a younger brother. I remembered how he cried when Mary had the miscarriage. I stirred my Blue Hawaiian and thought about that awful day, thirteen, fourteen years ago. Strange. I couldn't see it very clearly. It had been snowing. We were living in Indiana then. Or was it high summer in Montana? Mary slipped in the shower. On the stairs. The image just wouldn't come to me. I could see Josh crying though, bitterly, not under-standing at all. In my arms. Our house was a brick house with crawling ivy—no, a ranch-style wooden house—no, colonial—no . . . I drained the glass, asked the bartender for something else. "Something strangely colored," I said. "Green?"

"Grasshopper maybe."

"Sure."

Waiting for the next drink I suddenly knew that the memory was completely gone. It must have been truly traumatic, I thought. Poor Joshua. A few years later and the imaginary companion started to apear . . . then the notebooks in an alien hand . . . little things, nothing that would put the boy in a padded cell, just . . . unnerving things.

What sort of things? I couldn't remember.

I hated myself for being a terrible father.

My brother Theo . . . he'd say. And fret about Theo's bad jokes or Theo not flushing the toilet . . . little things . . . what little things exactly? Memory like a sieve. Stop drinking! Stop!

A truck squealed to a stop at the traffic light at First

and Oracle. The fat women slithered from the hot tub like the Slugs That Ate Texas. A jock dove into the pool. I downed my grasshopper and asked the bartender for something else . . . red maybe. Something red. Campari? No, redder, blood-red.

"Sir, I'm afraid I'm going to have to refuse to serve you. You're getting a little—"

The bartender stopped. A hand on his shoulder. A towering Chinese man stood behind him. I half recognized him. Where from? Memory like a sieve . . .

"Serve him." The man winked at me. He was tall. He was terrifying. His eyes were a window to the next world.

"Are you Death?" I said.

"Hardly, Mr. Etchison," said the Chinaman, "nor do I play chess! I fear you have seen too many Bergman films. My name is Cornelius Huang, and I am proprietor of this place. A *red* drink I believe you asked for, Mr. Etchison."

I mumbled something.

He poured a shot of vodka into a tall glass. Then he took a sharp instrument out of his shirt pocket—a sort of cross between a hypodermic and an astrolabe—and he jabbed himself in the finger with it. Casually, he let three drops of blood fall into the vodka. With the first drop the drink turned pink. With the second it became a milky maroon. With the third, the liquid was crimson and ringed with froth. He handed me the glass. I shrank. "Drink, drink," he said, nodding encouragement. "It is a fine drink for the composing of great poetry . . . for it dissolves boundary between reality and illusion."

I took the glass. I drained it in one gulp.

Theo . . .

Did Joshua realize the symbolism of that name? *ho theós* . . . God? Did he know that the illusion of a younger brother who always spoke the truth—no matter how great the pain, no matter what the cost—was a mad messianic metaphor right out of some nineteenth century novel?

Joshua wasn't just waiting for Godot . . . he was waiting
for God . . . and I had no God to give him, I with my
hopelessly humanist sensibilities and my incurable distrust
of higher authority.

I set the glass down on the counter. A dusty wind blew
across the pool and burned my eyes with chlorine and grit.
"A fine drink, Mr. Huang," I said. But he was gone, and
the bartender looked at me blankly, as though Cornelius
Huang had never been there.

I found Joshua in the hotel suite, poring through that
book of dreams. Mary was in the next room asleep and
drugged to the gills.

He looked up. The television was blaring. It was one
of those *Friday the Thirteenth* movies. "Dad, you've been
drinking," he said. And turned his attention back to the
book.

I said, "Son, I want to play a new game."

He said, "I don't know what to do! You're slipping
away from me, the whole world is sliding away from the
truth, what I know is the truth. . . ."

"Son, let's pretend—"

"He's gone. Sucked into a toilet bowl by an ocean
tempest. And that Chinese dude made you forget everything. Somehow."

"What Chinese—"

"Mr. Huang."

"You've never even met Mr. Huang. He's the manager
of the motel or something. I only just saw him today for
the first time—"

"Then how come I know his name?"

"Son—"

"I know what you're going to say. Schizophrenics are
devilishly smart. They'll do all sorts of secret research to
feed their delusions. You'll tell me I've been snooping
around looking for facts to trip you up, Dad . . . but it's
you who's losing his mind . . . look how drunk you are.

Jesus fucking Christ." He looked at me with a kind of
terrible pity and I was afraid for a moment, afraid that he
was right, afraid that *I* was the one who had lost touch
with reality. . . .

I had to be strong. Behind that mask of certitude was
confusion and illusion. I had to be his anchor, to be strong
for him. "Let's pretend it's all true, son . . . let's pretend.
For the sake of pretending." There was a part of me that
didn't want to play this game. For a moment I thought of
the alcohol dyed crimson with the Chinaman's blood. "I'll
try to believe I have another son who vanished mysteri-
ously when we were wandering in the desert. I'll try to
believe that black is white, son," I said, "because I love
you."

Behind us, the hockey-masked killer sliced another
woman to ribbons. The music welled up, distorted into
bursts of static.

Joshua wept.

"We'll start with the dream book," he said. "And we'll
go to the police. And track down the Chinese restaurant
with the river in the cave." I didn't know what he was
talking about but I played along. If I humored him, perhaps he would let slip some clue, some key that I could
use to set him free. Or I could learn what I had done
wrong . . . some scene of primal child abuse we might
have both repressed. . . .

"There's not much time," Joshua said. "Mom's due at
the clinic . . . when? next week?"

"We'll take all the time you need," I said, feeling my
whole past oozing through my fingers. Jesus, I wanted
another drink.

I wanted the Chinaman's blood.

chapter seven

King Lear

Theo Etchison

The whale-rock is deceptively close. It takes a good
part of another day to reach it. I can't tell how far anything
is, I don't know what size it's supposed to be, and the
horizon is too close . . . that's how I know we're not on
Earth anymore.

I sleep and dream a dream within a dream.

*It's spring break I guess. We drive down to Virginia
Beach. Everyone went to the putt-putt golf course and I'm
standing alone at the balcony of our room in the Sheraton
listening to the seagulls. It's unseasonably hot. I taste the
salt air and the gulls clamor and drive me crazy like a
heavy metal concert I can hear the seawaves pounding
and then* I'm not dreaming anymore. The seagulls are
warcries. Smoke in my nostrils.

But I *am* dreaming. . . . I remember the dream . . .
war . . . dust of a burning planet . . .

The ship collides with the beach. I look up. The whale

mountain fills the whole sky haloed with soft sunless light. The craft moves in sharp spasms and I realize that we're going onto the beach with some kind of pseudopods. The next spasm hurls me against the side and I see the battle raging at the foot of the mountain. I can make out figures in the blood-tinged sand-dust thrown up by their chariot wheels.

Elephant men in punk helmets. Glistening lizards with swords that glitter with laser light. Elves with pointy ears. Amazons mounted on robot horses. There's a mound of corpses sliding into the sea and a flock of carnivorous insects feeding. There's a smell of burning blood. The smoke makes me cough. It's a little bit like incense.

"Get a move on, truthsayer." It's Thorn, pulling me up by my teeshirt. "We're home now."

He throws his cloak around me and we kind of leap into the air. I'm holding on for dear life as we like hover a moment and then take off and soar over the battle toward the mountain.

"Afraid of heights?" Thorn whispers.

I open my eyes. We're descending. In the midst of the battle there is an old man sitting on a palanquin on the shoulders of about fifty dudes with reptile faces. I know the old man from one of my dreams. He is King Lear. He has long white hair and a face crosshatched with wrinkles and ice-blue eyes. He surveys the carnage. There is no feeling in his eyes. He is a madman. But we're alike. We are both lost. Adrift among the dimensions. Somehow I know we're in the same position, me and him.

He doesn't see us yet. The beach is on fire.

The old man clasps a scepter in his bosom. He stares wildly about, mutters to himself, and the reptile litter bearers stand, impassive, indifferent to the fire that sweeps along the sand and the cries of dying creatures.

Rolling toward us come gargantuan war machines, catapults that spew fire mounted on turrets. I try to look away, I bury my face in Thorn's cloak and choke on the smell

of blood and brimstone. And suddenly we've landed. My
feet hit something solid. Pain shoots through my ankle. I
yelp. Rudely I am thrown aside. We're on the palanquin.
I've been kicked onto the floor and my arm is dangling
between two litter-poles and I feel cold lizard breath on
my fingers.

I pull myself up. I'm crouching now, staying out of
their line of sight. My eye is level with the hem of the
king's garment. It's the kind of thing a Roman emperor
wears in old spectacles, but there seem to be people woven
into the cloth, shadowy people that you can only see out
of the corner of your eye, when you try to look at them
they kind of get siphoned into the folds of the robe . . .
yeah, the cloth is kind of woven out of humans souls I
guess. It flutters and flaps and throws grit in my face.

"Father," Thorn says softly.

"Call them off," says the king. "Don't they recognize
me? Don't they know who I am? Don't they realize I'm
the master around here?"

Thorn laughs. Very softly. When I look in his face I
see a little fear—not the fear of something he cannot
understand, as he felt with me, but the thrill that goes
through you when you are about to defy your parents.

"Call the buggers off, Thorn," says the old king.

Thorn looks around. A decapitated head lands at his
feet. He kicks it off the palanquin. There's a glint of
triumph in his eye maybe. "Herald," he says. He's never
raised his voice above a whisper, but I can always hear
him above the roar of the sea and the screams of dying
creatures.

Mr. Huang is standing beside him suddenly, Mr. Huang
in a business suit, dusting himself off with a handkerchief.

"Where were you?" says Thorn. "I need you to sound
a cease-action."

"I was pouring a man a drink," Mr. Huang says. "It's
what you ordered me to do, sire. Surely you don't expect
me to be in two places at once." He plucks the conch-

trumpet out of the churning air. He blows an eerie blast that echoes and reechoes against the mountain that fills the sky.

Suddenly the conflict ceases. The dust settles. A war-tower tumbles onto the sand and crushes some of the soldiers. The soldiers assemble in small groups, the lizard warriors gathering behind the palanquin of the old king.

The king stands up. He is every bit as tall as Thorn, though his white beard roils about his face like a cloud-bank. I'm a little bolder now and I sit up.

"Father," says Thorn, "King Strang."

King Strang's face is like the mountain itself, furrowed and craggy. There is a wound on his forehead, and something wriggles in and out of it . . . a maggot perhaps. I stare at him. He exudes nobility even though his forehead festers.

"Welcome to my castle, Father," says Thorn, but there's a hint of menace in what he says.

"Welcome? You call this a welcome?" Strang says. His voice is hoarse, almost inaudible. "A couple of hundred soldiers, war-towers, big guns?"

"Dark times, Father. You'd have done the same thing. A man can't be too careful."

"But I'm your king!"

"That's where you're wrong."

I'm piecing the story together in my mind from scraps of dreams. The king is the old man who was trying to give away his kingdom to his three children . . . that was in the dream. There were three children: a daughter, a son, and one I wasn't sure of. The son was Thorn and the daughter was Katastrofa Darkling.

"You may recall, Father, that you gave up the throne."

"On condition," says King Strang, his voice trembling, "that I retain the title and the style of king—"

"Poor fool; you should have listened to my brother, Ash."

"I have disinherited him. As you know." So Ash was

the third child—the one who wouldn't flatter. That was kind of like in the play we saw at Wolf Trap.

"Poor Father. Ash was the only one who ever gave you good advice."

I sat all the way up now.

"I bid you welcome, Father," Thorn says, and smiles a fake smile. Then he turns toward the mountain and claps his hands. "Open the damn gate, herald," he says. I hear three blasts on the conch.

Three times and three times again and the wall of rock like *dissolves* somehow. I gasp. But why should it surprise me? Nothing in this place is what it seems. The rock has become a kind of veil or force-field shot through with veins of colored light. Behind it I see level upon level of Thornstone Slaught . . . staircases that spiral up forever like the model DNA molecule in Mrs. Carter's biology lab. . . . It's like you took about fifty shopping malls and smashed them all together. As I look up and up the decor gets more and more Mediaeval-looking. I get the feeling that there was once this old castle on top and like they kept burrowing down into the mountain and here at the base it's more high-tech.

I feel movement; the litterbearers hoisting the palanquin high over their shoulders . . . turning.

"South wing all right for you, Father?" says Thorn. His voice is as sweet as a sugar-coated cyanide pill.

"Don't make jokes, son," says the old man. "I've already lost a dozen guards because of your security system. And I can't replace them, you know . . . not since the power failure at the clone plant." He's just mumbling really; I'm the only one who hears him. Suddenly he reminds me of my father for a moment. I start crying. I don't know why.

"South wing it is."

"I am still King Strang! You must house me in the Imperial Suite, as is my right!"

"You don't need all those rooms, Father . . . what are

you going to do, call a transdimensional summit meeting? Who'd come?"

I see the rage flare up in King Strang's eyes. He raises that scepter of his, the scepter I have seen in my dreams that can suck a man's soul right out of his body. He doesn't strike his son . . . he's looking around for someone to lash out at. That's when he notices me for the first time. I'm wiping my eyes with a fold of my teeshirt. I must look pretty fucking pathetic. His anger dims a little.

"Imperial Suite," he murmurs.

"Papa," Thorn says, shrugging, "this isn't a hotel, you know. And your credit cards have all been canceled." He winks at me. I don't think they use credit cards here—the joke must have been for my benefit. It occurs to me that Thorn is actually showing off in front of me, that he actually has this need to impress me. "You're just a useless old man, Father . . . might as well get used to it."

"Useless . . . old . . ."

I look around. The lizard warriors have all stiffened. They stand ready to spring, their javelins poised. The light from the burning beach makes the shadows dance on their faces. I see now that they all look exactly alike. . . . They've been manufactured somehow. The clone plant. That must be what Strang meant.

A moment of tension. I don't know if they are going to attack.

"Call off your clockwork dinosaurs, Father," Thorn says.

"My Imperial Guard . . . my most faithful retainers—"

"You never could get much loyalty, Father," says Thorn, "unless it was from some preprogrammed device."

Strang lifts up his scepter . . . makes as though to strike his son.

"Treason," Thorn whispers.

And clicks his fingers.

All at once the battle starts up again! Fireballs whiz

through the sky! Chariots charge! The lizard warriors are flinging their spears, which turn into shafts of laser light that set the war-turrets aflame. The litterbearers are still standing, ready to carry their master into the castle. The battle rages around us.

"You can't do this to him, Thorn," I say very softly. I don't know why.

He looks at me. Picks me up by the scruff of my tee-shirt. Stares into my eyes. "What are you talking about?" he screams.

I realize suddenly that what I've just said is part of my knack . . . my truthsaying gift . . . if you can call it a gift. "You can't treat your father this way," I say, "or things'll go bad for you, Thorn."

"What are you speaking up for him for, weasel?" says Thorn. He slaps my face. I taste blood. "Don't you know how many people he's killed, how many worlds he's destroyed? Look at him, boy . . . he's the enemy . . . he's the corrupt heart of everything . . . the one we're going to have to save the universe from. He's mad, boy, and when he's mad the cosmos goes insane and it's up to us to clean it up."

"He's mad because you drove him mad," I say.

He slaps me again, I go sprawling, my head smashes into the old king's knee . . . I feel his whole body give a little, like there's nothing inside. He feels like my mother, desiccated, empty.

Then I feel the old man's hand on my head.

I look up. I can't understand what I see in his face. It is not tenderness. I am too far beneath him for him to feel anything like that. "Who is this child," he says, "who speaks the truth however great the pain?"

I turn. Father and son glare at each other with the utmost hatred in their eyes.

"I have my own truthsayer now," Thorn says.

The king says to me, "I suppose you know why I can't set foot in Thornstone Slaught again."

"Your honor's at stake," I say.

"Goodbye, truthsayer," he says, and runs his bony fingers through my hair and makes me think of Dad for a moment. And I start crying again without knowing why.

chapter eight

The Uncertainty Principle

Joshua Etchison

A few hours after Dad's about-face, my mother's condition got really bad and we had to check her into the university hospital. There was a chance we weren't even going to make it to the laetrile clinic after all. But we'd always known that.

I didn't want her out of my sight. Maybe they'd come and take her away too and then Dad would forget she ever existed too. He was always drunk now and when he slipped away to drink he would come back remembering even less of our family's past. I struggled with the orderly because I wanted them to put a cot in her bedroom so I can watch over her all the time, but they gave me an injection and I woke up in the motel room in time to see my Dad feverishly throwing a few clothes into an overnight bag.

"Come on, son," he said. "We're going to get to the bottom of this."

"Humoring me again, Dad?" I said.

He looked around crazily, like a madman in a B horror movie. Then he went over to his big suitcase and pulled out a few books.

I recognized his latest poetry book, *The Embrasure of Parched Lips*. I've got you! I thought, and I sprang off the couch and wrested it from his hand.

"What are you—"

I turned it to the dedication page. Triumphantly waved it in Dad's face. "Wake up, Dad! Who'd you dedicate this book to? Don't you remember?"

He took it from me. A puzzled look crossed his face. "Dedication page's been ripped out," he said. "Did you do it?" And he showed it to me. It was gone.

He slammed the book shut. A Polaroid snapshot flew out of it and landed on the floor. "Look, Dad—it's us!"

We both looked at it as it lay on a heap of underwear above the tawdry polka-dotted shag. Me and Mom and Dad and Theo. Smiling stupidly. Uncle Tim had taken that picture.

We knelt down on either side of the dirty clothes. My father smiled. "Who's your friend?" he said. He really didn't know.

"Friend, Dad? You know I wouldn't hang out with any freshmen. . . ."

He took the picture. We peered at it. Slowly, like a mirage, Theo's image faded from the photograph. Dad laughed. He was uncomfortable. "There isn't another kid in the photo . . . trick of the light or something I guess," he mumbled.

God, I hated Theo. For making my Dad think I'm insane . . . for going away and leaving me to deal with all this bullshit . . . someone, some force was erasing all traces of Theo from the world, but it was taking time. Like with the snapshot. Reality was probably pretty resistant to change. . . . Whatever was "fixing" the world was changing as little as possible, and only at the moment when change was needed. If Dad and I had never looked at the Polaroid, Theo's face would always have been on it. That's how it worked. I once read an article in *Discover* magazine that said the whole universe works this way . . . that the act of observing the cosmos changes it.

Sometimes it wasn't quick enough.

Sometimes you could catch it just before it changed.

They called this the uncertainty principle.

Thoughts raced. If I could figure out the sort of things that would have to be changed and *catch* them a split second before they changed and arrange for Dad to see them too . . . but I knew that if I even *thought* about them too much they would start to want to change. . . . The reason for the Polaroid was that no one had been thinking about it, it had just slipped out of the book—had to figure out a way of focusing my thoughts on something else, on *tricking* whatever this really-changing phenomenon was. . . .

"Hurry up, son. Stop daydreaming." He'd always talked to Theo in that tone.

My Dad stood at the door with two overnight bags full of clothes. "We're going to do some investigating . . . you and me . . . get to the bottom of this. Missing persons bureau—we'll go back to that Chinese restaurant you keep talking about . . . anywhere you want." I got up. Got a whiff of his breath. He'd already been drinking, and lips were stained red as though with pomegranate juice . . . or blood. "Let's get us some cholesterol burgers before we go down to the police station."

"Dad, you know I only eat health food now."

"Bullshit, kiddo! You love Burger King more than life itself."

What other things did my father no longer know?

That clinched it. There were bugs in this alternate universe business. Leaks. They were trying to rub out Theo from the world, but sometimes they would miss and rub out something else.

For instance, how come *I* hadn't forgotten anything? Or had I?

Phil Etchinson

I drove my mad son down to the police station. There was a man named Milt Stone, a tall man of Indian descent. He knew who I was; apparently there'd been an article in the *Star* that mentioned my arrival in town. Apparently a Mr. Huang, proprietor of our motel, had told them that Phil Etchison, the world famous poet, was passing through, and . . .

"Matter of fact, Mr. Etchison," said Detective Stone, waving us to a sofa piled high with papers in his over-airconditioned cubbyhole of an office, "the wife, she's really looking forward to going to your autograph party. Reads a lot, you know. She likes Stephen King and Rod McKuen." I suppressed my impulse to throw up and smiled at him, wondering what on earth he meant by my autograph party . . . I didn't remember agreeing to one.

"Do you have . . . any alcohol?" I asked him. My son turned away from me.

"Don't you go blaming your father, now," Stone said to Joshua, not unkindly. "He's going through a lot." He rummaged in the little refrigerator behind his desk and pulled out a battered can of generic beer. "You say your boy run off?"

I looked at Joshua. Took a swig of the beer. It was still warm and burned my throat but it felt good. "Joshua will tell you about it," I said. "He's the one who . . . remembers it best."

"Well, I can surely understand how you wouldn't want to talk about it, sir," said Stone. "The wife told me how much you loved that boy. . . . She showed me what you wrote about it on that there dedication page."

Joshua tensed. What had he been trying to show me back there in the room? The dedication page and then the photograph that for a split second seemed to show an image of another boy . . . what did all that mean?

I'd dedicated *The Embrasure of Parched Lips* to Mary, hadn't I? And there was a little poem about . . . about her miscarriage, about Joshua's rage . . .

I didn't want to tell him he was mistaken, didn't want to embarrass Joshua, so I only said, "Joshua will tell you about it."

"We have a computer, Mr. Etchison, that links up all the missing person reports with all the information we can lay our hands on. But I imagine your boy'll turn up. Was there any . . . trouble between you?"

Joshua said, "He was kidnaped. By a man named Huang. The man who owns the Chinese restaurant on Route 10."

Stone looked up sharply. "The big restaurant with the façade that makes it look like the set of *The Last Emperor*?" he said.

A thin smile on Joshua's lips. "That's the one."

"Why, son, that restaurant's just an idea in the mind of a mad old Chinaman that came breezing through Arizona a hundred years ago. Go down to the county museum, there's an artist's impression of what it would have been like. Impressive as shit. But there ain't no restaurant like that on Route 10. Hell, there ain't no Route 10 no more; they turned that into an interstate."

Joshua was trembling. He got up and asked for the bathroom. I took the opportunity to tell Detective Stone about his problem. "Just humor him," I said. "Please."

"Strange," he said, "I don't see as how you folks could have known about the old Chinese restaurant, not unless you were experts on our local history. . . ."

I took another swig of my beer. Stale tobacco smoke lingered in the air. A spider crawled up the frame of a frayed college diploma.

"Detective Stone—"

"Call me Milt. Please."

"Milt, Joshua will go to any lengths in order to suck us into his private reality."

"Seems like a normal enough kid."

"He scares me."

And then Joshua stood in the doorway, wiping his hands on his hair.

"Want to see the computer now, kid?" said Milt. Josh nodded. "They always brighten up when I mention that computer. If you gentlemen would care to come with me . . ." He got up, straightened his shirt against his massive body, and motioned me toward the doorway.

"I'll handle the case now, Milt, if you don't mind." A woman's voice. Very low . . . with the velvet smoothness of a viola. Joshua paled, moved toward me. It was then that I saw her framed in the sodium yellow of the light from the hall beyond: a delicate-featured woman with long red hair. Even the unflattering police uniform she wore became her somehow. There was something reptilian about her face.

Milt Stone did a sort of double take. When he answered it was in a different voice; he sounded almost hypnotized.

"Of course," he said. Blinked a couple of times. Then turned to me and said, "Forgot to introduce you. Superintendent Darkling . . . Kathy Darkling."

"Katastrofa," said Joshua softly.

The woman laughed, a silvery laugh with a mocking edge. "It's an honor," she said, "to meet the celebrated poet." And inclined her head toward me, though she managed to make it seem condescending. "Many of my . . . people have enjoyed your verses, Mr. Etchison."

"I know you," said Joshua.

The woman seemed to notice him for the first time. Her demeanor darkened. "The young are such dreamers," she murmured. That's what I thought I heard her say.

"We'll find your brother for you," said Kathy Darkling. "I promise." Joshua's face was soaked with sweat, even though the airconditioning was on full blast. She took him by the hand. Like the detective, my son seemed mesmerized. "Our computers know *everything*."

We followed her down the hall. She didn't so much walk as glide. We lagged by the water cooler; she turned to look back at us. Her eyes had a yellowish cast. Somehow she didn't seem entirely human.

I caught up with her. I wanted to whisper a word or two to her about Joshua's madness. She merely said, "Reality is a shifty thing, Mr. Etchison. I've had a lot of experience with disturbed teenagers; let me talk to him for a while."

"Be my guest."

"Alone, if you don't mind."

She opened the door marked with her name, ushered my trembling son inside, stepped in after him. It slammed in my face.

"Women detectives," said Milt, shaking his head. "She's new; just got assigned here yesterday; women like that, they always gotta prove they're ten times more hardassed than us men."

chapter nine

Inside the Mountain

Theo Etchison

I blink and we're inside the mountain.

Thorn and I and the three-headed dog from the boat and Mr. Huang. Walking across a hall that just went on and on, granite columns stretching up out of sight, intertwining, statues, flashing lights; people hurrying, eyes downcast when they catch sight of us, creatures scurrying by, robots, little globes that flit through the air squealing and squeaking to one another, weaving in and out of the throngs of people. We're in the space I glimpsed before that I said looked like a fifty shopping mall pileup. It also looks like a mishmash of a dozen science fiction movies, except it's a whole lot more lived-in. The robots look battered, the people look dowdy, the columns are peeling, half the flashing lights are out of sync. There are a lot of sphinxes like the ones half-submerged in the bay. Little sphinxes lining the walls, a huge one poking up out of the floor that has about a dozen cleaning ladies swabbing at one of its paws with mops.

"Not quite what you expected, is it, Theo Truthsayer," Thorn says. He continues striding ahead. It's hard to keep up with him.

"Well . . . it was high fantasy when you abducted me, and now it's kind of a hokey space epic," I say. "Or the cover of one of those old pulp magazines."

"Or like the dreams of a lonely, overimaginative teen-age boy," Thorn says, reviving, for a moment, my flagging hope that this is all some wild nightmare that just won't end.

"You're right," I say. "Look—a bit of *Star Wars* here, a touch of *Blade Runner,* even a few decorations lifted out of *Land of the Pharaohs.* Sure I'm dreaming."

"You do not like my taste?"

"I don't like *you.*"

"And I thought it would make you feel more at home to be surrounded by images from your personal mythos," says Thorn.

"Don't do me any favors."

"Very well then." He shakes his head and suddenly it's all gone . . . all of it . . . and instead we're inside the ultimate vampire castle. Cobwebs stretching up as far as I can see. Sweeping staircases coated with dust. Mist roiling about our knees. There are people here too . . . gibbering corpses . . . misshapen mutants shambling through the mist.

"It's all mutable, you see," Thorn says, gesticulating grandly. "All the elements, all the beings we perceive . . . the fabric of the universe is the fabric of dreams . . . starstuff is the stuff of fantasy. . . ."

Is he trying to tell me that I'm dreaming? Maybe I'll wake up soon, but I'm not going to hold my breath waiting anymore.

"But you're different. You have no imagination, Theo Truthsayer."

We have reached a stairway that just goes up and up and up, but I know it's not to heaven. The air we breathe is foul and the steps are piled high with human skulls. Thorn kicks them out of the way and I hear them clatter, clatter, clatter down the steps, the echoes blending with distant cries of pain.

"No imagination?" I say. "No one's ever accused me of that before."

"I daresay they've been telling you you've too much of it, my boy. But that's not it at all. . . . You're a truth-sayer. Every person, every object, every event in the universe spins a cocoon of fantasy around itself, but you, you see the inner truth of things. You hear the inner music. That is your gift, your curse. You have no aura. You are transparent. You are—if I may use so corny an expression—pure of heart. That's why I've hunted you out . . . laid traps for one such as you in a dozen worlds . . . sent the one you call Mr. Huang to fetch you to me. . . ."

He takes the steps two, three at a time. It's hard to keep up. I don't know how many steps it's been . . . a hundred, five hundred. But it doesn't seem to tire him. He talks the whole time, obsessively, but I'm hardly listening because the last couple of hundred steps are so exhausting. The familiar is bounding beside us with the drool dripping from his three mouths.

"I, of course, I . . . being a ruler . . . am not pure of heart. But you will already have understood that. Power corrupts, you know. Yes."

In some inchoate way, I sense he is actually trying to apologize to me for slapping me around in front of his father. It was a matter of face, I suppose, having a truth-sayer to kick around. Or more than face.

"I didn't appreciate being treated that way in front of him," I say, "and I didn't appreciate the way you treated *him*, either." I keep thinking about my own family and how fractured it's become, and I wonder whether I would ever treat my Dad that way even though I know he doesn't understand anything about me.

"Keep your eyes and ears open, boy, but don't try to change the way things are. You're needed here, I tell you." The staircase turns, narrows, I see a vague light above.

"You wouldn't need me if you were so damned important."

"I'll have you thrown in irons."

"Big deal." Bondage is big with these people, I decide.

He's about to hit me again but thinks better of it maybe. He continues: "Things were good once, you see. My father ruled wisely. The three of us—Ash, Katastrofa, and I—we lived in a kind of paradise, isolated from everything ugly. The River flowed near my father's castle and through the River came travelers from distant worlds and my father too became a traveler. . . . He roamed the many universes with an old man who always knew the true paths from the false. . . . He reached the River's end, the ocean of oblivion. . . . He came back with the scepter that feeds on souls . . . he grew dark in his heart."

"You think you're not, Thorn?" I say.

"I'm a lesser evil!" he says. There is a despair in him, the same despair I have seen in the face of his father. "It's all a consequence of my father's act, don't you see? It's a disease that's infected us all . . . turned me against my family. . . . It's a cancer eating away at the entire cosmos. . . ."

"Sounds kind of melodramatic," I say. I don't want to believe him. But it's so like what's been happening to my own family. I can't help feeling something for him.

"So will you help me, Theo Truthsayer? And perhaps, if you are really good at what you do—"

"I'm not sure what it is I do yet!"

"—we can bring back your mother. That's right, little one. A little wrinkle in the transdimensional probability nexus . . . we can iron that sucker right out."

*   *   *

I don't know how much longer we climb those stairs.
I think there must be some kind of shortcut—they're just
doing it this way so they can impress the shit out of me—
it's working.

At last we reach Thorn's throneroom. It isn't so much
a room as a desolate heath, with the wind howling and
with twisted rocks jutting from the purple-gray wild grass.
There is a kind of sky overhead although I know we are
still somewhere within the castle. Alien moons shine down
from behind shifting wisps of mist.

A dining table appears. We have lunch. While Thorn
drains blood from the veins of a beautiful woman who
lies, naked, on the table in front of him, servants in black
serve me, on a gold platter, something that looks like a
Big Mac, fries and a chocolate shake. But it all tastes like
blood. I think they've just disguised it to look like things
I'm familiar with. Make me feel at home. As if I could.
But when I really concentrate I can feel the seething life
force in the chocolate shake and I don't want to drink it.

"You're not hungry?" Thorn asks me.

"I can't help thinking that if I eat the food around here
I'll be forced to stay here forever."

"Ah, how very mythic," Thorn says, laughing. Then,
winking, he adds, "Go on, eat, it's harmless. I won't give
you food that'll blind your mind. You're too important for
that."

I believe him. I eat the food hungrily. It seems that I
haven't eaten in a very long time.

"In any case, boy," Thorn says, "I should think you'd
best get some rest now. We'll start in the morning."

"Start what?" I say.

"As if you didn't know!" Thorn says. "Why, the des-
tinies of a million worlds rest on your slender shoulders,
and you sit around playing this game of childish naïveté
as though—"

I try to blot him out. I think about my parents and my

brother. They are fading . . . or are they? I see my brother
sitting in a little room. Talking to a woman. A snake-
woman! I've seen her in my dreams. Her name is Katastrofa Darkling.

Later they take me to my room. It's like the throneroom, an endless field of tall gray grass, shrouded in slow
mist. The sky is the color of Thorn's eyes and illumined
with the same dull sourceless light. Here and there are
weathered gravestones. In the middle of it all there's a
bed, a desk, a color TV, all the stuff from my room back
home in Alexandria. There's my favorite comforter on the
bed, the almost threadbare one that has a bunch of Ewoks
on it. The mist curls in and out. I sit down on the bed
and point the remote at the TV, but all the channels are
showing *The Twilight Zone*.

They've left me alone now. I know everything in the
room's an illusion. When I really concentrate I get a sense
of its real size. And all those objects I'm familiar with are
fake too. The TV turns out to be hollow. When I lie back
on the bed it kind of stretches out and envelops me and
suddenly I'm floating in utter soundless darkness. When I
sit up again it's the old bed shaped like a racing car and
kind of too short for me.

I look in the drawers in the desk and sure enough the
desk is just a façade and inside it are alien objects . . .
something that looks like a cross between a sea-urchin and
a stethoscope, a couple of spiny purple fruits, a kind of a
laptop computer, a . . . fountain pen. I take the pen and
touch it to the TV screen and *The Twilight Zone* disappears and instead there's like this map . . . in three
dimensions . . . a mass of threads of light, like a Tesla
coil, hanging in the air. I peer at the lightstrands. Forking
and unforking . . . I see that it's all one thread of light,
weaving, winding, spiraling, doubling back on itself. And
I get the feeling that the map is why I'm here . . . that
somehow I'm the only one who can read it.

I stare into the map for a long time. The map rotates; I see it from many angles. As I follow the twisting strands I realize that the map is in more than three dimensions. I seize upon one strand and trace it with my finger and I feel my whole hand being sucked into somewhere else, fading out of the real world. . . . It must be the river they're always talking about, I think. The river that is the path between all the different realities.

My concentration breaks; the map shrinks and drops into my palm . . . a marble.

Rod Serling reappears on the TV screen. I stick the marble in the pocket of my shorts. Then I start to get ready for bed. I'm filthy and there's nowhere to take a shower until . . .

I look up. There's a door standing in the middle of the field. It's like the door to the bathroom at the top of the stairs at my house. I get up and step inside. It's exactly like back home. A couple of fresh towels, my Alvin and the Chipmunks electric toothbrush with its batteries dead, my sci-fi trivia toilet paper and a poster on the wall of Traci Lords in *Not of this Earth* with a big brown mustache that my friend Tommy drew in anger the day we all piled in the car to leave for Mexico.

I draw the blinds and I can see all the way down Quantico to the corner with the condos the next block down and the snow melting and Tommy waving at me from across the street.

I take off my clothes and wash them in the sink. I put the marble next to my toothbrush. The clothes are matted with blood and green scum. It takes a long time to get it all off. I hang them on the towel rack, take a shower . . . as I'm drying myself I take another look through the window. . . . It's summer now and Tommy is older, taller, and he has another friend, a girl.

I close the blinds.

I clutch the marble and step through the door into the heather and the howling wind and the gray light filtering

through shifting mist. I'm naked but I can't feel the wind.
I get into bed and I fall asleep, gazing into the marble
with its microscopic filaments of light, staring at worlds
within worlds.

In the real world I always dreamt of this place, but here
I dream of the place I left behind:

*Joshua is sitting in a small room across from Katastrofa
Darkling. She wears a policewoman's uniform. Above
their heads, a naked bulb swings. Behind her face is a
poster for a death rock band. She holds a marble between
her thumb and forefinger and forces Joshua to look deep
into it. I can't tell what he's thinking.*

*"Stare into it! Stare into it! Tell me what you see! And
it better be right, or you'll never see him again. . . ."*

*I see my brother through the eyes of an insect. His face
repeated endlessly in the facets of my compound eyes. I
hear the snake-woman laughing. I see sweat on my brother's forehead and I'm beginning to feel what he feels . . .
not the passing lust he felt for pudgy Serena, but the real
thing . . . love maybe . . . an emotion so powerful he
doesn't have room for Mom and Dad . . . or me.*

*My insect-consciousness flits past them, shoots across
the room to the door and the keyhole through which I see
my father pacing back and forth, back and forth. . . .
He's reading and rereading my dream book, trying to
puzzle it out.*

A detective is with him. They are waiting.

*I turn around to see the fire glittering in the woman's
eyes. She is too beautiful to be human.*

*"Come on," she says. "You are his closest relation.
Surely you must have a bit of the ability."*

"What ability?"

"You know."

"I don't know."

*"Fool . . . when he drifts away from you, when it seems
to you that he's gazing into some fantasy universe, where*

*do you think your brother is? Hasn't it occurred to you
that you might have the power to follow him, to see what
he sees . . . if only a shadow of what he sees? Your
brother is already taken, and I must settle for what I can
get . . . though half-truths can be more dangerous than
lies.''*

My brother looks blankly at her.

''What's in the marble?'' she says.

*My brother shakes his head. Then, ''The River,'' he
says softly, with a kind of vague recognition.*

*''What is the meaning of the River?'' she says. And
touches his hand.*

*''The meaning of the River is . . . fuck fuck fuck oh
fuck oh fuck,'' he says and he can't control himself and
I know this is what he's like when I peer into his room in
the middle of the night and he has a big boner in his sleep
and comes all over the sheets and wakes up, gets all
embarrassed about it, and won't look me in the eye.*

*She holds his hand tight now, tight, and forces him to
look into her eyes. . . .*

Now we're in the throneroom again . . . me and Thorn
and the herald and some of Thorn's followers, with the
dog clawing at dirt at the foot of the throne. I'm wearing
these death rock kind of clothes they left out for me with
a silver skull in my ear and a black cape.

"I see you've found the map of the River," says Thorn.

I hold up the marble.

"Good," he says. "Let's see if you can read it!"

All at once I see that the throne is at the edge of a
brook that winds across his field of vision. I wonder why
I haven't seen it before. The sound of trickling gets louder.

"Feel the River . . . feel it run from the beginning to
the end of spacetime . . ." Thorn says, and already I can
hear the rushing of the waters, a timeless tuneless music.
With my mind I reach into the marble and grab hold of the

fragment of light that is the point we're standing at . . .
I step forward . : . I feel the water lapping at my feet.

"We're in your hands," Thorn says. I can tell he's not
happy with this arrangement.

"Where are we going?" I ask him. But already I know,
already I am plunging into the water, already it's up to
my waist and I still go on, following the thread, like
Theseus in the labyrinth, finding the safe stones to stand
on as the current begins to surge and—

We're hurled into the vortex now. . . . We're standing
in a bubble of silence as the water churns around us . . .
storms of colored light burst over us . . . mists whirl
madly . . . translucent creatures with gargoyle faces fly at
us . . . on either shore time races while in our pocket
universe time stands still. Vistas of alien worlds blur into
one another.

Slowly I see that we're on board a vessel, all glass and
metal, that I am standing by the prow with the marble in
my hand . . . that I'm thinking the ship into moving. . . .
I'm stilling the water. . . . I'm thinking easy now, easy,
as though I'm petting a frightened animal, and I'm calming the turbulence.

The water becomes gentle. We are borne by the downstream current. The raging light does not touch us. I know
it is illusory . . . that each person sees something different . . . that what I see reflects my own confusion.

"Having a good time, boy? Navigating becomes you."
Thorn looks at the vortex. I think that the river he sees is
a river of blood. He smiles grimly.

"You're just testing me," I say. "This is a well-
mapped part of the River. . . . You come this way all the
time. You didn't bring me here for this."

"Little by little, Theo Truthsayer," he says. "There are
places where my father has destroyed the gateways. The
worlds we rule are linked together by a thread. Easily
snapped. Easily cut off."

The River passes through an area where light does not

rage. There is nothing beyond the riverbank. Not even blackness. There is a sense of utter desolation. Like seeing my father forget I ever existed. These are dead places. I see what Thorn means about whole worlds being cut off from the River. Perhaps these places can be reached again. The River's always doubling back on itself. But the way isn't on my map. That's why they need me.

The River forks again and I will the skiff down the right fork. Just as we are turning I see the dragon.

At first it's just a chain of gold-scaled rocks that stretches upriver. Then the rocks lengthen, link up, and the dragon's head thrusts out of the water, confronting us head-on.

"Katastrofa!" Thorn exclaims in disgust.

The dragon's eyes are the eyes of a beautiful woman. The scales iridesce in the cascading water, clanking like bronze plates. Clinging to the dragon's neck is a young man. Joshua.

We see each other for only a second before the skiff plows on. His eyes don't give anything away. I don't know if he was kidnaped or if he came of his own free will.

"This ruins everything," Thorn says, shaking his head. "I wish I had some blood."

chapter ten

Katastrofa Darkling

Joshua Etchison

I was face-to-face with her at last. I couldn't control
myself. She held my hands in hers across the desk in that
shabby windowless room with the naked light bulb swinging back and forth, back and forth, like a torture scene in
a Nazi war movie. She was everything I remembered from
my dreams. Her long red hair streamed behind her
although I could feel no wind and the airconditioning was
off. She had almond-shaped eyes the color of summer
grass, and her features were perfectly symmetrical. My
hands sweated at the touch of her lizardskin gloves. I was
trembling. I was having kind of a waking wet dream. I
was full of desire and embarrassment and I couldn't look
her in the eye.

My throat was dry and I kept staring at the water cooler.
DRAGON SPRING WATER, said the logo, and it showed a
coiled-up crimson dragon breathing fire, but the fire was
misted from the condensation. She kept asking me ques-

tions. How long I'd had those dreams. Detailed questions about Theo's dream book that made me suspect that her knowledge of it was sketchy.

I told her what I could remember. The bit about the king and the three children—the King Lear part—made her tense. Her lips tightened. "It's not true," she said. "Not the way he tells it. It's too complicated. . . ."

"Where's my brother . . . Jesus Christ, what have you fucking done to him?"

She knew who Theo was all right. But not as much as she let on. She had nothing to do with his abduction. I could tell that right away because when she let go of me, when I slipped from her spell for a moment, I screamed at her, "I want him back—I want him back—I want everything to be the way it used to be."

And she looked at me blankly for a moment, then said, "Of course. Everything will be the way it was. If you come with me for now."

The room was filling up with smoke. The bulb swung back and forth and I could feel myself being hypnotized.

"You can't take me anywhere. . . . We're not connected to the River here. . . ." I whispered. What river? How had I known there was supposed to be a river?

She merely smiled and got up.

"Would you like a drink?" she said, and got a paper cup and went to the water cooler.

Dragon Spring Water . . .

She handed me the cup. I lifted it to my lips. The water was cool, so cool . . . and her hands burning hot as they brushed my cheek. She leaned over and pushed the water button again and let the water spill onto the floor and the water was gushing now, the water was spiraling round and round me like a lariat. . . .

"Can you become a truthsayer?" she said. "You have it in your blood. . . ."

"I'm not a truthsayer!" I shouted. "I don't even know what one is!"

"What a paradox!" she said. "When you say that you are not a truthsayer, it has the unmistakable ring of truth and makes you into a truthsayer anyway, which means you were lying which means you can't be a truthsayer. . . ."

She wasn't joking. The paradox was driving her crazy. *I* was driving her crazy because I wasn't Theo. But she still had to have me. I was the next best thing. I didn't know what it was for . . . she'd mumbled something about saving the universe, but, Jesus, give me a break.

"Come on," she said, "let's test the current."

Then she enveloped me in her arms and I guess I kind of came in my pants but before the embarrassment hit me I was being sucked into a whirlpool and the water was changing colors and Katastrofa was changing . . . bursting out of her cop's uniform, scales slicing up through her skin, her fingernails thrusting, curving into claws. . . . Still she held me tight in her embrace though I could feel the talons ripping my shirt and she kissed me and I could taste her tongue taste the brimstone and the myrrh in her breath sweet and bitter and sour and she whispered "Not so fast little boy slower slower slower there go go go slower slower you want to give me pleasure don't you taste me taste me" and she was hot to the touch, hot as the foam churned around us and we stood at the eye of the tempest and behind her the pendulum light bulb swung and I could feel her nails shred at my jeans now and feel the sharp tingle of her brush against my hair down there and I winced from shame but I was aroused again bursting again and still she whispered "slower slower do you want to rush headlong into hell boy? slower slower" and it was like those sleepless nights I had alone with my burgeoning new body sleepless thinking alone when the summer moonlight streamed into my bedroom in Virginia and the shadows on the walls embraced made love while the wind blew sticky through the open window hot and pregnant with impending rain, she—

Enveloped me in her arms like the sticky wet wind of summer as the water swirled around us—

Phil Etchison

—and I stood at the doorway listening. Pacing. I could hear nothing of what went on inside. Until suddenly there was a cry, an animal cry, like a prisoner being interrogated in a war movie. I looked down. My shoes . . . my socks were soaked. A pool of water had formed at the threshold of the inner room. More water was seeping out. Behind the door I could hear a rushing sound . . . a sound I used to hear a long time ago when Mary and I were newlyweds and I taught Eng. Lit. in Buffalo . . . when we would go to Niagara Falls for the weekend.

The sound lasted a split second. I blinked.

There was a brief discontinuity of some kind . . . a quantum shift. At that moment, the fellow I had met in the bar at the hotel came down the hallway.

"It's good of you," I said, "to let me tour the police station. I never know when I might need to use a bit of . . . atmosphere . . . a twinge of memory."

He looked a little perplexed for a moment, as though something I said didn't make sense.

"It's kind of you to offer to escort me to the autograph party, too."

"Think nothing of it. . . ."

Again, the bewildered look.

"What about Joshua?" said Detective Stone, and looked at the doorway the water had been spilling from. A Hispanic woman with a mop elbowed past me, swabbing at the floor.

"Joshua?"

Joshua Etchison

—and then we were racing downstream and she was changing into a dragon and I was riding the dragon as the colors of the vortex whirled around me—

Theo Etchison

—and the dragon sinks under the surface of the River and I scream my brother's name but I know he doesn't hear me and it's because the snake woman's holding him close—

"Concentrate, boy!" Thorn says. He grasps my shoulder and I bark in pain. "You must concentrate on your truthsaying. . . . My father has been diverting the River. . . . The maps aren't that good anymore. . . ."

"Joshua!" I shriek it at the top of my lungs. His name echoes along the banks of the River, bounds and rebounds over the twisted mountains of a thousand alien landscapes—

Phil Etchison

"Joshua?" I asked again, as I got into the front seat of the police car.

And again Milt Stone looked quizzically at me, and consulted the three-ring binder, with its notes written in some childish handwriting. And he said to me, "Tell me, who did you dedicate that chapbook to, I mean that *Embrasure* thing?"

"My wife. It was when we first found out about her illness."

"I suppose you know that laetrile isn't going to work?" he said, with infinite sadness in his eyes, as he started down Speedway, heading toward an exit to the 10. "I don't mean to be cruel," he said, "but we see our share of cancer patients in this town, heading down Todos Santos way, toward that clinic of Dr. de la Verdád's. They come back with nothing but memories and hefty invoices their insurance won't cover. I don't want to hurt you, Phil, but I hate to see you go through—"

"It's okay, Milt," I said. "She doesn't have cancer. It's worse than that."

I know he was waiting for me to say something like

AIDS, something fashionable. Cancer is often a coverup these days. But I trusted him. I couldn't help myself. "There's nothing wrong with her . . . not physically. . . . They thought it would be a good idea if I humored her . . . told her I was taking her over the border for a cure. . . .''

He looked at me expectantly. I started to weep a little. It was the first time I'd wept, really wept, since we set out from Alexandria, she and I, a desolate couple, each of us in his private bubble of reality. God, things would have been better if we'd had children. Maybe she wouldn't have gone all the way over then. But she had made herself barren.

The car moved swiftly past a shopping mall, a chorus line of service stations, a burnt-out hulk of a McDonald's.

"Mary's a paranoid schizophrenic," I said. "She hears voices. She believes she has been impregnated by the Holy Ghost. She believes she is about to give birth to God." I started to sob.

Strange, I thought . . . every time I tell someone about Mary, it seems like I'm telling it for the first time. It never gets any better.

"What about Joshua?" Milt Stone said.

I didn't want to talk to him suddenly. Even though he'd been such a friend to me the previous day, in the bar, coming up to me when I was on the verge of drinking myself into a stupor, letting me talk about my poems. When people see me the way I really am, it's an ugly thing, and I feel much better hiding my face behind the printed page. I didn't want to think about that scene in the bar. In fact, I discovered to my surprise, I had repressed it utterly. . . . I couldn't remember anything at all except that jarring moment, that disjunction, and the water seeping out under the doorway of the inner room in the police station.

I started to panic. "Mary . . . I've left Mary. . . . Where is she? She could have wandered off anywhere, God knows what she might have said to someone—"

"She's at the hospital. We're on our way to pick her up. Remember? To go to your autograph party."

I couldn't for the life of me remember when I'd agreed to that autograph party. My mind was overwhelmed by a single memory, a memory so sharply etched that it seemed to me almost like a scene from a play, something starkly artificial. . . .

I remembered the first time Mary had started to go off the deep end. At the maternity ward, holding our second son in her arms, trying to breastfeed him . . . stillborn. Squeezing the milk from her as though it would bring him back to life. And the nurse standing by, wringing her hands and looking from me to her and back again.

God, sometimes I wished that she were really dying.

I wished for the cancer to come down and eat her away . . . anything rather than the mad delusions that consumed her soul.

chapter eleven

Illusions

Theo Etchison

Something has happened, something has changed . . .
back there, in the real world, my world. The dragon sinks
into the stream and I start to realize there may not be a
world to go back to. Not the same world anyway.

"Soon," Thorn tells me as the River rages around us all,
"we'll have a big test of your truthsaying abilities . . . and
we'll all know whether my investment in you was in vain."

"What happens if—"

"I don't know! One thing at a time!" he says, and the
three-headed dog yaps viciously and runs in circles around
our feet. There's an ominous tone in his voice and I get the
distinct feeling that if I don't pass this test I'm totally history.

Phil Etchison

We went to the hospital; Mary had been sedated; apparently she'd had some kind of outburst. Every now and

then her mind completely reedits her vision of reality, and she has a seizure. Millions of bits of information fly madly around in her head and then they all fall into place at once and there's a cogent universe, with its own rules . . . but not *our* universe. They wouldn't let me see her. Sighing, Milt Stone drove me to the bookstore.

It was a kind of mom-and-pop—or rather, a pop-and-pop place in a small shopping plaza on an endless main drag that traverses all of Tucson. I usually don't agree to signings. They are mostly exercises in humiliation, unless you are someone like Stephen King. I didn't even remember agreeing to this one. But I was surprised to see a dramatic banner outside the store, with my name in pseudo-Mediaeval lettering, and that the window was piled high with a display of my latest poetry book . . . with a cardboard cutout figure of myself skulking professorially behind them. No wonder Milt Stone had recognized me. I peered inside, where I could see a wine and cheese table and the store's proprietors bustling about. Although we were early, there was already a big crowd, and I ducked to one side, into the doorway of a McDonald's, so that I could continue to look at the window display without being seen. Milt followed me.

A huge poster showed the book's cover painting, a lurid thing that looked like a composite of every B-grade movie I'd ever longed to see during my deprived Calvinist childhood. A spaceship soared over a tropical landscape where a dragon was breathing fire over an exotic alien princess chained to a throne. There were quotes from Gene Wolfe, Isaac Asimov, and Philip K. Dick, each one more fulsome than the last.

"Phil Etchison's latest sci-fi classic . . ." it said over the title of the novel. I began to feel . . . not quite myself. Possessed by someone else, some malevolent spirit. "There can't be a quote from Philip K. Dick on my book," I said. "Philip K. Dick has been dead for eight or nine years. And besides . . ." There was something else wrong too. Something I couldn't quite put my finger on.

"Dead?" said Stone. "Why, he was just on Larry King last night . . . that fourth book in the *Blade Runner* series . . ."

"There's no such . . ." I stopped.

Blinked. The poster was still there, but the Dick quote wasn't. I wanted another drink. My mind was playing tricks . . . or someone was playing tricks on my mind.

"Yeah," Stone was saying, "I seem to remember hearing he'd died. My wife reads a lot, she's the one who tells me these things. Come to think of it, Larry King wasn't even on last night. Because of the riots, you know. In China."

But that wasn't the worst of it. I knew who Dick was and I was pretty sure he had died, but I was also absolutely certain that the newly published novel I had come to sign was not my own.

I mean . . . seriously . . . *The Pterodactyls of Eternity?* Surely that wasn't something that could have been penned by the author of . . . of . . . I drew a blank. My own book.

Besides, I've never liked science fiction.

I stepped into the bookstore. Detective Stone followed me in. He was staring strangely at me, as though I had become a different person before his very eyes. Fans can be very tiresome sometimes, but I did not want to be rude; he had, after all, given up a day's work just so he could chauffeur me around Tucson.

"Would you care for a drink?" A Chinese accent; a tall cadaverous man in a dark suit, holding out a squat glass with a frothing red liquid. Smiling, I took it from him. I took a few sips.

It was as though I had awoken from a dream. The crowds were gone. The spread of canapés and expensive wines had vanished; in their place was a silver platter of wilted lettuce topped with a few forlorn chunks of Ameri-

can cheddar; the wine came in those milk carton things.
The stacks of science fiction books had shriveled to a
desultory pile of copies of *Songs about Embalming,* my
latest chapbook from that university press somewhere in
the Dakotas. A few of my other books lay next to them;
there were a couple of *Embrasures* that were probably
survivors of a Waldenbooks remainder table. I swiftly
downed the rest of my drink. The Chinaman, too, had
vanished. The drink had been sickly sweet, with an almost
sanguinary flavor to it; it tasted familiar, but I hadn't been
able to place it. I wanted more, but I couldn't see the
bottle it had come from.

"I've just had the strangest dream," I said to Milt.

"So have I," he said softly.

"What's happening to us?" I said. Before he could say
anything, a young man had thrust a copy of the book into
my hand, and was brandishing a ballpoint pen. I asked
the man's name, turned to the dedication page, and signed
right underneath the inscription to my wife. There was, I
noticed with some satisfaction, a line forming. Only two
or three people, to be sure, but attention was attention. I
forgot about searching for the mysterious blood-colored
drink.

"Mr. Etchison!" It was a teenage girl, a little on the
chubby side, with oversize mirror shades and a neon pink
teeshirt. "Like, how amazing you're here and everything
and I can get this book signed. . . ."

I looked at her blankly. She did a quick double take.
Our eyes met and I saw that she expected me to know
who she was. When I didn't react, she said, in a sullen
tone, "A couple months on the road, he sees me in my
awesome new hairdo, and he doesn't even know who I
am. . . . I sat up wtih your wife all night one time,
remember, when she was like, puking a lot."

My astonishment must have been plain. "Look, Mr.
Etchison, don't worry. I didn't run away or anything. I'm
in town with my mom, I'm like, doing this tour of the

college, you know, I don't know if I'm going to go to U of A, or ASU, but my mom totally agrees that I need to be out of Virginia cause, you remember, I quit that congressional page job because you know what a lewd old man Congressman Karpovsky is, with that scandal and everything, and him living two blocks away on Kirby. Jeez, Mr. Etchison, you still don't know who I am, do you?''

Some of the customers had gathered around. She pulled a copy of *The Embrasure of Parched Lips* from her satchel and presented it to me along with a gold Cross pen.

''I'm Serena Somers.'' She opened the book to the dedication page, which read:

> *To Joshua and Theo*

She added, ''I used to go out with your son, remember?''

''Sluglike,'' I said. I did not know what it meant or why the word had slipped out.

Serena laughed. ''I guess that nickname's always gonna stick,'' she said, ''even though I like, lost 17 lbs. on that Walter Hudson diet they show on late-night TV.''

''Who are you? Why do I seem to know these things about you?'' The situation was becoming steadily more Kafkaesque.

''What do you mean, Mr. Etchison? Oh, I guess you're in one of those moods of yours, where you like, seem to slip into another universe or something.'' She winked at Milt Stone, who shook his head ruefully. ''Sometimes, when he's writing poetry, he disappears for like weeks! And he doesn't even know his own name.''

''You don't understand,'' I said. ''I'm not the one who goes away. It's not me, it's—it's—everyone else, what can I say? Slippage. Yes. The universe is like an infinite mosaic of tectonic plates and they rub up against each other and wear away at the edges of reality and—''

I looked around, realizing that I had raised my voice several decibels above the acceptable level of rational discourse. Why did everything around me seem so *wrong?* I looked at the book I had just autographed for Serena Somers. Everything about it seemed wrong; the heft, the off-white of its binding, the point size of the typeface. Yet the words inside were unmistakably mine. Unless my whole life up to that moment had been a dream. Which did not seem unlikely.

"What a coincidence," said the girl I'd never laid eyes on before. "Us meeting like this, three thousand miles from Alexandria. The kind of thing you'd find in one of those, like, Dickens books Mrs. Pritchard keeps making us read." Nervously, she ran her fingers through her spiked blond hair.

"What a coincidence," I repeated. I signed one or two more books and downed a glass of the flat Asti Spumante one of the store owners had thrust into my hand.

"Do you think I could go and see Mrs. Etchison?" she said. "I know Joshua probably doesn't want to talk to me anymore, but I still think he's cute."

"Joshua?"

"Oh, Mr. Etchison, you really can be such a dweeb sometimes."

Milt was beckoning to me urgently. I felt as though I was drowning. He grabbed my sleeve and led me to another part of the store, behind a display of the latest Stephen King titles.

"Repeat after me," Milt said. *"I am not going mad."*

"I'm not," I said.

"Think back. Two or three hours ago. In the police station. You and me. Sitting across from each other. Were we just shooting the shit, was I just an admiring fan who volunteered to give you a tour of the station? Wasn't there something else?"

Yes. At the edge of my consciousness. Something else.

My consciousness. Streaming past me. You never step

twice into the same river. Facts beneath the surface. And every time I bent down to grasp them they'd swim away. Taunting.

"If you won't admit there's something fishy going on," said Stone, "at least tell me *I* ain't going crazy. I don't want to lose my job yet. I'm the only one of my people on the force here, you know. Affirmative action's a load of bullshit." I saw bitterness in his face for the first time, sensed that he was a man who did not easily reveal himself.

"You're not going crazy," I said, though I was starting to have serious doubts about both that proposition and the preceding one.

Theo Etchison

—surging around me. I stop. I hold the marble in my fist and feel it sucking all the warmth from my body. I close my eyes. Something's happening, something's shifting. Every time I use my power the universe buckles and I can change the course of the River. That's what it's all about.

Thorn is speaking. I can hear him above the roar although he never raises his voice. He says, "We're getting to a place, my boy, where the River goes mad. That's because my father's been storming around, sealing up the gateways between the worlds, doing everything he can to smash the links that hold the universe together. Don't ask me why. Perhaps he just regrets giving up all that power. But I don't have to tell you that without communication, there's no community. There's no family. The universe shatters into a million pieces and they all go sliding into their own private pockets of barbarism, their own private hells. I guess you understand why you're needed."

"I guess." But I am thinking of my own family and how Thorn and his herald have severed the links between us and how each of us is sliding into his own personal darkness.

"Don't think of them. Think of the gateway."

I clench the marble tightly. I can see it even with my eyes closed. I can see the filaments of light, twisting, untwisting. The threads are spun by my own thoughts. Am I a truthsayer because I can always know the truth, or because I *make* the truth happen by what I say? When I blurt those things out does it make me responsible for them coming true? This is a majorly horrifying concept and I don't want to accept it either way.

There's only one thing I know for sure. There isn't any River and there isn't any vampire named Thorn or any of those other things I've seen since I zoned into this parallel universe. These things are all metaphors. They're half-familiar things plucked out of the junkheap of my mind, out of the sci-fi movies and the Stephen King books and the gore magazines and my dad's awesome poetry readings. They're familiar things because they keep me sane. There isn't any fantasy world. Maybe there isn't any real world either. Maybe every man is an island after all. This is the most totally frightening thing of all.

Maybe I'm the only person in the universe and maybe I'm just imagining everything—

"And maybe you're God, Theo," Thorn says, and I can hear the smirk in his voice, "just like your name says."

"Can you read my mind?"

"No. But I've burned up a dozen like you. I know the stages you people go through. First the bewilderment, then the solipsism, then, maybe . . . enlightenment. But usually not."

I don't want to understand him. Instead I concentrate hard on what's in the marble. One of the strands of light needs mending. It's writhing like a snake, sparking, shorting out the threads that lie alongside. I know I can mend it. I can reknit the filaments and make the paths run straight again. I'm not sure how yet. It's something to do with vibrations or wormholes or . . . the fabric of space-time. I feel the River flowing all around me. My hair's standing on end and there's a coldness seeping into my bones and my hands are clammy from gripping the marble.

"The gateway that's been sealed off," I ask, "where does it lead?"

"Earth," Thorn says.

I open my eyes. "Earth."

"My father dogs our footsteps," Thorn says, "and tries to lock the gates behind us. He does it for spite, perhaps."

The ship that isn't really a ship pitches against the wind that isn't a wind. "I'll have to make a new gateway," I find myself saying. And thinking: Or I'll never see them again and it'll be my own fucking fault.

But how? "Say the words," Thorn says.

"What do you mean, say the words?" The three-headed dog is barking somewhere far away.

"I don't know! Who am I, a truthsayer? There's some kind of mumbo-jumbo you people do, and then we have a new fork in the River that links two more regions of spacetime. Speaking a thing's true name, I suppose."

"That doesn't sound very scientific," I say. No, more like a fairy tale, where a wizard can call something by its true name and gain power over it.

"You need long Latin words before you can believe in it?" says Thorn. "Very typical of you people. All right. Here are some polysyllabic utterances that will get you in the mood. *Transdimensional disjunctive node. Hypercosmic transsonic digital-to-analog superspatial simulations. Hocus-pocus.*"

I don't need the pseudoscience. It's all becoming clear to me. Kind of. I can't explain it except with cumbersome metaphors, but I know it's true: I just know.

Every man *is* an island. The universe splits off a million million times each millisecond, and each of us carries a private universe around with him wherever he goes. Where the universes intersect, that's when we think we encounter other people and we think they are our friends and our parents and the people we love. But we never really know them because we never cross from our little bubble of reality into theirs. When we part company with a friend, we can never know how alien the world he inhabits is from ours. We can never know. That's not quite true. *You* can never know. I can. I can cross over. It's a special talent.

There was one true world once, at the beginning of time. In the infinitesimal moment before the big bang, when the universes began to peel off, one by one, like the skins of an onion. They keep splitting off, each one one quantum different from the last, but they all contain within them an echo of the one true world. That's what my talent is. I can hear the echo. I can tune my mind to that echo the way a piano tuner tightens a string. Because I can hear it, I can also speak its language. Because it's a living thing, I can make it understand me.

Thorn is rambling on now, he's talking about the Uncertainty Principle or something, but I don't have any need for explanations. I can feel everything all at once. I'm at the center of the storm, the storm is me, I'm making it happen, I'm alone speaking with the heart of the one true world.

King Strang has left the shore where his son spoke treasonous words and where he looked into the truthsayer's eyes. He lifts his scepter and leads his lizard warriors into darkness. Rage goads him, blind rage with leathern wings and the face of a skull.

Time is running out for him. The dark thing that has pursued him since he snatched the scepter from the source of the River pursues him still.

He must dam up the River. Cauterize the pathways. He follows the trail of his son, skimming the stream on a lightning-wheeled chariot. Seal the gateways! Randomize the currents so that no one will ever know whither they flow!

Strang—the king who looked into my eyes and whispered, "Truthsayer . . ." It's him I'm fighting. He's old and he knows many secrets of the River, many hidden twists and bends and subterfuges. But he is not a truthsayer. He is only a king.

"Tell me what you see!" says Thorn.

I see King Strang, a hundred times human size, defending the great gates of a city. I am the giant killer. I wield a sword of light.

Behind the gateway come the cries of a besieged people, hungry, hopeless, out of control. Strang moves, jerkily, a massive stop-motion animated monster. His arms and legs are of clay.

I leap from the prow and my sword streaks behind me into the sunlight. My sword is a rainbow blur. I thrust. The Strang-monster shifts, gazes down at me, his feet pounding the rocky shore. He roars. "Despair!" he screams. Behind the gate, the crowd takes up his cry. I can taste the desolation in the wind. I feel like I'm going to piss myself again. Strang has four arms, and his nose has thrust upward into the horn of a rhinoceros.

Earth is behind the gate.

"Strang!" I shriek. My voice is tiny. The wind shrills. Salt fills my nose, my eyes. I run toward him with my sword held high, a tiny figure against a man-mountain, and all the while I hear Thorn's laughter in my ear. And all the time the landscape shifts. Mountains rise up behind the citadel. A waterfall gushes. I'm running uphill toward the portals that seem to recede the more I run. And still there's the giant, and the ground quaking with every footfall.

And suddenly I'm much younger and I'm swinging a plastic sword and wearing the Viking helmet that I bought from Toys 'R' Us and I'm running alongside the brook in

back of my grandmother's house in Spotsylvania County
and the monster is my grandma's fifteen-year-old cat Pizzi-
cato who's dying of feline leukemia although no one
knows it yet. I'm thrusting at the air and shouting imaginary Nordic curses. I'm maybe six years old and it's one
of the summers that stretches forever. My Dad has been
reading the *Völsunga Saga* to us every night before we go
to sleep in the attic among the antique chests and the
broken dolls and the bundles of faded love letters.

"You're nothing,"—I yell at the Strang-monster—
"You're just a scrawny old feline riddled with cancer!"
And I see an image of my Mom fresh out of the chemotherapy and I'm charging her with like this big old hypodermic needle and all the images are fusing and melding
and shifting in and out of each other and I know it's
Strang, trying to make me weak. But I can see through
him.

I lunge at him. Suddenly he's small and shriveling fast.
I slice his head off with a single blow and it flies upward,
shrinking still, buzzing, until it's no bigger than a fly.

"You're not really King Strang," I say to the head
that's circling my head, spattering my cheeks with blood,
"you're just a kind of afterimage that's trying to block
the path of the River. . . ."

And the gates burst into flame and I see people rushing
out, calling my name, falling to their knees in front of me
and acclaiming me as their savior I'm starting to feel like
a superhero in a comic book saving the universe and I'm
scared because I know that's not me that's just a dream
play—

I hear Thorn say, "You did it! You *do* have the ability." And I hear the dog yapping, barking and howling at
the same time from his three throats.

And I squeeze my eyes tight shut and I'm standing at
the prow of the vampire's ship, and when I open my eyes
I see the water gathering into a funnel, and at the end of
the tunnel I see . . . this is what I see.

My father, bewildered, autographing copies of his book.

My mother, sitting in a chair, rocking herself back and forth.

My mother's not dying anymore. But she's not cured either. Something has taken the place of the cancer. That's why I'm trapped. Forever.

They think she's mad but that's not what it is. She's been stranded in the universe the way it was before . . . many universes ago. The universe where there were two sons and my mother wasn't sick yet. Every man is an island. A desert island. They think she's mad but she's a universe unto herself. And I'm the only one who knows.

"You asshole," I say to Thorn. I'm so angry I can hardly feel it at all. I try to strike him, to punch him out, to kick him in the balls, but I just go right through him like he's not there. Which he's not, of course. "You've made it impossible for me to go back."

"I need you," Thorn says. He touches my cheek. I feel his weariness, his sadness . . . and his shame at having to beg for help from a lowly kid like me. His cloak flutters in the imaginary wind and I hear the creak of imaginary planking. "I suppose you know now that I can't stop you from returning. I can't keep you here. You're a truthsayer. One way or another, you could find your way home."

"If I go back, my mother will be dying again," I say. "As long as I stay here—"

He shakes his head. I get the feeling he almost regrets putting me through hell. But then again, maybe he's just manipulating me.

I say, "Why couldn't you have given me a better deal? Okay, let's say I agree to give up my freedom so my mother won't die. But did you have to make her into a madwoman? Couldn't you have just wiped me out of all their minds . . . remade their universes so that I never existed for any of them . . . so they could at least be happy without me? And what about Joshua? Why did your sister Katastrofa have to kidnap *him?* And isn't there a third child of your father? What about him? Nothing's guaranteed, nothing's safe. . . . We're pawns in a three-way chess match."

"Now wait a minute," Thorn says. "I can't edit reality that much. I did what I could. Some people can be shunted from reality to reality—as you say, just like moving a pawn from square to square. Some people cling to their private universes and won't budge. I can't just say, hey, zap, the world is another world. I'm not God." He looks me in the eye and adds, in all seriousness, "Are you?"

book three

the river styx

It doesn't take long for the experience of the
numinous to unhinge the mind.

—Umberto Eco

TO MY WIFE'S SONS

When she stands at the river's edge, sometimes
I watch her; sometimes
Knowing the things she sees, unknowable to me,
I cannot bear to watch; sometimes
I wish for the river to run upstream, back to the mountains,
Blue as the sky, as grief, as desolation.

She sees them playing by the river's edge; sometimes
I think I hear their laughter in the wind that shakes
The cottonwoods. I cannot bear to listen,
Knowing she suckles the stillborn, unborn
Gods, her dream-selves, drawn from the secret river
Inside. Oh, turn the tide, push back the waterfall, make her
    no longer
Cry out to me from the depths. In my heart I know sometimes
That the river has reversed its course; I know sometimes
That the river will not turn back till its watery end,
Black as the sky, as grief, as disillusion.

She is walking away from the river's edge; sometimes
I know she will never come home.
Better I do not look at all; for in the momentary closure,
The blink's breadth between two truths, two truths can both
    be true.
When I close my eyes I have two sons, and each
Is the other's shadow; she is the two-breasted madonna
Who suckles the dark and light, the quick and lifeless;
Red as blood, as desire, as disenchantment.

chapter twelve

The Third Darkling

Serena Somers

Actually, I had lied to Mr. Etchison. It wasn't, like, a total accident that we happened to be in Tucson at the same time. And I wasn't with my mother. I was with Ash. My mother didn't know where I was. Ash had taken care of her. He had put her in the state where she was constantly expecting me to come back from the mall at any time, but it didn't bother her that I had been gone for days. It was strange because in a way this was what I'd always like wanted.

I had already been to see Mrs. Etchison in the madhouse and talked to her. She was the only sane person on the entire planet, as far as I could tell. Apart from me, of course. I knew that the whole world was going to blow if I didn't do anything. It was that serious, but nobody knew, nobody would believe me, maybe nobody even cared.

I planted myself in the bookstore just so I could catch Mr. E. and maybe force reality on him. The book I thrust in his face wasn't part of his world at all; it was trapped inside a bubble of the old, true universe that Ash had conjured up somehow.

"Couldn't you just have put a bubble around the whole world?" I asked him, standing by the young adult rack, watching Mr. E. pull into the parking lot in a cop car.

Ash muttered something about the energy expenditure and quantum mechanics and Schrödinger's cat—a bunch of sci-fi clichés that didn't really satisfy me one bit. But there was nothing I could do. There was something about him that made me trust him. I *had* to trust him. He was the only one who believed me about the way things used to be. Him and old Mrs. E., but she was too doped up to notice much anymore.

Ash took me in to see Mrs. E. and it was strange to know that the three of us, two visitors and a madwoman, were the only ones who knew what was literally the secret of the universe. Of like, one universe in particular.

We sat across from her, talking in whispers, with a nurse hovering in the background with a little tray of hypodermics and mega-shiny electronic gadgets. Mrs. E. looked better than she had in a long long time. She didn't have the cancer anymore, you see. Schizophrenics do not smell like they're rotting away on the hoof—that's how she used to smell, the whole house reeked of it so that all I wanted to do was get Joshua out of there. Theo never forgave me because I never set foot in their house after I found out. I didn't mean to be cruel but death is just too much for me to take.

She wasn't dying anymore. Schizophrenics smell sweet. Ash told me that this is sometimes known as the odor of sanctity and that saints used to be schizophrenics oftentimes. Ash tells me many things.

Ash used to be my imaginary friend when I was little. Now he's real.

That's the one piece of reality that Mrs. E. and I don't share.

She can't see Ash. When I told her about him she smiled indulgently, shook her head; I knew she half-suspected I was another inmate and only play-acting about being a visitor from Virginia.

"Couldn't you . . . you know, like leave us alone for a while?" I asked the nurse.

"Regulations," she said. And sat down sullenly in the corner. "I'm surprised they let you in at all . . . not being a relation, you know." I had had Ash to thank for that. I don't know what he did, but somehow he had enchanted the secretary, the head nurse, one of the psychiatrists . . . and here we were. Sipping tea together in a madhouse in Arizona.

I just couldn't get used to seeing Mrs. E. with hair again. She lost all her hair from the chemotherapy; that's how I pictured her all the time, even after it changed. Her hair was beautiful. It was like Josh's hair. She was beautiful too. With Josh's eyes.

We sipped tea together and I told her, "I've come to make it better for you, Mrs. E. Everything is mutable. That's what Ash says."

She only smiled and nodded her head. "We can bring them back, make the world the way it was before," I said. "We can, Mrs. E. Somehow I don't know how but somehow somehow I—" Oh Jesus, I totally wanted to cry and puke at the same time.

"And make me sick again," she said.

I couldn't answer her. I knew that would happen if we turned time back to the very moment reality had branched off. Wasn't there any other solution? Only Theo would know. I'd already learned from Ash about Theo's mondo superpowers. I half expected him to burst through the window at any moment with a purple cape billowing behind him and lightning flashing out of his goofy grin.

"Get me out of this place," said Mrs. Etchison.

The smell of her madness . . . even above the medicine smells of the hospital . . . I turned to Ash.

He shook his head. "I can't leave her here!" I whispered to him. Mrs. Etchison was weeping quietly to herself.

"Reality . . . too much shifting . . . unstable," he said.

"How about," I said, "if we took her back to where it first happened . . . to that Chinese restaurant?"

"If the gateway is still there," Ash said.

He stood in the doorway's shadow. No one could see him but me. Oh, but he was beautiful. There was this unearthly light about him and his face was really pale and there were a few faint freckles on his cheeks and his hair was long and totally black, like a night in the country. This was how he had always appeared to me when I was a kid. I never knew that he was there to plant the memories in me so I wouldn't be afraid when he started coming back soon after I had my first period. He was preparing me for all these changes. Soothing me so I wouldn't go crazy.

Or maybe he had only just appeared to me last week for the first time but he'd edited my past so that I had always known him. What difference did it make? No one can be more than one version of herself at any one time, right? Except Theo. Always except Theo.

Thank God we're normal, me and Joshua and Mary and everyone else.

"Listen, Ash," I said, softly so no one could hear, "maybe we could help her escape. We can all go to the gateway and bring back Theo and change reality back to the way it was but maybe have Mrs. Etchison not be sick anymore, you know? And we could—"

The nurse was standing over me, staring strangely at me; I guess she saw me talking to myself and wondered why I wasn't an inmate myself. "Mrs. Etchison has to have her pills now," she said. "I'm afraid you'll have to come back tomorrow."

"Bye, Mrs. E.," I said, and kissed her on the cheek.

"Give the boys my love," she said. The nurse shrugged, not bothering to hide her contempt.

After that I saw Mr. Etchison in the bookstore, and I saw how he looked at the book I wanted him to autograph . . . not recognizing what he had written many worlds ago . . . and I knew something had to be done. I had to get Mrs. E. out of the loony bin and we had to go back, find the gateway, cross over to where the boys were, get Theo to do something.

I guess I must have been crying my guts out when Ash led me out of the bookstore. The old Nova was parked on Speedway. We'd stolen it from a used car lot. Ash put his hand on my shoulder and it was almost like he could read my mind, because he said, "He won't necessarily be able to fix things, you know. He's not God."

"But you say he's the only one who knows the true nature of things," I said, though it was hard for me to believe that Josh's kid brother, that introverted, moody boy, was in fact the physical center of the universe— which was one way Ash had been trying to explain it to me on the flight down from Washington.

We got into the car. The seat was boiling hot. I couldn't touch the steering wheel. The sun was in my eyes. I hate Tucson, I thought, I'll never go to college here, no, I want to go to New Hampshire or somewhere like that and ski my way to a bachelor's.

"The asylum's closed to visitors now," said Ash, "but Mary Etchison is not considered dangerous; there aren't any bars on her room or anything like that. We should be able to get her out quickly."

I pulled out. Ash couldn't drive, but he looked old enough to be in charge of me and maybe with my learner's permit we'd be able to bluff our way if we were stopped— assuming he could make himself visible.

We were about to be stopped now.

Siren. Blue and red flashing lights. I lurched, slammed

on the brakes, pulled over. I was really nervous. This had
never happened to me. Oh God I thought they've already
reported the stolen car, I'm ruined for life they'll send me
to juvie and I won't be able to get my license for sure let
alone save the universe or whatever it was I was supposed
to be doing. I looked at Ash, but his expression was hard
to read. You really knew he was from another world at
times like this.

I turned off the engine and the airconditioning went off
right away and I was just burning up. I forgot to roll down
the window for a moment. I just sat there. I couldn't
breathe.

"What's the matter?" Ash said. "Is there something I
can do?"

"I don't know what I did wrong—I don't think it was
that left turn, and I'm not speeding."

Finally I rolled down the window. There was a tall
Indian policeman standing there. I looked up at the rear-
view mirror and saw Mr. Etchison sitting in the passenger
seat of the police car.

"You're not in trouble, honey," the policeman said,
although he didn't seem pleased. "Even though you look
a little young to be driving."

"You'd never have thought that last year, officer," I
said, "but with the Walter Hudson diet, and me losing all
my chunkiness, I turned out to be only a wisp of a human
being, really and—" Running off at the mouth. Because
I was nervous. "Oh, Ash, say something, please!"

Ash sat immobile, face like an ancient Greek statue,
staring.

"Just who are you talking to, Miss?" said the
policeman.

"Can't you see him?"

He scratched his head. For a split second, I knew that
he could see *something* in the passenger seat . . . perhaps
a blur, a mist, a flash of rainbow-colored light. Whatever
he saw was beautiful. Ash is always beautiful, no matter

how he is perceived. He has a softening effect on people. The policeman smiled.

"The name's Stone, dear, Officer Milt Stone." He showed me his badge. "I wouldn't have stopped you, but you see, Mr. Etchison, the famous poet—oh, I know you, you were at the signing—he suddenly thought you were someone else, it seemed so important for him to talk to you—but—"

"He's right," I said. "I *am* someone else."

I think he saw Ash again, because he looked nervously at the seat next to me, then grinned again, showing a mouthful of uneven teeth. At that moment, Mr. Etchison came up behind him. Over and over he said one word: "Sluglike."

It seems that when one is crossing from reality to reality, fading in and out of existing and having-existed and about-to-exist, it really helps to be easily remembered for some undesirable physical trait. I started to mention the Walter Hudson diet, but Mr. E. was so weirded out I knew we didn't have time to discuss eating disorders.

"Disjunctive fugue," Ash whispered in my ear.

Mr. Etchison stared wildly, walked around the car in a steady clockwise motion muttering "sluglike" every few paces. It would have been funny if it weren't—

"Disjunctive fugue occurs because reality doesn't just shift all at once," Ash said, "it kind of snaps, like elastic, and some people have a slower rate of reality inertia. Of course, Theo's rate is zero. He's a constant, like the speed of light. Mr. E.'s his father and he must have the truthsaying genes in him so maybe he does have a little of the talent . . . if we could only open his eyes. . . ."

"Oh my God," said Officer Stone. "Oh my God, I do see someone there . . . someone shimmering a little . . . half man, half kachina."

"Welcome, Mr. Stone," Ash said. "I'm generating a small bubble of our reality so that you'll see me and you won't think Serena's gone insane. Please take Mr. Etchi-

son by the hand and we'll see if we can't bring him out
of disjunctive fugue.''

His eyes glowed. He was totally beautiful, like one of
those teen idol stars. I felt safe with him because he didn't
seem quite a man . . . that's why I started dreaming about
him at night, the night I had my first period and my parents had gone to the store and I was so alone. God I loved
him, not the way I loved Josh, which was always thinking
oh my God is he going to touch me how am I going to
feel if he touches me is he going to kiss me will his breath
be bad how will his lips feel Chapstick against the purple
passion flame lipstick from Dart Drug and then pulling
away, stopping before he can touch, so deathly afraid of
being loved by him because he's all boy, all hormones,
raging. Not Ash.

I was safe with Ash.

So safe. It was even okay to stop being fat.

chapter thirteen

The Harvester of Tears

Theo Etchison

And so Thorn has challenged me to be God, like my name says. I hate my name. I wish they'd named me Chris or Mike or David. Names do make a difference. I know things by their true names. I *know*.

It scares me.

I've changed my room—my prison—about twenty times now. Sometimes I make it exactly like I remember from when I was real little. I make the bed a giant crib, I make the doors gargantuan, I make every sound that steals in through the window seem never-heard-before. Other times I give it a far future flavor like in a *Star Wars* sequel or rig it up like the cave of a fearsome dragon, but I know it's all one featureless place, the reality of my room is a kind of psychic playdough that they've given me to mess around with. To shield me from the truth. The one thing they can never hide from me.

After my big test, Thorn is anxious for me to start work,

as he calls it. He calls me to his throneroom where I watch him drinking blood from jeweled chalices. I tell him I'm tired from that test and he threatens me but I can tell that I have the upper hand in a way. I start making demands. He tells me that planets are being blown up and whole societies are falling into oblivion just because I'm sitting around acting like a spoiled child. I can't really grasp what he's saying and I just tell him over and over that I want to return home. It's been like that for days or what passes for days in this buttfuck Egypt of a universe.

I tell him I need more freedom.

I want to be able to travel around without being watched all the time by the herald who is also Mr. Huang who is the man who will blow the conch and summon all the storm troopers if I just try to look at something I'm not supposed to.

I need to see, hear, feel what my parents are doing. . . . Yeah I can feel them all right, I can know things that are going on but it's way at the edge of my perception, like hearing the CNN Headline News from a television set in your parents' bedroom while you've got a heavy metal band blasting from the boombox on your desk.

That's what I tell him, and I can see him squirming, but eventually he relents and he lets me roam unguarded through the palace. That's how I learn so many new things.

I'm getting used to the way the images shift around—in my own room I can control it completely now. I keep the marble that's really a map of the universe in a little pouch that hangs around my neck. Usually I still wear the clothes I'm used to but some days I try on their clothes—cloaks that flutter without wind, high pointed collars that swell up behind your head, halos, spiked breastplates, glow-in-the-dark ear cuffs. Or sometimes they seem to wear nothing at all. You have to stare at them for a long time to see the wisps of iridescent smoke that curl around them and slowly change color according to their moods. It's kind of a bracelet thing that generates the smoke.

The third day of my freedom is when I see the harvester of tears.

I'm all wandering through the castle. People don't notice me much or when they do they won't look at me, they just shuffle past me with their eyes downcast, not making a sound because mostly the castle is carpeted with thick rich muffling tapestries. One day I did a hundred rooms, I counted them one by one, one room with a hundred stringed instruments built in the shapes of outlandish animals all covered with cobwebs, one room with vases, thousands, laid out in rows, chipped, dusty vases, one room with music copyists dipping their quill pens in inkwells made from the skulls of whales and dinosaurs, one room all black, featureless, one room where women danced naked through fire . . . I counted them and forgot them except for quick impressions . . . like when I was a kid leafing through one of Dad's poetry books and letting the images tumble through my head like the leaves in autumn. That was the first day. The second and third I'm more selective. I don't go into every room anymore, just the ones where the doors seem somehow more inviting.

Jesus but I feel alone, I wake up wetting the bed sometimes and I think that this is kind of an embarrassing thing to do considering I'm supposed to be like the messiah or something. I want my family. I even want Josh to beat me up or something. Jesus I'm lonely. He's counting on that, Thorn I mean, counting on me wanting someone to talk to, anyone, even a prince of darkness. But I don't want to give in yet.

I wander.

Around the two or three hundredth level of the castle I find like these parapets that open out into gardens. The gardens seem to just hang in the air; you can't see what holds them up. I step out into thin air. I'm thinking, so what if I fall to my death . . . it's so far down anyway I won't feel a thing. But no, I'm walking on air.

Many of the plants are what I'm used to. There is a row of cottonwoods that remind me of the time we were staying in Colorado at our cousins' place next to the Arkansas River and my dad wrote a poem about us, a sad poem about how we were going to grow up and leave him.

Well we didn't really grow up that much but we did leave him.

I'm walking on thin air breathing in the fresh scent of the foliage that weaves in and out of the cloudbanks, while far below me the sea beats against the rocks, the sea that leads to the Chinese restaurant back in the other world, my world. Jesus I'm alone.

I try to feel my family. I feel Josh least of all. He's like completely drowning in these sex emotions that I really don't quite know how to deal with. I kind of see my mother sitting at the edge of a hospital bed. My dad is in a car. A police car I think. I hope he hasn't done something foolish. Mr. Huang is dogging him. Keeping him drunk so he won't see the world change shape. They all seem so vague, so many realities ago. To feel them I not only have to reach across space and time but also across alternate worlds, alternate spaces and times. I feel tired, so tired. I'm burning up from the effort. I lean against what seems to be the trunk of an oak tree.

"If only plants could talk," I say under my breath, wiping my brow with a fold of my teeshirt. "I'd at least have someone to talk to besides mad princes and their minions." I'm talking to myself. It's come to this.

All at once I'm conscious of the grass whispering. I think it's calling my name. I crouch down. The grass rustles. Clouds stream through me. I hear it for sure now: *Theo, Theo, Theo.*

I think about the talking flowers in *Alice in Wonderland* or was it *Through the Looking-Glass,* the flowers that get pissed off and ask Alice "What makes you think we *can't* talk?" and speak in conundrums like everyone else in the Alice books, like everyone here too.

I put my ear to the grass. I hear voices. Rustling. Tinkling. A kind of lullaby. My name, over and over.

What makes you think we can't *talk?*

Theo, Theo, Theo.

"Why are you whispering my name?" I ask them.

Vanity, vanity, comes the surf-shatter whisper of the grass. *Not any name of mortal being. We call on God. God. Theo, Theo, Theo.*

I tell them I am Theo.

They are singing to me now.

I hear my name in the ceaseless rhythm that is the grass the desert the station wagon moving inexorably toward my mother dying.

"The flowers lie too much, Theo Truthsayer."

I look up. It is Thorn. I haven't seen him coming; he doesn't come and go like ordinary men.

Thorn stands beside me on his own little cloud that tendrils around his ankles. He stands in a private wind that blows his cloak away from where the wind I feel is blowing.

"Are you ready to come with me now?" Thorn asks me. "There is so little time. If only you knew, if only you understood how troubling the affairs of the universe are. . . ."

I know that he will say anything and do anything to get me to cooperate. I flinch from him.

"You're going to tell me you're not ready to start work yet," he says. "But my patience is wearing a little thin. We've worlds to conquer . . . lives to save . . . madmen to catch before they destroy the universe . . . all the things heroes are supposed to enjoy. And let's face it . . . you're starting to like it here. You're even warming to me a bit."

"It's the kidnaping syndrome I guess," I say. "You

know, the one where the victim starts to feel sympathy
for the abductors.''

"Very good.'' Thorn laughs, a dry, uncomfortable
laugh. "You're the kind that follows the TV news, you're
up on the latest psychobabble.''

I don't look at him.

I only hear the grass, which whispers always, *You are
God, Theo, you, you, you. And you alone. Alone. Alone.*

"Come on, Theo,'' says Thorn, "let's see how you
cope with the real world. The world as it is. The thousand
worlds. The world of which all you've left behind is so
infinitesimal a part that it saddens me to think you want
to cling to it. . . .''

He takes me by the hand. We step from cloud to cloud,
upward toward the sun. The ocean stretches toward the
horizon that's far too near to be the earth's, and the water
is far too gray, like dull steel.

"I want you to know that I am not that bad,'' Thorn
tells me. He sounds to me as though he's trying to con-
vince himself . . . or perhaps his father, who isn't here
but who I know obsesses him. "Hold my hand tight. It
will help you to see. Look! Into the face of the sun.''

I stare upward at the sky. "Time for a ride, Theo Truthsayer,'' Thorn says. "Let's go, little one. Stare into the
sun.''

I stare. Pain makes me want to squeeze my eyes shut
and draws tears. When Thorn throws his cloak over my
face I feel relief and blessed coolness. We are moving.
The wind is rushing at my feet and the cry of the grass
becomes more and more faint. Darkness is moist and cold;
the cloak keeps off the sun so I'm feeling it only as a
vague tingling in my face.

I can hear Thorn's voice: "You think I enjoy drinking
the blood of my subjects, little boy? How little you
understand.''

"Of course you enjoy it!'' I've seen that look of lascivious pleasure, I've seen his lips twist into the special smile of the paingiver.

He doesn't answer me. I think about Thorn's father. I know Thorn is thinking about him too, and that he's already starting to regret that confrontation beneath the cliffs of the gray sea.

We're moving. Not across the desert with the thunk-thunk of broken airconditioning and the smell of death. I can hardly feel movement. I'm wrapped up in Thorn's cloak. I'm his creature, clinging to the cool fabric.

Presently I try to peer through a fold of his cloak. The wind blasts me. It's already sunset. I don't understand how the day and night work in this world, so I don't know how long we've been in flight. But we're still over ocean. The air hums. It's hot, with a sweet smell, something like chrysanthemum tea.

I flinch from the wind, but soon I bunch up the fabric so as to make a peephole for myself. The wind makes my eyes smart and at first I can only see vague shapes. They're ice-trolls rearing up from black waves. They're statues of moon-pierced marble, smashed pyramids, megalithic faces half submerged, staring at the moon with eyes that are crystal mountains or lakes of still water. Jesus this is beautiful, I'm thinking, but part of me knows I've made this world myself, out of bits and pieces of my Dad's Sunday poetry readings, and that what I see may have nothing to do with what *is* at all. They have been telling me that I'm the truthsayer, the only one who can see the one true world behind the quadrillions of phantom universes, who can know the true names of all things and control their very existences; but how can this be? I ask myself. How? When everything I've seen, touched, smelled, has been dredged up from things I've dreamt?

From the dream book:
I'm in the forest and I see the Red King, sleeping against the trunk of a tree. I know that the tree is Ygg-

*drasil, the tree of the universe. My guide is Alice, and I
know I've somehow been transported to the set of a movie
version of* Through the Looking-Glass. *Among the trees I
can see cameras moving over well-greased dollies and
lizard men making notes and pulling foci. I watch but I'm
not quite there, because I'm somehow in the cameras as
they slither around the periphery of the clearing.*

*"Silly Alice!" says someone. It's the voice of the Vam-
pire King. "You're only a sort of thing in the Red King's
dream."*

*Another voice: the voice of the dragon princess: "You
wouldn't want him to wake up now, would you?"*

A third voice: "If he wakes up, we'll all disappear."

*The cameras titter among themselves like seventh grade
girls in the school cafeteria.*

*I walk over to the Red King. He's snoring. He's a giant
red chess piece with diamonds for eyes. As I walk toward
him I realize that I can go right into him. I can fuse with
him, become him . . . and if I do he will regain his soul
and awaken.*

I'm being pulled into him.

*I'm not even real, I'm more like an astral projection or
something, a kind of a hokey New Age thing people like
to talk about on late night TV shows.*

*I'm swirling into the Red King . . . swirling . . . swirl-
ing . . . and so I scream and scream to make myself wake
up . . . but if I wake up and I am not inside the king will
he wake up too? I don't think about these things I just
stand there and scream and scream but no one can hear
me and . . .*

"We've arrived," Thorn tells me.

I feel soft grass against my ankles. I twist free from his
cloak. We're standing in a courtyard. And there are like
these gargantuan columns covered in hieroglyphics all
around us, so tall that their tops disappear into mist. You
can hear wailing in the distance. I can't tell if it's birds

or women. They sound lost. Another sound too, a whip cracking perhaps. I'm scared. I want to leave.

"You can't," says Thorn, reading my mind. He must have seen the cosmic marble clenched between my fingers, flashing, as I stand there thinking to myself *If I run down to the river I can find my own way home*. Roughly he grabs me by the arm and pushes me forward. The hall is huge, like the Roman Forum in *Fall of the Roman Empire* and the Forbidden Palace from *The Last Emperor* and the Ishtar Gate from *Intolerance* all rolled into one. I stumble forward. The air smells salt, like the sea, like women's tears. I pause to look at the hieroglyphics on the columns. They are the usual Egyptian sort of things, with vultures and reeds and hippopotamuses and ankhs . . . and also my face. A thousand times my face staring down at me from sandstone columns. The sighing comes closer now. It's definitely human . . . a mob of humans, maddened by grief.

A creek runs alongside us, bordered with mosaic tiles. It's the creek that smells of the sea, of human pity. He pushes me along the edge of it. I look away from the glyphs.

"Good," says Thorn, "no need to read the inscriptions that foretell your coming to salve the world's suffering. Don't want to give you a swelled head or worse, some kind of a Jesus complex. Come on."

Our footsteps barely skim the stone floor, but already the columns are rushing by on either side like the palms along the avenues of Beverly Hills that you always see in movies when you're driving through Lalaland.

The creek gets narrow. We come to a wall that seems to have condensed out of the sky of Thorn's gray world.

The creek flows from an opening in the wall. The opening is encircled by a stone dragon that swallows its own tail.

In my fist, the marble flashes. I'm very scared now but Thorn pushes me along the tile bank, through the opening, into a chamber hollowed out of rock. The water splashes me. It is salt. There is a smell of lemon freshener. Suddenly I realize that we have come, by a curious circumnavigation of dimensions, to the bathroom under Mr. Huang's restaurant in Arizona. I can see myself and Joshua fighting . . . I'm leaning over the sink, bleeding into the running water. It's me and not me, another me, and behind me there's a shadow-me and another and another. . . .

"Too many realities . . . I can't see," I say softly.

"Look harder, Theo Truthsayer," says Thorn.

My other selves begin to melt. I'm focusing hard now. The other times and places that are in this room start to dissolve, and now I can't hold on to them, they're like a dream that slips away when the sunlight comes on you suddenly in the morning.

That's when I see the altar and the woman.

She's the mermaid I saw on the open sea, the one Thorn drained of life and flung back into the water. She's lying on a black altar cloth with candles at her head and feet and incense burning from braziers at the four corners. Behind her I can see women with bare breasts, wailing, pounding their fists against their hearts, weeping. I can't tell how many women there are because it's dark. Their tears are dripping onto the dead mermaid and a little rivulet of tears trickles down the side of the altar, down seven stone steps, becomes the creek that flows out of the room into the grand temple into the courtyard into the stream that joins with the gray sea.

Now and then, behind the weeping women, a tall man lashes at them with a whip. I wince. Their tears are wrung from them. How can their grief be real? But I know it is. I know their pain because I see what is in their hearts.

"Go up the steps," Thorn says. He gives me a little push. "I'll be right behind you."

I walk up to the altar.

Where the tears drip down onto the stone, there are

flowers and strands of grass that spring up from cracks and crevices.

I'm standing over the dead girl, gazing into her eyes. She doesn't seem dead to me. The greenish hue of her skin is like new grass peering out of the snow.

I know that she died willingly. That these women's lamentation is a willing thing, not wrung from them with threat of torture. It is how the world works. The living fling themselves into the death-giving embrace of their king and their death gives birth to the grief from which spring the tears that make up the water that girds the kingdom and gives life to the earth. It's all one process: the love, the kiss of death, the sorrow of the sisterhood, the water of live.

So I know something more about Thorn now.

I know that he's unhappy.

"In this place, they call me the harvester of tears," Thorn says.

I know now that Thorn has done a very difficult thing by kidnaping me and exposing to me his need for me, his vulnerability. I can't see him as evil anymore. He's arrogant and spiteful and full of cold asides, but it's because he has to live with himself all the time, and I know that he hates himself.

It's because I know all this about Thorn that I finally say to him, "I'll help you if I can, Thorn. You didn't choose to be who you are or how the universe works. I want to get home to my family. But maybe the reality I came from will never come back. Until I find my way home, I'll stop struggling against what you've shown me to be. I am a truthsayer. I know it's true and there's nothing I can do to make my powers go away. I'll help you if you'll help me. We have to establish some kind of a working relationship."

He turns away from me. Perhaps he is weeping. But I know he is too proud to show it to me, a precocious little shit from Virginia.

chapter fourteen

_____

Seeking Asylum

Phil Etchison

So there we were: a policeman, a teenage girl who
seemed to know everything about me and whose image
in my mind seemed inextricably linked with that of a
slug . . . and a supernatural being I couldn't even see at
all except, now and then, as a kind of dappled light against
the torn red vinyl of Milt Stone's police car.

We were going to rescue my wife from the madhouse.

Once I had accepted the idea of my own insanity, I was
able to enjoy myself after a fashion. The girl spoke to me
often of disjunctive fugue, a concept even the deconstruc-
tionists and semioticians might have had trouble defining.
She was being prompted by her invisible companion. I had
yet to see this Ash, but Milt claimed to be convinced. Maybe
it was just that he was a Navajo and lived closer to the spirit
world than us chairs of poetry from Northern Virginia.

Serena and I were in the back seat peering through the
security glass at the back of Milt's head as he drove. We

had abandoned the other car. It had been stolen, but Milt was curiously unmoved by this. As we turned onto Speedway he merely called it in and turned it over to someone else to pick up, identify, retrieve.

"Can you show me that book again?" I asked Serena. I meant the book that was mine and not mine, the book with the wrong dedication and the wrong binding. She held it out. There was something fluid about the book, something shifting.

"I can't let you touch it. Do you understand why?"

I played along. "Reality contamination," I suggested. "Particles of my reality infecting it, converting it . . . reality as virus." What a great metaphor; maybe even the title of my next chapbook.

This is what I read:

> They are standing at the river's edge; sometimes
> I watch them, sometimes
> I cannot bear to watch. . . .

"What is this?" I said. "It seems almost like a kind of parody of my poem. . . ."

"It's not a parody, Mr. E.," Serena Somers said gravely, "I remember when you wrote it. You had just come back from Colorado . . . a holiday in the country. I saw it on your desk."

I reached out to touch it.

"Oh no, you don't," said Serena.

"One home for the perpetually confused, coming right up," said Milt Stone, and we pulled in.

The sun was setting, suddenly, as it always does in Arizona.

Joshua Etchison

I flew on the back of the dragon woman, through clouds of fire, following the course of a sulphurous river.

"How far are we going?" I shouted.

She didn't answer me. We flew on.

The vortex swirled. The fire filled the sky. The fumes choked me. The wind was hot, searing. I felt like I was going through a kind of death. But when I couldn't take it anymore there was suddenly a chilled glass of ice water in my hand, and the glass bore the logo of the Dragon Spring Water Company and the face of Katastrofa Darkling smiled up at me from the water and I drank and drank and the goblet never seemed to empty, I drank death and oblivion and Katastrofa, and with each gulp I thought less and less of the other world. . . .

Phil Etchison

. . . and then it was dark. I longed for a drink and I knew I couldn't have one, especially fizzy red drinks prepared by overbearing Chinamen. There was a soft breeze and the oleander bushes swayed. The oleanders were what stood between me and Mary, Mary who stood at the window of her prison looking out at the wrong universe.

I could see her framed in the window. The window was open; she stood with parted lips and the wind made her hair move, strand by strand. "Mary," I said, "Mary, look down at me."

She said: "Phil. Serena, you brought Phil with you."

Joshua Etchison

I kissed the dragon, I was inside the whirlwind dragon. She was all woman and all dragon and one by one she plucked the memories from me:

Mother Mary in the woods smelling of death by the stream with no hair and three blankets shivering in the summer and—

Phil scribbling in his notebook, never looking at us kids, and—

Theo, his back to me, biking down the dirt road in Spotsylvania County away from me away from Grandma's house and—

She kissed away the memories. And I said, "I can't live without the memories, without the memories I'm just a sort of a thing in someone else's dream."

And she said, "You don't have to live. You're already dead. That's what the crossing did to you. You're not the real truthsayer and to you the gateways are dim and dangerous. You've crossed the boundary and it's killed you. But I will love you, dead or alive. It doesn't matter to me. Half-truths are better than no truths at all."

It made no sense but it didn't matter because I was kissing her inside the whirlwind inside the dragon.

Phil Etchison

I said, "We're taking you away. Because somehow . . . everything's changed. Maybe you're not crazy."

"Of course I'm not."

Serena said: "I'm going to create a diversion."

She began running toward the front entrance, screaming. Milt turned on the siren. He ran after her. I saw the two of them on the steps. She was doing a very convincing job of struggling hysterically. I heard an alarm go off and I saw a couple of orderlies running out of the front entrance.

"Open the window all the way," I said. It had gotten cold along with the vanished sun. Mary struggled with the window. She reached for the bushes, slid down. She was in my arms. I tasted bitter poison, the sap of the oleander, spat it out. "Come on," I said. I held her hand and steadied her. Her hospital gown billowed and when she looked back at me her eyes seemed focused on another world. A faint sweet smell came from her; behind the sweet smell another odor, like a stale locker room. I remembered that it was the smell of schizophrenia that I had grown used to in the long years of marriage—

—but then I remembered another smell too, a smell of dying, and I knew that *that* was the smell I had grown used to, not this, and I teetered on the brink of two realities, thinking this is not my wife and where have the children gone and why are we in Tucson not in Mexico heading toward the laetrile clinic at the speed of light and—

Tire squeal. Milt backed up the police car. Serena leaped up on the hood. The orderlies tripped down the steps in front of the hospital's baroque façade, bathed in yellow radiance from floodlights mounted on cactuses that lined the driveway.

I opened the door, shoved Mary onto the back seat, followed. The police car backed up all the way down the drive, then stopped so that Serena could climb in the front. There was someone else with her. I could see him clearly now.

"Is that Ash?" I said.

No one answered me.

The car careened up the avenue. I thought somone would be pursuing us, but we were not even noticed. Ash became clearer. He looked to me like a boy barely past puberty, delicate-featured, a mischievous smile, and the same unfocused gaze that Mary had.

The other cars in the streets become blurred. Street lights were streaks of rainbow-fringed light. The road turned, twisted, knotted itself into ribbons. The weirder the landscape, the clearer Ash became to me. Suddenly I intuited that we too were a blur, a thing seen from the corner of the eye, quickly dismissed as a trick of the light.

Ash spoke to us. He had the power to make us calm. His voice was a quiet music that stilled my unease and filled me with the sense that I stood at the edge of something huge and wonderful and ungraspable; you get that feeling sometimes when you go to the symphony and you arrive there late and you have to stand outside until the first intermission and from the foyer you hear a huge mysterious music muted by distance, muffled by velvet and marble. Yes, that's what he sounded like to me, though all he said was "Phil, Phil, Phil, be still, be still."

I was sandwiched in between Ash and Mary. In front, Serena clutched the book with my wrong poems to her chest. Milt Stone drove on; we took the 10 I think, because I saw the freeway sign float past, unless it was a sphinx or a brontosaurus.

I said, "Why are we here? Where are we going? Milt, you're a policeman, aren't you? . . . Don't you have a job to do?"

"Not anymore," he said. "I've heard a voice that's calling me to an ancient place. I've called in at the office and they all understand. I'm on vision quest leave, that's what you could call it. Where there's a lot of Indians, the white men's rules gotta give a little."

He began to sing. Ash kept time by slapping his thigh, but soon the slapping sounded like the pounding of a drum, and when he began whistling it was like one of those wooden flutes, shrill and haunting as the wind on the high mesa.

I squeezed my wife's hand and she squeezed back, tentatively at first, and then with a whole lot of pent-up passion. "I thought you'd never come," she said. I thought she meant coming and rescuing her from the madhouse, but suddenly I knew she also meant come inside her universe, step away from the world I still believed to be the real, sane world, into the cosmos of her lunacy and my two lost sons.

"I love you," I said. I wondered how long it had been since I had told her that.

The street lights whirled. The headlights of oncoming eighteen-wheelers stretched and stretched until they lassoed us with ropes of yellow radiance. Cactuses danced in the air.

"Where are we going?" I shouted.

Ash said, "Back to where the realities first diverged. It's the best way to get our bearings."

I kissed my wife with a passion I had not felt since the birth of my lastborn. . . .

What lastborn? Were not our sons illusions, creatures of her madness? Yet now I was being pulled into her dream world, now I felt as though it were I who had been mad, I whose body reeked of schizophrenia. But the passion that swept over me was not insanity. I kissed Mary and she kissed me back and it seemed that the whole world whirled with us at the whirlwind's center.

Joshua Etchison

And she said to me, "How does it feel to be dead," and I said, "It doesn't matter if we can be together, like this, at the eye of the storm," and I was thinking fuck Theo fuck my parents fuck all of them because I've gone beyond where they are, I'm dead but it's as if they were dead and I was alive for the first time. And kissed her.

Phil Etchison

As we broke away I saw the outline of the Chinese restaurant against the kaleidoscoping desert. What Chinese restaurant? Yes, there had to have been a Chinese restaurant. Where we opened up fortune cookies and Joshua had punched out—

Joshua. *Joshua.*

"How did we get here so soon?" I said.

We were in a howling duststorm. Dust pelted the windshield, pebbles clanked against the fenders and the hood. The wind screamed. In the middle of it all stood the Chinese restaurant, like a Mediaeval castle on a cliff jutting from a storm-tossed sea. I saw the castle too. I saw the

clashing rocks and heard the song of the mermaids. I knew
we were driving through universes in collison.

Suddenly the storm ended.

The Chinese restaurant melted into sunrise.

We were parked atop a mesa. There was no visible
roadway down to the 10, which snaked below us. One by
one we got out of the car.

"This isn't the place," I said.

But I knew that it really was the place after all. The
same coordinates at any rate. The identical spot in an
unidentical world.

Mary smiled.

"Jesus, I wish I could have a drink," I said.

Ash said, "It's the drinks that have addled your mind.
Drinks in fantastical colors, weren't they, drinks served
by a tall man with a jaundiced complexion." I could see
Ash almost clearly now, the way you see a ghost; he was
translucent; he refracted the dawn so that he seemed
haloed in a rose-tinted iridescence.

"Yes," I said, "I seem to remember that there were
always these drinks, and that they were brought to me
by—Cornelius Huang, he called himself." Every time I
had had one of those drinks, hadn't I felt somehow more
comfortable with the way things were?

"He calls himself Corny," said Ash, "because he is a
herald. He works for my brother Thorn. My brother is
a vampire. My sister, Katastrofa, is a weredragon. You
understand, they were not always this way. They became
worse, you see, after my father divided his kingdom—
each became an outward image of his inner self."

If this was how things really were, was it all that sur-
prising that I found the drink-induced realities more
credible?

"No more drinks," Serena said, "please, Mr. E. Even
if you go into withdrawal or worse."

As though I were emerging from a dream state, I found
my vision clearing. The wind was brisk and cold. There

was no Chinese restaurant at all here. No gilt pavilions lined with gaudy dragons. No tall Chinese man in a mandarin's costume.

There was, improbably, a well.

Around the well was a circle of stones, each one as tall as a man, each one covered with faded pictographs.

I saw Serena conferring with Ash. I saw Milt Stone go off toward the cliff's edge and stare into the rising sun.

Mary said, "Is it all coming back to you now? The Chinese restaurant? I was dying of cancer then; do you remember?"

An image: Mary wrapped in a Navajo blanket, bald from chemotherapy, her eyes sunk, always cold even in the blazing desert daylight—

Theo who always spoke the truth—

"But these are your fantasies. . . . I've seen the drawings you did in the asylum, I've seen the transcripts of the stories you told the analyst back in Virginia. . . ."

"Then why have they become so vivid, Phil? You never shared my fantasies before, did you?"

"I've always wanted to have children. The children you spoke about so often . . . acquired an inner reality for me." That was the explanation I had set forth in the dedication poem to *The Embrasure of Parched Lips*.

Mary laughed and suddenly I remembered the smell of her dying.

And knew that it was a true memory. Because eyes can deceive you; but smells never lie. I was coming to terms with disjunctive fugue, I supposed.

We followed Milt Stone as he strode toward the well. He seemed to know what he was doing. As he walked he seemed to shed everything that bound him to the white men's world—his walk became more measured, more in time with the timeless music of the wind; he sang a wordless melody; his hair streamed, his arms moved in an arrhythmic flapping, like the wings of a circling bird of prey.

"What are you doing, Milt?" I shouted to him.

His walk took him perilously close to the edge of the precipice. He did not stumble. He did not look down at his feet. His gaze was fixed on the well.

"Hey, policeman, you're gonna like fall off," Serena said. "This is no time to practice your Wile E. Coyote imitation."

Milt began to sing. I know the words of the song by heart now, because whenever I relive these moments the words come to me, alien and jagged as the desert rocks:

Piki yo-ye	*Dsichl-nantai*
Piki yo-ye	*Saa-narai*
Piki yo-ye	*Bike hozhoni*
Piki yo-ye	*Tsoya-shich ni-la*
Piki yo-ye!	

It was a joyous song, and though the sand seared my eyes I knew that the mountain was my friend. I wanted to dance as he was dancing, to give in to the wind's music, but I was afraid. I did not think I could give up so much of myself. I was fearful of every footstep. Far below us, along the 10, cars drifted like dead leaves in a stream.

At length he stopped. We others went up to him. We didn't want to get too close to him. It felt as though if we breathed on him he would topple to his death.

He said, "This is one of the openings through which the first men came up into the Fourth World, the world of sorrow in which we now live. This is the entrance to the underworld which is also the labyrinth of dreams. The people were driven out of the underworld by a great flood. Once upon a time, when I went to Arizona State and took the courses that would help me live in the white men's world, I would have called the place the Unconscious. Dr. Freud would say the Unconscious is like a vast and sunless ocean. Dr. Jung, more to the point, would probably agree, though he would be less likely to see a sexual connotation in every large body of water. Perhaps that is why we are all experiencing this gateway in the form of a well.''

I am not a fan of New Age blandishments, and I didn't particularly enjoy Milt's speech. As an undergraduate, I had sat through a whole series of Joseph Campbell lectures, so I was familar with the mythic underpinnings of psychoanalysis.

So I was a little annoyed when the creature Ash nodded knowingly. Of course, Ash was quite probably a figment of someone's Unconscious himself, and, with archetypes, it takes one to know one.

And as for Serena and my wife—they were as rapt and glassy-eyed as Catholics at mass. I was alone in my doubt.

I elbowed them all aside and stood at the edge of the well. I leaned down. The shaft went down, down, down. It was like Alice's tunnel to Wonderland. I could hear the ripple of moving water. It was the echo of the flood that had driven Milt Stone's people up from the ancient void. I heard it the way astronomers hear the Big Bang echoing still on their radio telescopes eons after it happened.

I could hear the sea. I could see lights: the gold vermilion of a seaside sunset, the silver glitter of a moonlit lake. I thought I could see a face.

More than a face. I could see a teenage boy enveloped in the embrace of a firebreathing dragon.

The boy was dead. I knew he was dead because of his eyes. They stared up at me without recognition, though I knew that he ought to know my name, that I belonged to him.

I whispered, ''Joshua.''

Mary gasped. She stood next to me now, and I felt her cold fingers skimming the hand that clutched the edge of the well.

''All right, Mrs. E! You see, he *is* starting to come back now!''

''Do you see anyone else?'' Mary said.

''Not yet.''

Joshua Etchison

—and kissed her, and turned away from the memory of my father's eyes—

Phil Etchison

"Not yet," I said. Because I had not yet given in to the wind's music. Because I still felt impelled to anchor myself in a single reality. Because I did not easily trust my emotions. Because it was hard for me to acknowledge the truth of elemental feelings: grief, faith, love, disillusion.

chapter fifteen

Blood and Circuses

Theo Etchison

My first day at work: there's a whole fleet of Thorn's ships, triremes, longboats, galleons, all of them with gargoyle prows and black sails and ghoulish crews, but I'm riding in the flagship of them all, sitting at the right hand of Mr. Death himself, with a three-headed dog yapping at my heels and Cornelius Huang making his conch sing somber music.

I'm standing right by the prow with the marble in my hand and I guess I'm kind of piloting, even though this path is so well worn that the fleet meets no resistance from the reality stream. We move through a thousand universes in a thousand seconds. I scarcely feel them blipping by.

The fleet puts in at like this island that's in the middle of a lake where a lots of streams converge. It's neutral territory. I can feel it. The dog has stopped barking and Thorn paces about the deck unconfident of his authority.

A harbor comes into view and Mr. Huang blows seven earsplitting blasts in seven directions.

I can see a city. A *Blade Runner* city gone cancerous, skyscrapers piled on skyscrapers, smokestacks belching, pillars of fire, traffic on the ground and in the air. We've stepped from fantasy into science fiction. I've left the Mediaeval kingdom of vampires and mermaids and arrived at another world.

I don't get a chance to look at the city for long. It hurts me to look. The city seems to be breathing, writhing, spewing out people who scurry through streets and skyways and slidewalks like hive insects.

We stand by the prow of the ship but no shuttle comes to pick us up and we make no move to go ashore. The timbers creak and ooze dark blood.

"Let the map guide you," Thorn says. I hold up the marble. It catches the light of an alien sun. "Do you know where we are going?"

"I think it's something like an arena or conference room," I say. Although what I'm seeing in my mind's eye is more like a kind of mega-Nintendo game. But that's ridiculous, isn't it?"

"Yes, something like that."

I close my eyes. Seize the pathway with my mind. Call out its name in the secret language of truthsaying. And we are there, all at once, Thorn and I and a couple of hangers-on. Once again I should have believed my instincts. The place we're in is kind of like the Colosseum in Rome, with tier upon tier upon tier enclosing a kind of arena. But what's in the arena—except that it's in 3-D or maybe even 4-D and surround-sound, *is* a lot like a Nintendo. Well, that's all right. I'm not intimidated by video games, even ones as big as a thirty-story building. After all, I'm a kid. I haven't yet traded in my lightning reflexes for the hormonal imbalances of adolescence, not like my brother Josh.

"Well," says Thorn, "we're all waiting."

"Lemme get this straight," I say. "You tore me away from my family, dragged me across a jillion spacetime-lines, fed me a bunch of bullshit about compassion and saving the universe like we were in some third-rate Dungeons and Dragons game . . . just so I could set a new high score on—on—"

"It's the fate of the universe all right," Thorn says. "Remember, boy, you may be the messiah or whatever, but you're still filtering the wonders of these myriad worlds of ours through that pubescent little brain—you see what you know."

So what do I know today, my first day on the job?

The herald blasts away on his conch. They announce my name. I look around at the tiers of guests and I see all kinds of species. There are humans in outlandish costumes with their hair piled into pyramids and obelisks. There are these giant calamari-creatures flopping around in glass tanks, staring down with unblinking eyes. There are aliens of every description, reclining on couches, drinking, gobbling up little rodents that scurry back and forth under the furniture. There are bipedal vultures in ecclesiastical robes and there are hive-beings that look like baskets of flowers. As Mr. Huang announces my name to the four directions I can feel them all tense up. My coming here has changed everything.

"Maybe you'd better watch for a while, sit the first couple of matches out." Thorn gestures and we're suddenly on a balcony that juts out from the first tier.

There are four of these balconies protruding from different parts of the amphitheater. Ours is packed with sycophants. It's cold here. Fumes rise out of clefts, and the walls drip with blood that coagulates into squishy stalagmites. A stream flows down the center aisle. I know that it's fed from the same source as the stream in the place where the tears are harvested.

Thorn ascends his throne. Sits down and points to a cushion at the bottom of the steps where he wants me to sit. I can hear them whispering all over the hall but I can't catch the words. The brook's murmuring covers up their voices. I shiver.

"Watch carefully," Thorn tells me.

I concentrate on the swirling 3-D video game thing that right now looks like a swirling mass of stars and planets and comets. Everything in it symbolizes something in the real worlds. Each twinkling speck of dust is a real place— a star system, a pocket universe, a chain of dimensional gateways that must be controlled. As I watch, I see people swimming through the simulacrum. This part's a little bit like lasertag I guess, because I think the people are blasting away at each other with like toy weapons. As they do so, some of the stars change color. They're falling into different spheres of influence.

"It's all really happening," I say. "It's not a game at all."

"A very astute observation," Thorn says. "Keep watching. You have to learn the rules."

I watch. It's a real power trip, I can see, for the contestants. They dart in and out of the starfield. They grab planets and hurl them at each other. One of the players is better than all the others. He moves like a robot. He has lightning in his eyes. He somersaults through the vortex, dodging comets and spitting out stars and moons. There's something about him that really frightens me. He can't be human. He's too swift, too mechanical, too perfect.

I can't help staring at him. The way he arcs up. Like a high diver in reverse. His leaping leaves faint light-trails and makes the audience sigh. He's a beautiful thing but there's death in him somehow.

I'm jealous of him the way I'm jealous of Josh, who's always handsomer and more self-assured and who always says the right thing and never shows me any weaknesses except maybe for the time he told me he had never had sex with Serena Somers.

Someone comes spiraling out of the starfield. It's a blur

of flesh and glitter and it tumbles toward the distant ground
and hits it with a thud. The audience jumps to its feet—
those that have feet—and a throaty roar echoes through
the amphitheater. A bloodthirsty sound. They're hungry
for death. The sound goes on and on until it about shakes
the walls and I look away from the arena for the first time.

"A casualty," Thorn says. "They are rare, but it does
happen when a combatant of unusual skill comes into play.
It's probably my sister's doing."

A distant fanfare from all the way across the
amphitheater.

"They're calling for time out, I imagine," Thorn says.
"How about some popcorn?"

Joshua Etchison

I think I *killed* someone.

I closed my eyes. The screaming went on and on. My
blood was racing. I didn't know how I could have killed
him. I hadn't even touched him. That wasn't how the
game was played.

I blinked. I was floating in a huge black void. I was
seeing stars. Maybe it was from the pain behind my eyes.
No. It was a miniature cosmos and I was in the middle
of a *shenjesh* game and I'd just killed someone just by
thinking at him.

The roaring was being to subside. I closed my eyes
and I was transported back to the pavilion of Katastrofa
Darkling.

She was leaning over the edge of the balcony, her hair
billowing in an artificial wind. She was a shadow against
the streaming starlight. Her eyelids were dragonscales, but
otherwise she seemed to be all woman.

She smiled because I'd defeated the last opponent, but
her eyes didn't smile at all. All at once I felt exhausted. I
sank down on the nearest couch. An attendant immediately
started to rub me down with an oily, pungent fluid.

"It smells disgusting," I said. "What is it?"

"It's like, embalming fluid," the attendant said. She went on working me over while others loosened my tunic and brushed my hair. A slave girl—the kind you see in Biblical spectacles, wearing nothing but chains and tattoos—was rubbing my feet. Now and then she squeezed out a maggot and tossed it into a silver bucket.

Katastrofa sat beside me. "You really made the last one fly," she said. "You're not afraid of anything."

"No," I said.

She kissed me. Abraded my lips with her scaly tongue. I felt a piece of skin tear loose. I didn't care. She spat it out into the bucket of maggots.

"You're really coming apart," she said. "But on the whole, I love you better this way."

She kissed me again and I felt desire stirring but it was more like the memory of desire, a ghost of what I felt when I was still alive. She kissed harder and I opened my mouth and it was like a transfusion. I felt the animation. I felt my limbs twitching. It was all dim. But I knew I was dead and I should be grateful to have any feelings at all.

She bit me gently on the cheek. I felt a twinge of remembered pain. Enough to know that I still wanted to be able to feel those things. And then the pain was gone.

"You're strange," I said. "I feel your arms and I don't feel them. I think I'm dreaming but I never seem to wake up."

I heard a distant fanfare. The game would start again soon. I did not know how long I had been playing. It was a game of life and death, a game that maintained the balance between the many worlds over which the Darklings ruled, but it never occurred to me to care about what the game meant. I knew I was good. I knew that when I played I was rewarded with a few moments of remembrance. Each time the high was less and less and each time I became more desperate. I wondered if all dead people feel that way. Maybe when you're lying there all dead and a second lasts a hundred years and then a few drops of blood seep into the earth and touch your lips and you go insane with remembering how it used to feel when the blood rushed recklessly through your veins.

Katastrofa had enslaved me. Death had not released me; it had only tightened her control.

She embraced me and I felt her dragonfire through the chill of my dead flesh.

"Only a minute or two until the next match," she said softly. "You have to win this one for me. Something has changed. There's a new factor. My brother Thorn has found another champion. He's going to be hard to defeat."

"I can kill anything," I said.

"We have visitors," she said. "Be careful. Remember what you have become, and don't think about turning back time. Can't be done."

"Whatever you say," I said. I was a lifeless puppet and she held all the strings.

There was a thunderclap and a cloud of smoke, as if someone had let off about a dozen of those extra-strength Hong Kong firecrackers. Then I saw the tall mohawked Chinese dude in the weird robes, the one who had abducted my brother. He had a conch-shell in his hand and he lifted it to his lips.

He blew three blasts. On number three my brother came through the puff of smoke. We saw each other at the same time.

Suddenly I felt frighteningly, overwhelmingly alive. I was bursting with hate and grief and the smell of Katastrofa confused my nostrils with nausea and desire and I could feel my family's love wreching me apart ten different ways and I knew that all these feelings came out of Theo, that he too could make me dance at the end of his string and make me forget I was dead. And while Katastrofa was good at creating the illusion of power, Theo was the power itself.

And I saw that Katastrofa was afraid of him.

Theo Etchison

We're on the balcony of the dragon-woman and there I am staring at someone who seems to be Joshua yet doesn't give off any of Joshua's vibes. I know the woman; I've seen her in my vision interrogating Josh at the police station. She's the one who brought him here. She's the enemy of Thorn, and she's his sister.

She's slowly turning into a dragon as she argues with Thorn, her voice becoming more metallic, her wings unfurling. I'm burning up and the sweat is pouring down my back.

"Stay away from my turf," she says. She doesn't so much say it as belch it out with accompanying smoke rings and sulphur-smelling fire. Her wings snap open with a steel-factory kind of clanging.

Thorn says, "This is neutral territory, sister, you know that. This is where we learn to sublimate our destructive passions."

"Get away." Her breath hangs in the air.

"Who's your new boyfriend?"

"Someone important."

"I know you have kinky tastes, sister, but I didn't know you were into dead people."

"You didn't? But you were the one who taught me." Her wings flap. The floor of the pavilion shakes. The heat penetrates the soles of my feet and I stand there hopping from one foot to the other and it's like dancing on live coals.

"I'm not . . . dead. . . ." Josh says softly. I think that's what he's saying.

I look into Josh's eyes and I think, he's beyond salvation, I can't reach him. I go toward him, I go on tiptoe because the floor is glowing from dragonfire. I touch him on the cheek and his cheek peels off in my hand.

"Joshua," I say.

I don't know if he recognizes me.

He's trying to say something. It sounds like *I'm not dead*, repeated over and over. It's the dragonwind whistling through snapped vocal cords.

"Pay no attention to him," Thorn says. "We've a mission to accomplish. We've a vision to fulfill. He's no one anymore, he's just a shadow of what you are."

But I'm a truthsayer and I know better. I know that everything that made him alive is squeezed into a tiny ball inside him no bigger than the marble that holds the key to all the universes. I'm the only person who knows his true name and his true self and I'm the only person who can lead him back out to the world of the living and I can only do it if I plunge my mind into the hell he's hidden in to pull him out.

Trumpets are sounding again. An alien with a Howard Cosell–like voice is floating through the amphitheater on like this big flying disk. He declaims and his words are punctuated by brassy discords.

"Gentlecreatures! Generals! Ambassadors! Delegates, Senators, Neutralities, Principalities, Angels and Archangels!"

A hush falls. I can hear the dragonwoman breathing. I know that to Joshua she appears simply as a beautiful woman. He can't tell the beast from the woman. It's something to do with sex I guess. Also something to do with our mother. He sees her through the blur of mixed-up emotions through the tangle of conflicting realities through the one-way mirror of death.

"The Princess Katastrofa has graciously consented to sponsor the next challenge," the announcer says. There are scattered titters. The starfield whirls. "Who will take it up? Who will answer the challenge of the champion of the Princess of Fire?"

Joshua stands up. He's glowing. Katastrofa breathes on him and he's on fire and he's forgotten who he is. "No!" I scream and I try to grab his arm and pull him toward me but his arm comes off in my hand and blood sprays

my face and he looks at me with unseeing eyes and I
know that all he can see is the woman in the dragon
darkness.

The emcee goes on: "The Duke of Shendering has
formed an aliance with the Queen of the Stone Lizards.
The Empress of the East has unveiled the spear-tips of the
stars and smashed the nebulas of night." And all kinds of
bullshit like you might hear if you were eavesdropping on
a table of young nerds majorly caught up in a fantasy
roleplaying game.

Katastrofa (she is suddenly a woman again) scoops up
Joshua's arm from the smoking floor and snaps it back
into its socket like a Lego piece. The skin knits together
and the blood and pus are slurped back into the flesh. "I
can keep you together for a long long time," she says as
she embraces him. She blocks him from seeing me and I
scream out to him with my mind but he has closed himself
off to me even though I know there's a part of him deep
down inside that knows me and wants to hear me.

My brother is bathed in crimson light. The crowd is
shrieking out his name and his name is a warcry. My
brother turns away from me completely and disappears in
a cloud of smoke and the next thing I know he's walking
slowly toward the heart of the churning starfield across the
sky to the accompaniment of drums and blaring trumpets.

He stops for just a moment. Perhaps he's heard my
silent cry. He's listening for something. He's a tiny figure
poised at the edge of the Nintendo of death.

"Who will take up the challenge?" says Howard
Cosell, his tentacles trailing from his hovering platform.

Thorn says to me, "This is the moment, Theo Truthsayer. This is why I've brought you here."

And I'm thinking: In the heart of the simulacrum it'll
just be me and him and who's to know what passes
between us?

If I can get him alone . . .

"At stake! The seventeen worlds of the Westerly Riff,

once allied with the kingdom of Ash, now fallen into obscurity with the damming of the River!''

''I will be your challenger,'' I say.

A dead silence falls.

Then I hear Katastrofa wailing—it's a sound like a mountain wind and like a police siren—and I hear her wings slapping the dense air. Thorn laughs. I do not think he will be laughing long. Maybe their game is to control the universe, but I have my own game and the stakes are the lives of the people I love.

''You are not . . . ashamed . . . to be making war on your own flesh and blood?'' Thorn asks me softly.

''Isn't that what you're doing?'' I say. ''Anyways, me and my brother're always fighting.''

I think about the time Josh bloodied my nose and we're in the bathroom of the Chinese restaurant and he told me the truth about Serena Somers.

chapter sixteen

Mesa of Lost Women

Serena Somers

Mr. Stone made a fire beside the well, in the shade of
one of the standing stones. He brought out this three-ring
binder from the police car. It was full of notes in a kid's
handwriting, tiny disjointed letters.

Evening was falling. Soon it would be below freezing.

Mr. E. and Mr. Stone pored over the notebook by
flashlight. I knew what it was, of course. It was one of
Theo's dream books. Theo always kept some kind of notebook where he'd write down his secret thoughts. I'd snuck
a look at it once when I came over to study with Josh
when Theo was out there somewhere communing with
nature or whatever it was that he always did all by himself
in the woods by their house. It was full of stories that
Theo would write down after he woke up every morning.
I think the two men were trying to find clues in Theo's
notes: clues about how to get from world to world. They

squatted in the shelter of the stone with their heads touching.

"I could hear someone in the well," Mr. Etchison kept saying.

"The well is the key," said Milt Stone, "the passage through the labyrinth of dreams." Mr. Stone is strange because sometimes he talks like a redneck and sometimes he talks like a college professor. I think that the way he talks is a kind of camouflage. I know all about that because all through junior high I hid my intelligence behind layers of blubber and geekishkeit. So I understood him. That's why I never called him "chief".

Mr. Stone had blankets and sleeping bags in the trunk of his police car. Mr. Stone had everything in that trunk, I mean he must have been a boy scout or something once because he was more prepared than anyone had a right to be. I mean, getting blown into another universe isn't like your everyday crisis, but he had that trunk crammed: tools, food, butane tanks, even a spare car battery and a couple of Stephen King books.

Mrs. E. and I lay down to sleep next to the well and were lulled to sleep by the water's whispering and the wind's wuthering. There was no sign of Ash, but that didn't surprise me; he had a way of coming and going and blending with the scenery until he felt like showing up again.

When I woke up it was still night. I could hear the men snoring. Mrs. E. wasn't lying beside me. I saw her silhouetted against the full moon, looking skyward at the stars, so many stars, so many more than I'd ever dreamed you could see. I picked up the blanket I'd been lying under and wrapped myself up snug and made my way toward her through the ice-cold wind.

"There's really just you and me," said Mrs. E. softly, "because Phil doesn't really remember. And Milt is in it because of some spiritual need that doesn't have anything to do with us."

I stood there and listened. Mrs. E. always used to talk to herself a lot in the days when she was dying of cancer.

"In the end," she told me, "it always comes down to us women. We're the anchors. We're strong, we can hold on to reality while for them it just keeps slipping through their fingers. That's the real difference between men and women. They *want* to know but we just *know*."

"But Theo knows," I said, "if you believe the things Ash has been telling me, I mean about his superpowers or whatever they are. According to Ash, everything we see or think we see is just a shadow of what he sees."

"When he grows older he'll probably lose it," she said. "The truth will become a dream to him. And he'll be just like the rest of the men, hopelessly trying to grasp something that's always out of reach." It didn't seem at all strange to me that a woman fresh out of the loony bin should know about truth and reality and the things that separate men from women.

I could see that she had been crying. I didn't want her to stand out here in the cold. I said, "The fire's still warm, Mrs. E."

"Won't you call me Mary now, Serena?"

"Sure," I said. We were, like, fellow journeyers now.

"I seem to remember," she said, "you used to be kind of fat once."

"A regular Pillsbury doughgirl," I said. "And you were kind of thin."

She smiled.

"If we come out of all of this with our family intact," she said, "I'm going to be getting thin again, real thin."

"I guess so," I said. This was what was hanging over her. She could have her family back maybe, we could turn back the wheel of the worlds, and she'd be dying once more and maybe I'd be fat again. I guess we both had something to sacrifice to bring back Josh and Theo, but for me it wasn't anything like slow painful death. I marveled at how strong she was.

She turned her back on the moon. The wind whistled.
I could feel my cheeks flaking.

"Do you know what Phil said to me this evening?"

"What, Mrs. E?" I couldn't quite bring myself to call
her Mary yet.

"He said he loved me."

I knew that Mr. E. hadn't said that to her in a long
time. Maybe not since the illness set in. Oh, he'd shown
her time and time again—this whole cross-country journey
was a kind of proof of his love, since they all knew that
the laetrile treatment was just a bunch of bullshit—but I
never remembered him ever telling her. Not that I'd been
around much after she started to, you know, smell bad.
Jesus, I love those death scenes in hospital soap operas,
but they don't make TV in smell-o-vision.

I envied her too because Joshua had never said anything
like that to me. I dreamed about him in secret.

"There's a kind of magic on this mesa," said Mary
Etchison. "We're struck between worlds and anything can
happen. I feel almost like we're in the middle of *A Midsummer Night's Dream*. And we can sleep and wake up
to find ourselves different people. We can lose our own
names. We can fall in love with—"

"Dudes with donkey's heads," I said, remembering the
movie we saw in Mrs. Lackland's Shakespeare class. "I'm
not surprised you can't sleep."

"Yeah. The wind has this haunting music to it. Can
you hear it? Listen, listen."

What I heard in the wind was Ash's voice, the voice I
always heard when I was a little girl tossing and turning
and being afraid of the pattern of leafy moonlight through
the Venetian blinds in the steamy summer Virginia nights.
A voice that tickled me, you know, down there, before
I'd learned the words for desire, before I'd learned to
touch myself and rock myself to sleep against the rolled-
up comforter with the smell of sweat and goosedown in

my nostrils and the image of Joshua dancing in my squeezed-tight eyelids. That's what I heard in the roaring of the wind. "Yes," I told her, "it *is* magic."

"The first time I made love with Phil," she said, and she wasn't really talking to me anymore, although she was pressing her hand against my cold hand, "was in a barn at his parents' country place."

"That's intensely romantic," I said, thinking about the drive-in and the one time I'd gotten close to relieving Josh of his uptightness.

"Not that romantic." She laughed. "Horseshit you know. But there was something magical, like tonight. I think there was someone else with us. I think he was standing over us or maybe sitting beside the bed. He was my guardian angel. I never saw him but when I dreamed of him he was a slender boyish creature, not quite a man or a woman. I think I've seen that person again. He came with you to the psychiatric ward, I think. That *was* him, wasn't it? I think he's with us now but I can never be sure whether he's really there."

"Ash?"

"His name doesn't matter."

In a way I was even a little jealous. Ash was my childhood secret. But it was exciting too, knowing that we'd shared this experience. Maybe all of us women have someone like Ash in our lives and we spend all our time repressing the memory.

"It's because of him that we haven't slid from universe to universe like the guys have," I said. "He told me that. How he even went back in time to whisper in my ear when I was four years old, so I'd recognize him and not be afraid when I saw him again."

"I think it was when I stopped seeing him that I started to die," Mary said. She wiped her eyes. "Jesus God Serena I don't want to die. But it has to happen for things to come out right."

"Maybe not. Maybe Theo knows something we don't know."

"No. There's no magic really," she said. "It's just wishful thinking."

"No magic?" I said. "But you said so yourself! Listen to the music of the wind, you said! You even made me hear it—you made me hear—oh, so much awesomeness!"

The wind howled. The moon was radiant, wreathed with a wisp of cloud. I could hear coyotes, I thought. The magic was still there.

"Come on, Serena," she said. "Maybe we can toast some marshmallows or something while the others search for the truth."

"Yeah, Mary, yeah." A satisfying moment of female bonding.

"Did you know you're getting beautiful?"

But to me I'm still sluglike Serena, I thought.

A helicopter crossed the moon. Abruptly the spell was broken. We both looked back at the standing stones. Mr. E. was waving at the helicopter with a big white cloud tied to a branch.

"Does this mean we're being rescued?" I shouted.

We ran toward him. He was gesturing wildly at the sky. Mr. Stone was squatting on a blanket in some kind of loincloth. He didn't seem to notice the cold at all. He was a little withered-looking but beautiful, like one of those sepiatone postcards of olden time Indians that they sell in souvenir stores along the Arizona highways.

"No, no, not rescued," he said excitedly, "not rescued at all—*we're* going to be doing the rescuing."

"I radioed for supplies," Mr. Stone said. "Tents, pickaxes, canned food, portable generator, you know, stuff."

"You must have a lot of clout," I said. "I don't quite swallow the business about, like, vision quest leave."

"Sometimes I surprise myself. We're going to be here

for a while. We have to get the rituals right. I'm having a few anthropology books delivered along with our canned corned beef.'' He pronged a marshmallow with a twig and brandished it at Ash.

Ash was back. I could see him in the flickering firelight. Meanwhile the chopper was landing about a hundred yards from us. Mr. Stone got up and sprinted toward it, yelling for help carrying the supplies. Mr. E. followed him. I crouched down by the fire while Mary tended to the half-cooked marshmallow.

I found Theo's notebook lying half-open next to the fire. I leafed through it. I read about dispossessed kings and rivers guarded by lizard warriors. I read about a building-sized video game that controlled the fate of the universe. There were a lot of pages crammed in that three-ring binder and it seemed to me that even while I was reading the number of pages got bigger. When I turned to the end I saw the words forming one by one on the last sheet. As each word formed it seemed as though it had always been there. The universe was in flux and editing itself the whole time I was watching.

The pieces were starting to make sense for me: the river linking the known worlds, the old king, Strang, who had divided his kingdom, the siblings squabbling over spoils, King Strang haunted by a dark bargain he'd made so he could control the river, Ash dispossessed for speaking the truth. In his dream book Theo compared it to *King Lear*, but I had to admit I'd never seen it—I had a hard enough time with *A Midsummer Night's Dream*.

The chopper moved off. Mr. Stone and Mr. Etchison were jabbering away to each other about ancient Native American peyote cults. Mary was asleep, wrapped in a blanket. I grabbed the marshmallow before it burned and handed it to Ash. He munched it very slowly. The light danced in his eyes and the shadows striped his face and he looked kind of like a lurking tiger.

"Talk to me, Ash," I said. "Tell me the things you used to tell me."

He whispered to me in the secret language of my childhood.

chapter seventeen

Joshua

Theo Etchison

The emcee has a glowing baseball in his hand. The ball is one of the worlds they're fighting over. He hurls it into the spinning void. The cheering crescendoes.

My brother has already dived after it.

"Go on then," says Thorn. Katastrofa glares at him. She has become a woman again. She's only all the way dragon when she's near Joshua. He excites her somehow and she changes.

I take the marble out of my pocket. Concentrate on it and through it into the heart of the simulated cosmos. I clamber up onto the edge of the balcony, on tiptoe, right on the railing. I sway. I can hear the crowd catch its breath. I close my eyes and I can still see the marble with my inner eye, even more clearly than before. I keep my eyes closed and I leap. It is a leap of faith. And before I know it I am caught up inside the game and I can feel the

starwind and the stars themselves hurtling past on pathways within pathways.

I'm flying. The game has become huge. I can't see the
crowd. The outside world is meaningless. But in the distance I see Josh. He's good. He flits about, rolling his
body up into a ball and catapulting himself forward by
sliding through the gravity wells of the heaviest stars.

At first I don't do anything because I'm totally overwhelmed by what I'm seeing and feeling. This mega-video
game is an analog of reality but it also *is* reality. I know
this because I can zero in on any part of it with like a
zoom lens in my mind, and the more I zoom the more I
see, there's never a moment where I realize that it's all
just dots like it would be if it were a computer screen. I
turn up the amplification on one cold blue dot and find
myself shrinking until I'm a dot floating high above the
atmosphere of a windy planet where the ice mountains
spurt blue liquid fire and in a detached kind of way I feel
the searing cold of it too.

I look at another dot and it becomes a crowded world—
a world of countries and wars and—zooming closer—alien
creatures thronging the streets and—closer—a furry mam-
mal being sacrificed to a fire-breathing god. Priests with
demon masks and acolytes with censers standing all
around. I think I'm in one of my dreams because the
outlines are all blurry but it could be from the incense that
burns my eyes. And I can feel the animal's deathscream,
so quickly—

I unzoom myself because the long view is more
detached and less full of pain.

I watch Joshua in pursuit of the glowing baseball. There
are other players too but he's better than all of them. Well,
he's good at sports and shit. He zeroes in on the ball
as it spirals through octopoid nebulas and careening star
systems. No one can keep up with him. They are shadows
dancing against the starstream.

I follow him. I cloak myself in clouds of galactic dust.

I shadow him as he chases the ball and dodges his opponents. I'm close to him but he doesn't see me.

I stretch myself out so that I'm huger than a star system and more attenuated even than the emptiness of space. I stretch out. I tuck myself into the curvature of the universe and thread myself through the wormholes that interconnect the spaces between spaces. I can do all this because I can see the essences of things and to see truth is to become one with it. I am the web and the worlds warp through me as the cosmos weaves itself into a tapestry of seamless becoming.

This is no video game. The Nintendo of death is just another metaphor that my mind has been using to screen out the flood of data. Everything is a metaphor. Reality is a metaphor for a deeper reality that's a metaphor for a deeper reality. I wrap myself around the cosmic egg. I'm the incubator of all life. I'm God.

Just when the megalomania is getting to be too enjoyable, I hear a gnat-voice buzzing in my ear.

"You're drifting, boy! Your mind is wandering!"

It's a little Thorn-thing, flitting in and out of my ear. He's in here with me, riding me. I try to throw him off but I can't dislodge him. "Leave me alone!" I scream. But I'm so spread out that my screaming has little effect—a few more subatomic particles collide at the hearts of a few stars, a backwater planet experiences an unseasonable rainstorm.

Thorn laughs. "Stop bucking and start saving the universe," he says.

He goes on talking—it's dull stuff about maintaining the illusion of control and the integrity of the body politic—it makes no sense to me. I grit my teeth. Jesus! I've got my own agenda, even if it means saving a few universes on the side.

I can see Joshua now. He's outstripped his opponents. I'm right behind him but he can't see me because he's concentrating so hard on catching the runaway planet.

Suddenly I sprint ahead, ricocheting off the gravity of the black hole at the heart of a nearby galaxy. I stand in the path of the fireball. I reach out my hand to catch it. It grows into a baseball glove. The planet smacks into my hand and I stagger back for a moment. It's like a live coal. The glove is gone suddenly and I'm treading water in mid-space and juggling the world like a hot potato.

Josh rears up in front of me. He rushes at the planet. His eyes are lifeless. "Oh no, you don't," I say. We fight like this all the time, over a baseball, over a game cartridge, over the last slice of pizza. But I've never seen him so vicious except for the time he punched me out over what I said in the Chinese restaurant. I see that he's wearing a dragon in his ear. It looks like a little silver earring but I know it's part of Katastrofa that's along for the ride.

I keep dodging his punches. He hurls a white dwarf star at me and it grazes my cheek. It's not like Josh to play dirty.

"Don't you know me?" I cry out. Thorn laughs in my ear. Maybe there's a glimmer of recognition in Josh's eyes, maybe not. He pauses. I compress myself tighter and project myself at him and butt him in the stomach and then, as he folds back on himself, I stretch myself wide, wide, wide, until I'm like a cloak wrapping him up in myself like a wind seeping into every pore and before he can react I rip the dragon earring from his ear and throw it into the nearest star . . . then I start shrinking with Joshua inside me, and the planet that was in my hand starts to balloon and balloon and . . . I orbit the planet like a crazed comet until I can feel Thorn losing his grip on me and then I swoop down onto the surface of the world. . . . The black sky turns to brilliant blue and there's a yellow sun glaring at us and we're falling, falling toward the desert below, our arms and legs in a tangle. . . . We're falling toward what looks like Route 10 and Arizona. . . . I spread my arms out and my arms sprout wings held together by wax that's starting to run in the searing sun. . . . Josh! I cry out to him with my mind and he clings to me, dead weight that's making me plummet toward the sand and . . .

I open my wings. I catch the wind. I remember how Thorn carried me through the cloudbanks of the vampire planet and right away my wings become leathern bat-wings. I slow down. We're circling a mesa. In the center of the mesa is a well and around it there are people. My father! and my Mom and a girl who looks like Serena but can't be because Serena was fat. And an Indian dude in a loincloth who's dancing up a storm around the well. And a police car parked beside standing stones.

Is the baseball we've been chasing after Earth?

How did the police car get up on the mesa? There's no road. Below it I see the traffic on the 10. I see that the well is a gateway. It's the same gateway that I came through the first time. Only the world has changed. It's not the same world and they're not the same parents I had before. Those parents are lost in a far-off branching-off of spacetime.

I'm circling closer. My Dad is waving a branch with a shirt tied to it. The wind is roaring but I can hear the Indian guy singing in a wheezing falsetto. Mom and the girl who looks like Serena are talking, waiting. Mom looks different too. I've seen pictures of her in my mind before, I know she's exchanged cancer for madness, but actually seeing it in the flesh makes it come home to me.

Joshua stirs. His skin is blue. He smells of dead things, of meat left out too long. Three digits are missing from his left hand and chunks of flesh from his cheek. He's trying to speak to me. A maggot crawls out of his mouth.

I realize that Dad is trying to attract my attention.

"I'm here, Dad!" I shriek. "I'm still alive, I'm still your son—and I've got Josh here too—"

He waves frantically.

Suddenly, seeing through his eyes, I know that he can't

see me at all. What he is seeing is a helicopter. When I cry out to him he hears the rattle of a chopper's engine. They're waiting for supplies. I hover right over their heads. Josh flails a little and another of his fingers breaks off. I see where the other digits land and are transformed into sleeping bags, piles of food, a cooking stove and a generator. Pieces of their dead son are sustaining my parents and they don't even know.

At last I reach the ground. My brother's still holding on tight. I call out to my parents a couple more times and then I realize that we're not stopping at the ground—the ground has no substance—we're falling right through the fabric of the mesa. We go on falling. With my head still poking above the rock I shriek out, "Mom! Dad! Serena!" over and over. But they just keep on gathering up the provisions and piling them up beside the well, and when I look up I see the helicopter that was me streaking up into the sky and I know that for them it is night. So I know that although our worlds are intersecting they aren't the same world. And then I sink into the rock with my brother in my arms. He's dead weight, pulling me through the soupy stone like a ball and chain.

We're falling softly down an endless tunnel. I'm not scared. Our fall is just fast enough that I can't really see what we're passing. The walls are covered with graffiti kind of like the New York subway. Now and then I think I see things half-buried in the rock. Skulls. Zombies. A condom dispenser. There's music in the distance, just a buzz, as though from a pair of abandoned earphones. It sounds a bit like a heavenly choir and a bit like heavy metal. We keep falling. Joshua never speaks but just goes on staring at me with empty eyes that are starting to weep a thick and bloody pus.

The tunnel becomes dark. I can hear water. The music echoes up the stone well. We're still falling slowly. I look up and there's a tiny pinhole of light at the top and I think I can make out my Dad's face peering down.

I think I hear Josh murmur something. Yeah. Something about "falling to Australia." When I look down at him his lips are frozen half-opened in an unformed syllable.

Suddenly we hit the ground and we're running.

Joshua's running with easy smooth steps. I've always hated how he can run. There's nobody home inside his head and still he leaps across boulders and dodges stalactites with the grace and strength of a wildebeest while I sprint and huff to catch up with him. The cave slopes downhill. Along the walls there're like old Egyptian tomb paintings but they show people we know—Mom wearing the moon on her horns, Dad dressed like Osiris. Some of the pictures are kind of pornographic. It smells of sex and death in here. I'm choking as I run.

Josh turns a corner. I make a superhuman effort and sort of tackle him and we go sprawling against a pillar of salt.

"Don't run away from me; don't you know me, me, me?" Something is oozing from a wound in his scalp. I shake him. I don't care if I hurt him because I don't even think he's inside. I slap his face and slick my hands with his thick cold blood. My hand stings with the ice of his cheeks. The caves grow darker. "I know you're in there somewhere. Wake up. Come back from the dark place you've run away to!" But I'm thinking, only God can raise the dead.

Then, abruptly, there's a flicker in his eyes.

Joshua Etchison

I woke slowly. I had been far away. From the moment Katastrofa slaked my thirst with dragon spit I had been in another country, a gray country where shadow was substance and substance was decaying memory. I had been dead.

I thought I would be dead for ever. I'd been playing the game for a long time. I had become a robot, living only for the times when Katastrofa would touch me, waken me a little . . . and then Theo had been there in the balcony and the spark of me that was still alive inside my body was suddenly kicking and screaming in my mind. Theo had called me by my true name, the name that held my essence before I was even an idea in the minds of my parents. . . . He had summoned me from the dark country . . . though I had forgotten my name or that I even had a name. . . .

I woke in a cold cave looking into my brother's eyes. He was all shaking me and slapping me and finally I said "Stop it already, I'm here, I'm here, Theo," but what came out was a parched murmur. I looked down and saw that I was still coming apart and there were pieces missing and what was left wasn't pretty to look at.

"Fucking Jesus, Joshua, what's happened to us?" I could see he'd been crying.

"There's no time," I said. I could hear the beating of dragon wings. I knew that as soon as I saw Katastrofa I would fall under her spell again. "When they find us it'll all be over. They'll control us again."

Theo said, "We can get home."

"I don't even know where we are," I said. Everything had been hazy since the police station in Tucson. I had made love to Katastrofa and then I started playing the game and the universes kept changing.

"A while ago we were on Earth, I think," Theo said, "because I saw Mom and Dad and maybe Serena Somers and this Indian dude. Jesus, Serena looks totally different if it *is* her. I mean she's rad-looking now, like thin."

I listened to the water dripping down the stalactites, pinging on the damp stone floor. Our voices echoed. I was reminded of the last time I had seen Theo—I mean, before we came here—somehow I didn't think we were that far from the marble bathroom beneath the Chinese restaurant. But we hadn't passed through any Chinese restaurant to get here this time. "So where are we now?"

"We're on an alternate Earth I guess," said Theo. "The Earth that came into being when we vanished. Earth is a pawn in their power struggle. Something to do with controlling the gateways that lead to the River."

"Yeah, the River that connects all the known worlds," I said. "And it's not a real river, it's a metaphor within a metaphor. . . . Sounds like bullshit to me but I guess it's true. Even if it all came out of your dream book."

"I just wrote down my dreams. . . . I didn't *make* any of this happen," Theo said. But I could tell that he wasn't sure about that. He was kind of enjoying the notion that he *did* dream all these universes into being somehow. It's good to be God; I know; Katastrofa had shown me that I had a little bit of the talent too—well, about as much talent as Theo had in his little finger anyways.

"How did I die?" I was certain of my death at least. It was an effort to animate my arms, my legs. I couldn't feel the maggots slithering. My body and I weren't part of the same entity at all. Getting it to move and talk was like trying to make a hand puppet do Shakespeare.

"It was something in the water," Theo said. "You drank water out of the cooler . . . Dragon Spring Water . . . maybe eating and drinking their food and water is bad. . . ." He didn't sound too sure of this part.

There was some kind of myth, I seemed to remember . . . a beautiful goddess abducted into Hades by the king of the Underworld. . . . She ate six pomegranate seeds and so was doomed to spend six months of the year as Queen of the Dead. "*You've* been eating and drinking," I said, "and you don't seem to be dead."

"I don't have all the answers. . . . I see things, that's all. I see them without understanding them. That's why I always blurt out the truth and fuck up everyone's life for them. I'm kind of an idiot savant, I guess. I catch reality and hold it in my hand and then it's up to *them* what they want to do with it."

I felt it again—the overwhelming memory of having

once been alive—God I wanted so much to flow into every cell of that cadaver and start pumping the lungs and pushing the dead air out. . . .

"Save me, little brother."

"I saw what she did to you. I saw it all the way from beyond the gateway. Hell of a way to lose your virginity."

"I should punch you out for that."

"You can't. You told me your heavy secret, remember? I know all about what you didn't do with Serena Somers. But you'd change your mind if you saw her now."

"Listen." The wind in the cavern died, rose, died, rose, and I knew it came from the flapping of leathern wings.

"She's coming. And Thorn can't be far behind."

I was scared shitless. I knew that only my little brother could bring me back to life—my brilliant, socially challenged, ratfaced little brother with the attention span of a gibbon on speed and the power to see through bullshit. I held on to him. He was the only thing that anchored me to my past and kept me from sliding still farther into the abyss. Jesus I hated him sometimes, like now when he was flaunting his knowledge of my sexual secrets, which were deep and dark to no one but myself. "You know how to get us out of here, don't you?" I said.

"Kind of." He pulled out a marble. "This is it, I guess." It kind of glittered and I could see that it wasn't a marble at all but a round thing woven from a million strands of light. "Look, you know there are three of them—Thorn's the oldest. Katastrofa's the middle child. Both of them want it all for themselves. That's what the game is really about. We play at hurling toy planets around but what we play is what really happens. Worlds blow up. Fleets of starships crash into the hearts of suns. You know—real *Star Trek* kind of shit. And we're making it happen. Well there's a third one too. His name is Ash, but no one ever talks about him. He was disinherited. He seems to have vanished. He's the only one who refused to flatter his father. That's Strang, the king. I met him once. He's mad. He goes from world to world trying to undo what's done. He has a scepter that can catch people's souls and in it are the souls of trillions of beings—everyone who's fallen victim to his hunger for power. He pulled this scepter out of the source of the River. Every moment of every day it tortures him, but he can't give it up. The scepter is the thing the others want; without it it's really all video games—cosmic video games—not absolute power. But to have it is to go insane, I guess."

"Am I in the scepter too?" I said. I didn't know how I could be in more than one place at the same time, but then that was what the River was all about—it was *everywhere* and *everywhen* at the same time.

"I think you are, Josh," Theo said.

I could see that he knew of a way to make me whole again . . . to bring us all home . . . maybe even to cure Mom . . . but that it was something fraught with dangers, something he didn't want to contemplate.

"I've faced King Strang before," he said. He didn't look at me. He sounded so frail, so vulnerable. Painstakingly I unclenched one hand and stroked the nape of his neck. I couldn't feel the sweat. I couldn't feel him at all. But I knew he was struggling not to recoil from my dead flesh. "He's haunted but he's not really . . . evil. Maybe we can deal with him somehow. If I can find him."

He got up. Held the marble in his palm, gazed into it until he seemed to be hypnotized. The threads of light coiled and uncoiled and the marble started to unravel and soon there were strands of light spinning all over the cavern, lassoing the stalagmites, spiraling, corkscrewing, twisting, lancing the darkness . . . and I realized it was all a single connected thread that reached back all the way to the primordial moment a split nanosecond before the Big Bang was scheduled to go off. . . . The light spun around and around us until we were cocooned in it. . . . Theo held out his hand to me. I made my fingers close

around his. . . . He pulled me up. The light circled us
and filled me with painful memories. . . .

—We were standing at the river's edge beneath the
shade of the cottonwoods. It was autumn. My father was
inside writing a poem—

Theo twisted a strand of light around his right hand.
"Hold on tight, Brother!" he said. I felt the light tugging
at us, then suddenly we were moving so quickly that caves
were blurring, the cave paintings animating themselves
like a gigantic flipbook against the stone formations—
home movies of our early childhood played as I was pulled
along. My gut churned with the acceleration but at least I
was feeling something, knowing some part of me still
lived. . . .

Then I became aware of the River. We were moving
upstream. The River was the strand of light and Theo was
reeling it in so we could fight the current. Cities flashed
past us, cathedrals of ice, jungles where dinosaurs battled,
futuristic wastelands, walls with Babylonian bas-reliefs.
We were sitting in a raft woven from the threads of light
from Theo's marble.

"How did we get here?" I said.

"We're like *inside* the marble, I guess, and the marble
is inside the baseball and the baseball is inside the video
game that's inside the City that's beside the River that's
the strand of light inside the marble."

It wasn't too comforting to know that we were riding a
kind of Möbius strip, shuttling endlessly between truth and
metaphor. I guess it was just one of those concepts that
only Theo could grasp, him being a truthsayer and all.

"Where are we going now?"

"To find Strang! Who's wandering up and down the
River, closing off gateways . . . before he permanently
closes off the way home."

"What about the game?" Wasn't I supposed to be in
some kind of competition to catch a baseball that was
really a planet?

"We're still inside the game," Theo said. "It's just, like, a higher screen of it that you never reached before."

And I was feeling more and more alive. I could feel the wet wind whipping against my arms and face. I could taste the wind, salt and sugary and bitter. We raced, churning up the water on either side as if we were waterskiing.

Theo Etchison

But I know that we're not going to escape that easily, because from behind I can hear the beating of great wings and I can feel the distant fire against the back of my neck. And I know Thorn can't be far behind. They're following my trail even while they're still up there in their balconies overlooking the arena, sipping their blood cocktails and feeding on the frenzy of the audience.

chapter eighteen

Pictures in the Sand

Phil Etchison

After we had brooded over the dream book all night, Milt Stone got up at the crack of dawn and went over to the edge of the mesa. He started to sing. I was wrapped in a sleeping bag and had three blankets wound around my head because of the cold. I made a slit to watch him out of. Mary and Serena were awake too, piling brushwood on the fire.

Milt wore a loincloth and he had bells on his wrists and ankles and when he danced they tinkled. He pounded his feet on the rock and sang—it was all in Navajo I supposed—and it seemed as though he were addressing his words to the mountains, the sun, and the well. I wondered how he could do all this seminude dancing when the temperature had to be no more than about 35°. Sometimes I saw Ash—a ripple in the sunlight, a wavering shape—who appeared to be pounding on a drum. Sometimes there was the sound of a flute, unmistakable even above the whistling wind. Sometimes there were other voices, harshly warbling, coming out of the very air. There was magic in this place, no doubt about it. Reality itself seemed tenuous, stretched thin like the skin of a burgeoning balloon, perhaps on the verge of bursting.

Why was Milt dancing? Why didn't it seem to matter that we had gone off in a police vehicle and I never saw him report back to any superior? I just couldn't buy the idea of vision quest leave, not even here in Indian country. I guess I was just too whitebread a kind of person.

Milt Stone was beautiful against the rising sun with his hair flying and his jowls quivering with every stamp of his feet. But after a few hours I was beginning to wonder when it would stop and what relevance it had to our predicament.

Mary and Serena stuck by each other. They made coffee and fried up a batch of bacon and eggs and did other stereotypically female things; it was a moving sight to me, because Mary hadn't done anything simple and domestic since our second child was stillborn and she had retreated into her schizophrenia . . . no! . . . since the cancer . . . no . . . I was deluged by warring sets of memories.

It got warm . . . the wind burned us and the sun scoured our faces. Milt Stone danced. Mary and Serena brought me breakfast and we sat around the dying fire, not speaking to each other.

Until I couldn't stand it anymore and I said, "There's something really fishy about Detective Stone." And I told Mary about my doubts. (Serena I didn't really talk to that much, because though she seemed to remember me perfectly, my recollection of her was still more or less confined to the inappropriate adjective 'sluglike.')

Mary said, "Maybe you should call the police station yourself."

"Yeah," Serena said. "Mr. Stone looks like he's barely halfway through his dance routine."

The women were right. I was going to fuss until I knew

for sure. I went over to the police car, which was parked
about two hundred yards from the edge. There were still
bundles of supplies from the chopper visit last night. I
looked inside the car, expecting one of those car radios—
they always have them in cop movies—but instead found
a futuristic looking cellular phone, the kind that looks like
a Japanese robot toy. It had flashing LEDs and a backlit
LCD screen that displayed rows of arcane symbols which,
on closer examination, turned out to be the alien starships
of Space Invaders, moving back and forth in orderly ranks,
tentacles twitching.

There were other things about the car that seemed not
quite right either. For example, the gearshift wasn't your
usual PRNDLL but read something like PRNDBQZLL—
the "Q" seemed a little bent out of shape. Also, the
steering wheel was on the left, which indicated that it was
the kind of car that you drove on the right side of the
road—but in America we drive on the left, don't we? Did
we? I panicked. It had always been left. No, no, it shifted
to left during one of those crazy reality shifts when everything became a mirror image of the last world and we all
wrote backwards and got younger. Younger? How could
that be?

Left or right? Why couldn't I remember something as
simple as that? I stared at the dashboard and its crazy
hieroglyphics, and I realized I was having a fullblown
attack of disjunctive fugue. And that phrase hadn't even
been in my vocabulary two days ago.

I gulped. Took a few deep breaths. Listening to Milt's
falsetto wheezing faintly over the wind seemed to calm
me down a little. I picked up the phone and saw, to my
relief, that the handset sported the usual Day-Glo green
lighting and the familiar digits as well as the # and the
*. I dialed 911 and asked for the Tucson police.

"Detective Stone, please," I said. "There *is* a Detective Stone there, isn't there?"

Static.

"S-t-o-n-e," I said, spelling it several times for an air-headed-sounding receptionist.

"Stone? Sir, we have no Detective Stone here. You wouldn't mean Stein, would you? There's an Angela Stein in homicide."

So on our way to the top of this mesa to which no roads led, we must have been treated to yet another shift in reality. This world contained no Milt Stone; Milt Stone was not what he appeared to be; perhaps he was, like so much else I'd been experiencing, a figment of someone's imagination . . . my own, perhaps.

Fucking wonderful, I thought. Maybe when I go to sleep tonight I'll wake up in the body of Stephen King. I could sure use a $15 million advance for *my* laundry lists.

I had a wild hunch. I picked up the phone again and dialed home.

A teenage boy answered. "Who's this?" I said. I was terribly afraid of what he'd say.

"Josh, of course," said the boy. "I didn't realize you were out, Dad. You need me to pick you up or something?"

"I need to speak to your mother," I said.

There was no answer for a few beats. Then the boy said, "Look, Dad, where are you? I'd better pick you up. You know you're not supposed to be wandering too far from the institute."

"Where's your mother, damn it?"

"Stop ragging on me, Dad . . . Dad?" I heard someone talking in the background. "Dad? It's some kind of fucking crank, Dad!" Josh said. But he wasn't talking to me. Someone else came on the line.

"Philip Etchison," said the voice.

"Philip Etchison," I said.

"I got an echo," I said.

"Who the hell are you?" I said. "Is this some kind of prank call?"

"Jesus Christ, you sound just like . . ." I said.

I couldn't be talking to myself. Surely not. I realized I'd broken out in a sweat. Someone touched me on the shoulder and I just spazzed. It was Mary. "Jesus Christ, Mary, talk to this man," I said, "tell me I haven't gone over the edge."

"I would hardly be a good judge of that now, would I?" she said. She looked at the phone—she didn't seem at all fazed by its futuristic design—and twiddled with a lever. It turned into a speaker phone and she put the handset back down. "Hello?"

"Mary?" I said on the speakerphone. "Oh my God, it can't really be you . . . oh God, oh God . . ."

"He's crying," I said.

Then I heard Joshua's voice again. "Listen," he said, "I don't know who the fuck you prankers are, but leave us alone. My Dad's been in therapy since Mom died. . . . He's been hearing her voice. . . . He can't sleep, he can't write. . . . You're fucking perverts to call us. . . . Just get out of our lives—leave us the hell alone."

"Put Theo on," Mary said.

"Who's Theo?" Josh said. And hung up.

I started to dial back but Mary put her hand on mine to stop me. "This isn't our world," she said. "We're trespassers. They've a right to be the way they are just as we've a right to go back to our own reality."

It made me uncomfortable to know that there were two of me here and that I was the one who didn't belong, who'd vanish in a puff of smoke as soon as the world was restored.

"Let's go back," Mary said gently.

It was past noon and the sun was blazing. Milt was still singing and the drums were still pounding out of the empty air.

Serena Somers

At around one or two in the afternoon Mr. Stone stopped as suddenly as he'd begun. He went back to his car and got out a kind of a tarp from the trunk and started to drape it over the standing stones, across the well. Mr. and Mrs. E. got back from their phone calls. And we just stood there, not knowing what he was going to do next. I tried to ask Ash about it but he was nowhere to be seen.

In about fifteen minutes he had turned the circle of stones into like this tent, maybe the size of our family room. The tent-flap faced the cliff edge. Mr. Stone looked carefully in the four directions, mumbled a few words to the tent-flap, then he slithered in and sealed himself off. I heard banging and crashing noises, like a dog shambling through a junkyard at midnight.

The three of us from Northern Virginia, we just kind of stood there looking at each other and looking totally stupid. I guess you don't run into many weird Indian rituals in Fairfax County. Last year I'd been to a Thanksgiving powwow in a church hall in Bethesda, but it hadn't been anything like this. Mostly they sat around selling like all this junk jewelry.

We stood a while longer. No more banging noises, but I could hear a flute playing softly. The flute reminded me of Ash. Ash was in there. He was responsible for all this somehow.

The tent-flap opened a crack. Light flickered inside. "You can come in now," said a voice. It didn't belong to anyone I knew.

We filed in one at a time. Mr. Stone was in the shadows, his back to us. A fire burned in a crescent-shaped hearth he'd put together from a pile of stones. The front end of the police car poked into the tent through tarp walls. He motioned us to sit in a semicircle. There were places for each of us, little pillows. We squatted and waited.

"He's made this place into a *kiva*," Mr. E. said with an air of academic authority, "a Navajo sacred place." The well murmured and made his words all blurry and echoey.

Mr. Stone emerged from the darkness. But it wasn't Mr. Stone exactly. It was a woman.

Mr. Stone was wearing a buckskin dress with fringed edges. It was covered with beadwork. He had let his hair down. His face was painted white, and he had on bright red lipstick and heavy mascara. He walked toward us. Even the way he walked was different. He swayed back and forth. This wasn't like a scene from *The Rocky Horror Picture Show*. Mr. Stone didn't look like a guy dressed up as a woman. He *was* a woman. Well, maybe his tits weren't that developed, but Jesus, I could empathize with that. This was getting intense.

"Well," he said. That voice! It was pitched an octave higher, it had the lilt of a woman's voice, but it was kind of unearthly too. Like one of those disembodied spirit voices they have in old black-and-white horror movies. "You may have noticed that I'm not quite the man you thought I was."

"My God," Mr. Etchison said, "you're a *berdache*."

"You ain't ignorant, that's for sure," said Mr. Stone. "You've taken some of the same anthropology courses I did when I was in white people's college." He sat down across from us, on the other side of the fire. "Yes. I am a *nadle*, a sacred man-woman, and a powerful shaman. My pueblo sent me to the white people's college so that I would absorb as much knowledge of alien worlds as I could. After all, my job is to commune with alien worlds, so it's only right I should be sent to live among aliens. Would you care for tea?"

"With pleasure," Mary said. I could tell that Mary trusted him completely. I'm not sure where the teakettle appeared from, but what Mr. Stone was pouring into these Japanese teabowls was a greenish fluid that didn't look much like tea.

"Don't drink it!" said Mr. E., but Mary had already drained the entire bowl.

I looked at the man-woman, like totally confused, and

he said gently, "I suppose I should give you the condensed version of Anthropology 101, since you haven't
been to college yet. . . . When I was little older than you,
Serena, I went up to the high mesa to seek a vision. When
I came back I told my parents, 'I am a woman.' That's
what the vision told me. When a boy has a vision like
that, the parents celebrate with a feast, because the parents
of a *nadle* are always blessed with good fortune. Their
son will be able to talk to the gods. I have been doing
that since childhood, and yes, it's a living."

"What's in the tea?" I said, staring deep into the bowl
and seeing . . . I don't know what . . . someone else's
eyes stare back at me.

"Peyote!" said Mr. E. "Drugs! Be careful!"

"Oh come on, give me a break, Mr. E.! You went
through the sixties, you can't tell me you never tripped, I
mean, you used to go to those parties with Andy Warhol
for God's sake . . . like, don't be such a tightass."

Mr. E. looked really pissed off, but when Mary started
to laugh he couldn't help laughing a little too.

"Listen. This is a sacred thing we are doing now, my
children," said Mr. Stone, "but laughter too is sacred . . .
something that you white people have forgotten with your
crystal cathedrals and your televangelists. Laugh, children,
laugh. . . ."

And we did. We laughed ourselves helpless. And suddenly I noticed the sandpainting. How had it gotten there?
We had been sitting around it the whole time. It was
drawn in brilliant colors and the smoky firelight dappled
the ochers and turquoises so that it seemed alive. The
painting showed all of us . . . Mr. and Mrs. E. and the
two boys and me . . . very stylized . . . standing in line.
There were gods with frogs' heads holding our hands and
leading us towards a well. Ash was standing in the well.
His eyes glittered. As I stared at the sandpainting, I could
have sworn that he winked at me. I thought I was going
to shit myself. Music filled the *kiva*—the wind was like

children laughing and gnarled wooden flutes and drums
made of human skin and—my flesh was crawling, I was
thinking Jesus, I really want to go home, there's a sale at
Garfinckel's this Saturday.

"Drink the tea," Mr. Stone said. His eyes were big
and empty like the sockets of a skull. He was crying into
the fire and each drop made the fire sizzle and sent up a
cloud of blood-tinged mist. I took a sip. It was bitter and
I made a face. Mr. Stone's eyes grew wider and I felt that
I was going to slide right into them, into the well that led
into the country of dreams. I looked back at the sandpainting and Ash was beckoning to me. His fingers were definitely moving. No, it wasn't just the flames.

"What's the plan then?" Mr. Etchison said slowly. He
lifted the bowl to his lips. But he didn't drink, not yet.

"Well . . . I have made a study of Theo's dream book,"
said Mr. Stone. "He talks about another country . . . a
kingdom inside his dreams that's in some ways more real
that this one we're in now. He's in that dream country,
Phil, and so's your son Josh. There's a war going on
there. He's got it all explained away in sci-fi terms—
planets and lizard warriors and starships—but I have to
use the metaphors I know, and I have to explain it by
saying that the forces of the universe are in conflict—that
it has lost its *hozhoni*—that is, its harmony is broken.
And it is because the eternal order of things has been
disrupted."

"Oh," said Mr. Etchison, and then, as he always does
at moments of totally intense epiphany, he began to quote
Shakespeare: "You mean:

> *'Take but degree away, untune that string,*
> *And hark what discord follows.'* "

"Well, yes, something like that," said Mr. Stone. "We
must come to a state of *hozhoni* ourselves before we can
resolve this problem. We must feel love for one another.

We must drink the peyote tea together. There are many ways of traveling to the shadow world. Some, like Theo, have never left it. He is the lucky one. Others, like this *nadle* who speaks to you in the words of Yeibichai, grandfather of all the gods, can journey to the shadow world by sending forth our spirits from our bodies. But that takes training, and you people have no time. You must find the two boys before the universe is torn asunder by disharmony. Or else . . . we may find ourselves in a world cut adrift, spiritually barren, the gateways to the other worlds sealed off forever.''

"Come on, Mr. Stone," I said. "You're not telling us that if we sit here and guzzle hallucinogens and like do a bit of transcendental meditation, then Josh and Theo will just come floating up to us through the well?" There's only so much New Age jargon you can swallow at one time. I tried to blink the soot out of my eyes.

"I'm afraid it won't be that easy." Mr. Stone fluttered his eyelashes at me. God he was beautiful! He made me feel queasy, and I quickly downed the rest of my peyote tea. "We will have to find them. So drink up, and I've got a whole kettle brewing so you'll get plenty of it . . . because when we're through drinking and meditating we're gonna pile into my police car and just drive ourselves on down into the well."

I saw the car's front end aimed right at the well and realized that Mr. Stone was dead serious.

book four

ama no gawa:
the star river

Drunken, I walked to the edge of the moonlit stream.

—Li Po

FROM MY SONS

When I stand at the river's edge, sometimes
I feel you are watching me; sometimes
I think you cannot bear to watch me,
Knowing the things you know, unknowable to me.
I can only know the things I have touched and seen,
Not rivers that run upstream, back to the mountains,
Not truths within truths or dreams within dreams,
Gray as the sky, as loneliness, as love.

But you can know the laughter of the wind that shakes
The cottonwoods; and you can know
The milk that suckles the unborn, stillborn gods,
Your dream-selves; you can drink from the secret river
Inside. Oh, turn the tide, push back the waterfall, let me
    hear for once
The voices from the depths; for in my heart I know
These things are real; the river has turned backwards;
The river will not turn backwards till its watery end;
Black as the sky, as night, as self-destruction.

Don't let me walk away from the river's edge. I know
I will have to enter the water to come home. I know
That in the blink's breath between two truths, that I must
    grasp
Both truths and make them one. I have two sons. I have
    heard them.
I have seeded the two-breasted madonna who suckles the dark
And light; the quick and lifeless; the transient, the eternal,
Red as the sky, as desire, as death.

chapter nineteen

Death and Transfiguration

Phil Etchison

I drank deep. My mind began to unclog. I knew now that my memories had been drowned in drink. Those strangely colored drinks, so often handed to me at just the right moment by a tall Chinaman who had professed to be a fan of my poetry. . . .

We all drank deep. With each draught I found another memory. Like Theseus in the labyrinth, I had found the end of the ball of yarn and was stepping backward through the convolutions of my past.

I saw Milt Stone sitting with his eyes closed, murmuring softly. He was entering a trance I supposed. We all were.

Mary said softly, "Where are we going?"

And Milt said, "We are going to die."

I knew what he meant immediately. He was talking about the shamanistic experience—the loosening of the soul from the body—to travel into the spirit world. It was a familiar idea but not one that I had ever thought I would experience. I said, "We can't go . . . where Theo is . . . because we don't have the power that he has. We can only go by dying."

"I don't care," Mary said. "I've been close before."

"I'm afraid," Serena said, and Mary comforted her. "Why do we have to die? Ash doesn't die when he comes to see me. Thorn didn't die when he stole Theo."

Milt said: "I don't know who these people are. Perhaps they are a kind of kachina then. But I haven't heard of them. Even though I am a shaman, and a sacred man-woman, you can't expect me to have heard of everybody in the world beyond."

We drank. I felt myself sinking, sinking.

I began to dream with my eyes wide open. In the dream I saw myself standing at the edge of a stream fringed with cottonwoods. It was like a place in Colorado I used to visit, where the Arkansas dwindles to a creek; like my parents' place in Spotsylvania County too. I was squatting under a tarp beside a fire guzzling hallucinogens in a slo mo replay of my college days, but across the fire I could see the river clearly. I was alone. The sky was brilliant blue and I knew it was summer, the eternal summer that belongs to boys who are out of school, the summer of sneakers and swimming holes, Ray Bradbury summer; standing outside myself, seeing myself look soulfully at the trickling water, shying a flat stone at the stream and unable to make it skip . . . conscious of a terrible aloneness.

Then Mary was beside me at the river's edge. I looked at the Mary sitting on the ground of the *kiva*. I squeezed her hand. She smiled at me. The man-woman who was our guide and shaman threw a handful of herbs and sweet-smelling dry grasses onto the fire. Through the incense smoke I saw the other Mary, healed and free of madness. She raised her hand toward me in benediction. Water gushed from her palms. The odor of sanctity filled the *kiva*; I almost choked on its sour sweetness.

"Mary," I said softly. And the Mary beside me held my hand tightly, and the Mary beside the river kissed me and with each kiss—just as with each swallow of the peyote tea—I regained a lost piece of myself.

Serena was lost in her own dreams. She was crying out "Ash, oh Ash," and giggling like a little girl. Perhaps she was seeing a scene from her childhood. At one point she cried out in pain.

I heard the laughter of young boys. They were playing in the shallow water. Leaping the stepping stones. Little children. I had been told their names many times since suffering the selective amnesia of shifting worlds, but now, when the littlest one looked at me from the far bank, and I saw his eyes—Mary's eyes—the color of the sky flecked with the murk of the river, I called out his name: "Theo, Theo."

"Be calm. Be still." It was Milt. "I know you want to burst with the joy of rediscovering yourself. But you must hold it all inside."

We drank again. "I'm afraid it's time now," Milt said at last. I don't know where the bow and arrows had appeared from but suddenly he was standing next to the well, wrapped in a blanket of many colors, and he was drawing an arrow from this quiver. He licked the point of the arrow and nocked his bow and took aim at me. "Do you wish to make the spirit journey with me?" he said to me. I hesitated. "You have to say yes! Quickly! I can't kill you without your permission!"

The youngest boy looked at me from the far side of the river. I knew I belonged to him. He raised his arm toward the sunset in a manner reminiscent of the last lines of Thomas Mann's *Death in Venice*, and I cursed myself for the over-intellectualizing fool that I was. "I do," I said very softly.

He asked the same question of the women and one by one they nodded their assent.

The arrow flew straight and true. The pain seized me

all over. I was on fire. I was shaking, sweating, weeping tears of blood. I clutched my heart and found it in my hand and it was a rose whose thorns stabbed deep into my palms, my scalp, my side. I stared and saw the women writhing on either side of me. In the corner of my eye I saw Milt fastening a rope around his neck and thrusting one end up at the sky, saw him kicking, saw his tongue loll from his parched blue lips, saw him fall lifeless to the floor of the *kiva*, saw him sprawl over the center of the sandpainting.

It was then that I died.

I knew it was death because I had become quite still, quite feelingless. Darkness blanketed me, and a cold beyond coldness. In that darkness I glimpsed the light that hides itself in the thickest darkness, and I knew that the dark and the light were one. I was on the verge of becoming part of the flame, part of the prime mover of the universe. It is not something that can be explained, only intuited; and I, who had spent my adulthood far from intuition, even though I professed to be a poet—I who had hid behind the walls of the university rather than live and love and swallow fire, as poets must—I was ashamed of the sham my life had been. I wanted to dive into the source of the river and forget everything.

Now I knew why, when I'd looked into the well and seen the half-remembered image of my son Joshua, I had thought him dead. If he had been pulled across without warning, without the shamanistic ritual . . . it would have been hard to resist the seduction of the light.

God! I wanted to give myself to it completely! To become a drop in the eternal ocean . . . God!

But then I heard a voice. Theo's voice. Calling me from the brink. I felt his hand on my shoulder, pulling me away from the light. And saw him—yes, in that *Death-in-Venice* pose, poised at the river's edge, at the boundary of life and death . . . and he only said, "Dad, not yet."

And then it seemed that I saw him walk toward the well

across the glassy sea . . . turning back now and then to look back, wistfully, at the reality we were leaving behind. And I started to follow.

He stepped into the well and disappeared.

Then Milt rose from the ground—with infinite slowness it seemed—and walked toward the driver's side of his police car . . . which was somehow more than a police car . . . it was wreathed with strands of laser light. The others were rising too. A soft blue radiance haloed Milt's face. Mary followed him to the car, swimming through air thick as water. Serena walked shyly behind her. The car was glowing. Shafts of golden light pierced the incense clouds. When I looked up I saw that a full moon was shining even though the sky was a black tarpaulin. There was flute music in the air. The women were seated in the back now, and Milt went around to open up the passenger door for me.

I got in. Milt was already sitting beside me. The gearshift still had all those unfamiliar letters. He saw me staring at it and said, "You'll see what they're for soon."

The inside of the car was awash with light. I realized that the light was Ash; that Ash was with us, that he had never left us. In fact, I distinctly remembered Ash . . . a young man who'd stopped by and given me a jumpstart one morning when I was stalled in the winter snow . . . one of my poetry students who had dropped out after one class although he'd written the most brilliant poem I'd ever seen, scrawled it on scratch paper and made it into a paper airplane and sent it zinging toward my desk my lectern my pulpit and the airplane hovered above my head like the proverbial paraclete before nosediving for the trash can. Oh I knew Ash all right. Why had those memories never surfaced before? There was a mythic polish to them that made them seem almost planted . . . but I had no time to worry about it anymore. Milt had put the car into Q—whatever that was—and he was concentrating so hard that the sweat from his forehead was making his mascara run.

I could hear something revving up. The car was shaking. The light was deafening. The car's vibrations filled me with warmth and assailed my nostrils with the fragrance of musk and civet.

I looked out of the window. I saw myself then, and Serena and Mary, still sitting there in our trances . . . we had left ourselves behind. I looked away. It is not good to gaze on yourself without a soul.

The well was ahead. The well was the mouth of a serpent. I could see down the gullet . . . down to the bubbling lava. . . . Milt Stone pumped the accelerator and the engine pounded like a human skin drum and screeched like a bird of prey and we were on fire and . . .

The car spurted! Swelled! Was propelled toward the well and the well threw itself wide open to receive us and . . .

"Make sure your seatbelts are fastened!" Milt shouted urgently. I scrambled for the strap. Serena screamed.

I could feel Mary touching my neck. Her hand was sweating.

We were spinning! Falling! Down the oesophagus of the dragon! Milt shifted gears. We were in Z now. It was a gut-wrenching sensation.

As we plummeted I saw that car we were in was . . . unfolding itself . . . turrets were unfurling, antennae pushing up from the hood, the hood ornament ballooning into a pagoda . . . with terraces of hanging gardens. . . . The seat belt was writhing as it snapped away from me and became a tower of light reaching up into the height and crowned with circling stars. . . . The front telescoped out into a throne. . . . The interior of the car became huge and numinous, vaulted like a Gothic cathedral, with stained glass panoramas depicting mythological scenes of war and ravishment. . . . The incense came from braziers set against Ionian columns . . . from somewhere in the

distance came the soaring melismas of a boys' choir, arc-
ing across vast smoky spaces, canyons in marble, mosaic-
stone skies inlaid with jewels and dusted with gold. . . .
The figure of Milt was changing too, growing. . . . His
fingers shortening into talons . . . his aquiline nose becoming even more hawklike . . . quetzal plumes sprouting
from his scalp and the nape of his neck. . . .

And still we were falling, falling, still I could see,
through gaps in the cathedral walls, the well-wall glistening with wetness as we plummeted. . . .

And then I heard—it seemed to be a wind at first, before
I started to make out solo voices—a huge collective roar
as from a crowd at a political rally, a crowd at a rock
concert. . . . What was it? The hall we sat in—was it
cathedral or throneroom? At the far end a curtain was
whisked aside and sunlight streamed in and the roar of
the crowd became deafening. . . . Serena took the lead,
clambering over the backseat—which had become a long
velvet couch with gilded human feet—and running across
the smoking marble floor to what seemed to be a huge
bay window opening onto a parapet that overlooked a
city. . . .

I looked down and saw myself transformed. I had been
rather conservatively dressed before—having come more
or less straight from my autograph party—but now I found
myself wearing some kind of chain mail—it looked like
chain mail at least, but it hugged my body like tight
sweats. Mary's getup was not unlike that of the goddess
Isis, while Serena resembled a Salvador Dali interpretation
of a Valley girl, complete with earrings that appeared to
represent a pair of golden phalluses.

Where Milt had been driving appeared now to be the
bridge of a starship which occupied what could be con-
strued as the antechapel of the vast chamber, at the oppo-
site end from the terrace where the sound of screaming
multitudes had crescendoed so that I had to shout to hear
myself talk.

"Serena, hold on a moment. . . . Where do you think you're going? Don't you think we should be a little more careful? . . ."

It was useless. She stood at the edge of the bay window and turned to me and shouted, "Hurry up, Mr. E.! The whole city's turned out to see us! And now you'll get to meet Ash at last—all of him—not some half-real projection into our dimension. . . ."

I hesitated. Detective Stone now seemed far from human as he supervised a dozen crew members in garish trekkie-clone uniforms. He was pacing up and down, a flask of bubbling blue liquid in one hand, back and forth along something that looked like a cross between the bridge of a starship and a Mediaeval torture chamber.

When he saw me move toward the terrace he levitated toward me, flapping his wings now and then and squawking. Mary cried out with pleasure, for though he had changed his shape he still moved with the same strange grace he had exhibited while dancing on the mesa's edge, while pouring peyote tea in the garb of the man-woman.

"My memory has come back now," said Milt.

"You're not a Navajo shaman anymore? You were just faking, I suppose," I said. But the memory of death and transfiguration would not be dismissed. I knew it would never leave me and that I was forever changed.

"A shaman? Why, sure enough." He punctuated his statements with chirps. "But that was in your world. Here, you see, I am someone else. I am Corvus Ariano, High Pilot of the flying citadel of Ash. My duties consist mostly of conserving our supply of the water of transformation." He indicated the flask of blue liquid. A similar blue liquid seethed along a creek which seemed to run down the middle of the chamber. "When Prince Ash sends me to other worlds to perform diplomatic missions on his behalf— helping you to stay in touch with reality was one such mission, I might add—when I leave the homeworld, I have a lot of trouble remembering who I am. With some people, universe-hopping is second nature; with people like me it's a necessary evil, and when you do hop the results seem more or less unpredictable."

"Come on, Mr. E.!" Serena shouted. "It's time for you all to meet someone in the flesh—someone you've seen only as a shadow before."

We stepped out through the curtains. We were on a parapet overlooking a city. The place I had thought of as the cathedral was perched on a huge structure, perhaps a pyramid. I took Mary's hand. It was cold. I turned to look and saw that she was moving slowly, ever more slowly . . . and that her eyes had stopped blinking.

She was turning to stone.

I didn't have time for the crowds gathered in the plaza below, who were shouting out our names and calling for Prince Ash to appear. Serena was leaning over the balcony, waving frantically and blowing kisses. Milt—or Corvus, as we were now to call him—was standing rigidly at attention, and Ash, his master and our host, was slowly taking shape on a dais overlooking us all, an androgynous youth of surpassing beauty. . . . The crowd prostrated itself as one man and whispered the name of Ash. . . . I could not enjoy the spectacle, because my wife was hardening in my arms, and as I kissed her lips I tasted marble.

Wildly I tried to call for help. No one was paying any attention to me. They stood at the edge of the parapet acknowledging the cheers of the crowd. Milt—Corvus—held up something at the sky which looked like a TV remote controller. He pushed a button and the sky dimmed. Another and the fireworks began. The light rained down and colored my Mary's whitened face with garish greens, harsh blues, flashing vermilions. Only her eyes remained alive. They stared, time-frozen, with an expression of timeless compassion, like the eyes of a Madonna. Her hands were outstretched and her Isislike headdress displayed an image of the moon between the horns of a cow.

I stayed, clasping the image to me, until the cheering had subsided, the fireworks had quieted, and a soft music began to play from, I supposed, concealed speakers somewhere on the veranda. Servants had brought in a table and chairs and it seemed that we were about to be served a traditional English tea. The situation was so incongruous that I began to laugh. . . . I laughed until, without warning, I found myself in tears.

Ash touched me on the shoulder.

"You must be done with grieving now," he said. "We have a lot to do."

"What's happened to her?"

I looked at Ash. Ash was not tall, but an aura emanated from him. He looked at the statue that had been Mary. Then, beckoning to two of the servants clad in black who always seemed to appear when he needed them, he said, "Place the image of the Mother of Waters back in her votive niche." They carried my wife away. "The people are happy," Ash said—his eyes danced in the light of the now-silent fireworks—"because she has been restored to them; they are always sad when she is forced to leave us."

"Leave you?—But she's my wife," I said.

"She has always been much more than that," Ash said. "You will see, Truthmaker."

"Truthmaker?"

"It is our name for you; it has been, since the most ancient stories were told about how you fathered Theo Truthsayer on the Mother of Waters, who caused herself to be born in the world of humans. . . ."

"I don't understand."

"Surely you of all people should, Philip Truthmaker. You've spent your entire life mythologizing the mundane. . . . Is that not the function of poetry?"

I bowed my head in shame. "Ash, I've betrayed the

very idea of poetry. . . . I've settled for a cushy chair of poetry at a second-rate university. . . . How can you expect me to understand about Mary?''

But wait, I thought. In different worlds, we sometimes took different forms. . . . I knew that. Corvus Ariano was some kind of pilot in this universe, while in ours he was a transvestite witch doctor. Could it be that Mary, the madwoman (or cancer victim, depending on which set of memories I trusted) was some kind of godlike being here? But she was also a statue.

''Not a statue,'' Ash said, reading my mind, it seemed, ''but a creature who lives in a timeframe so dilated that a single breath she takes can start with the birth of a sentient race and end with the fall of its last civilization. Later, tonight, we will worship her together. But first, let's have tea. Corvus!''

''My Lord,'' said Milt Stone.

''Open up the sky.''

We sat down. The tea was peyote tea, brought to us in a silver service and cut with milk and sugar. There were cucumber sandwiches, and I half expected the March Hare to come leaping over the balcony and the Dormouse to be found snoring among the sugar-lumps.

Presently the sky folded up like the roof of a convertible, and beyond it I saw a glittering starscape—comets, planets hurtling, nebulas, constellation on constellation, constantly shifting. Serena had hurled herself upon the cucumber sandwiches. . . . I think that she probably felt long overdue for a break from that Walter Hudson diet . . . and Corvus was doing things to his TV remote. I didn't feel at all hungry, but I didn't dare ask any questions for fear of having my mind blown beyond repair. The sandwiches tasted more like seaweed than cucumber, with perhaps a hint of chocolate.

''You want to know what's going on,'' Ash said, ''and you're too polite to ask.'' I nodded. ''Corvus, what's our position?'' Corvus murmured a string of coordinates; Ash smiled. "We are on our way to rescue your sons," he told me at last.

"Yes." I thought I must have sounded stupid.

"I'm sure you know the general situation from Theo's dream book: Theo and Katastrofa are quarreling over my father's kingdom, I'm in disgrace, and my father is doing his King Lear thing, wandering around a blasted heath somewhere, doing a passable imitation of Paul Scofield on acid." Behind his flippant tone I had a sense of a relentless tragedy playing itself through to its preordained dénouement. "Theo has found Josh and they are traveling upriver together. Perhaps they are looking for my father. Perhaps Theo will be able to reach him; everyone else has tried and failed. My father's pride is a terrible thing and, since the demons in the scepter of life and death have begun to possess him . . ."

Downing more tea seemed to make this outlandish universe more and more credible. Only the idea that I had been married to some kind of mother goddess for the past eighteen years seemed hard to swallow, but even that was not too bad after the fifth cup.

"By the way, in case you hadn't noticed, this city is also a gigantic starship. We had to do a lot of fantasy transdimensional space folding to get the city to look like that police car, let me tell you . . . but I think you'll agree that it was the only possible getaway vehicle."

I wasn't counting, but it was at about that moment that I think I surpassed the White Queen's record of believing six impossible things before breakfast. I was rapidly coming to the conclusion that Charles Lutwidge Dodgson—Lewis Carroll to the uninitiated—must have been responsible for designing this universe. He was as believable a demiurge as my boy Theo.

"We are now closing in on where I think your sons have gone to, at a sizable fraction of the speed of light . . . which is why the sky seems restless," Ash went on.

"And as soon as we find them we'll scoop them up,

bring them home, sweep my wife off her pedestal and live happily ever after?'' I said.

''Intense!'' Serena said, awed.

''It sounds like a plan and a half,'' I said.

''It's the only course of action left to us,'' Ash said, ''if we are to preserve the integrity of the universe.'' And again I felt the sense from him of hurtling towards inevitable doom.

''Jesus,'' I said. ''And until a few days ago I didn't even know I had any sons.''

''You know it now,'' Ash said. ''It is as though you had awakened from blindness.''

''Yeah, Mr. E.,''' Serena said between mouthfuls, ''you *know* it.''

''Do I?'' It occurred to me that, in my entire life, I had never taken anything on faith before. What kind of a poet was I? ''Why should I risk my sanity to save people whose existence I'm not sure of?''

''Because you love your wife,'' Ash said.

Later that evening, as I lit incense sticks in front of her shrine, watching the stars streak by through the observation window set into the dome of her cathedral, I realized that Ash was right. Choristers mounted on mechanical clouds flew overhead, eulogizing her with spirited anthems; thousands of the city's inhabitants lay prostrate on the floor of the cathedral, their palms pressed together, now and then murmuring their private prayers to her so that their voices melded with the mushy resonance of marble; children strewed flowers and lit candles; widows beat their breasts and pleaded for their husbands' resurection; Ash, too, prayed, kneeling in a private pew, with four acolytes wielding censers and a fifth to asperge him with water to which a drop of the Water of Transformation had been added, sanctifying it. But I alone loved her as a man loves a woman. I alone was the consort of the goddess.

I place a wreath in Mary's hand and kissed her on the

cheek. I backed down the thousand steps, thronged with
worshipers. I entered something that looked like a confes-
sional booth, to be magically transported to the bridge of
the starship, where Corvus was directing his staff, striding
about and flapping.

Serena looked up from a terminal where she'd been
doing her Lieutenant Uhura thing. "Mr. E.!" she said.
"It's awesome—Big Bird here has located them."

Corvus didn't seem too affronted at this nickname. Perhaps he was not a big fan of children's television. Person-
ally, I did not see the resemblance. Most of his feathers
were blue-black, and there was still enough of the sacred
nadle about him for me to feel a little . . . well, sexually
uncomfortable in his presence. "Put them on the screen,"
he said to Serena, who began pushing buttons in earnest.

Corvus whipped out his remote, pointed it at the air,
and clicked. All at once I saw them. They were life-size
and three-dimensional; it was almost as though I were
standing between them. They were riding a raft of light,
and Theo was standing just as I'd seen him in my peyote
vision, with his arm upraised. Joshua was a decaying
corpse, moving jerkily as though by stop-motion animation. Around them was the River; I knew what the River
was by now.

"It's like a scene from *Huckleberry Finn*," I said.

"Oh, come on, Mr. E.," said Serena, "these boys are
going upriver, not down: . . ."

A shadow fell over them. There was a dragon overhead,
about to swoop down. "Don't you panic now, Phil," Corvus said. "We'll be there any minute."

chapter twenty

Upriver

Theo Etchison

The dragon's getting closer. Thorn's closing in. We're
straining to go upriver. The river slopes upward and it
takes all my strength to keep on the path. We're cocooned
in our million strands of light and anyone who pursues us
can see us, burning on the water like a captive sun. I can
tell that Josh is still in Katastrofa's power. She's close.
He can feel her. He has enough of my ability to be touched
by her across this distance. She's making him uncomfortable, she's stirring up all those adolescent emotions he
has—the only feelings she allowed him to keep when she
killed him so she could bring him across to her side of
the river.

We're shining so brilliantly I have to close my eyes.
And still the light streams in through the closed lids, a
like of crimson fire. I have to move forward on instinct
alone. Maybe—

Joshua screams. It's too bright for him. The fire is rag-

ing and his body, drained of the water of life, is starting
to char. I can smell singed hair. I don't know what to do
except . . . maybe . . . I start to think about safe places,
places where I used to hide from everyone when I was
little . . . the attic at our grandparents' house in Spotsylvania County. . . . One time when I was maybe six and
Josh was eight and we hid inside the great oak chest all
night, popping up now and then to surface and breathe the
moist mosquito night . . . rummaging through old love
letters by flashlight. . . . The chest was like a doorway to
another world. . . . "Josh," I say softly, "think about the
old oak chest. Think hard. Think security. Think how safe
we are, just you and me, alone with our grandparents'
past. Can you see it?" I hope against hope that I can force
this old memory out of him. If we're thinking the same
thing, focusing on the same moment in our common past,
maybe I can move into his thoughts, amplify, breathe life.
Maybe.

"Yeah," Josh says slowly. The fire is cooling. I can
feel a veil of darkness dropping over us. I open my eyes.
Yes. We're still on the raft woven from light but we're
also together in the wooden chest bobbing up and down
on a sea where the cockroaches are pirates and the mosqui-
toes are circling albatrosses . . . and there's a salt breeze
fragrant with the scent of crushed pineapple and banana and
coconut. "You still remember that?" he says. "Jesus."

"You rang?"

He laughs—a feeble laugh, but enough for me to know
he is still there, trapped somewhere inside his own dead
animated flesh.

We move on. High in the air, flashes of lightning from
cloud to cloud show that we're still inside the light-cocoon
inside the river inside the marble inside the video game
inside the inside out. "Ahoy," I say, and wave the marble
like a cutlass. "Ahoy, ahoy," and "great white to star-
board" and "south-south-west" and "fifty lashes, then

keelhaul him!'' and other stock phrases out of late-late-night pirate movies. Joshua smiles.

"Shiver me timbers," he says weakly.

I can feel the planks groan from the weight of our cargo . . . breadfruit trees . . . gold . . . ivory . . . tawny slave women . . . yeah. I wrap the illusion more tightly around us like a down comforter on a winter night. I pull together the pieces of the sky so it is one seamless blue and you can't see the lightning of the paths of light. For a few moments Joshua seems almost human. I do love him a lot really, even now when he's not really here at all.

"Hey, little brother . . . an island."

"A whale maybe." That's what always happens in cartoons.

"No, an island, really an island, palm trees bending, monkeys dancing on the beach, girls with nothin' on under their grass skirts." And he points. I see something else. I see a tall round glittery mound burst from the ocean . . . covered with like thousands on thousands of gold-green-fire-red tiles. Yeah. And the water starting to seethe around the island like there's a volcano about to erupt out of the depths. They're not tiles, I'm thinking, they're scales.

"It's no island, Josh," I say. "She's tracking us. The dragon woman."

He's starting to shake now. All over, like someone about to have an epileptic seizure. His eyes go all glazed. She's touched him. Grabbed him where he feels it. Jesus it pisses me off. I'm just standing here on top of an old chest bobbing up and down in the ocean facing maybe two hundred tons of fire-breathing lizard and I don't know what to do.

And then she rears up out of the water and the illusion splits in two and the sky is sheared and crashes down like a tarp and she's ripping the sky apart with her fangs and—

"Give me what's mine," she says. It's a tiny voice for

me alone, a whisper in the wind that whips us as she lashes the water with her tail and—

I have to sustain the illusion. I reach back into our past again. Try to conjure up the smell of the dust as it dances in the moonbeams that slide down the chinks of the roof. . . . "Go away now," I whisper in a six-year-old's voice, "go away now, monsters." But the dragon doesn't hear me. She plunges and breaches again and her screech tears open the sky. Josh is still shaking. . . . She has a hold of him.

"Don't listen to her!" I say.

But he says, "There's something else . . . you wouldn't understand."

And then, all at once, the illusion shatters. We're on the river and cocooned in light. The dragon's circling us. She's coiling around and around and squeezing us back into the marble. And Joshua is giving in to her. I can feel him slipping from me, feel the life go out of him. . . . I've got to do something. I shake him.

"No . . ." he says. "Don't worry about me. . . . You're dead to me now . . . they're all dead to me, Mom and Dad and everyone else in the old universe. . . . This is the thing I belong to . . . when you grow up and your hormones kick in you'll understand . . . yeah. . . ."

There's only one thing to do. I've got the marble gripped tightly and I hold it up over our heads. "I am the truthsayer," I scream. "I'll forge a new pathway. I'll bend the course of the River—I'll go where you can't follow."

I hear the dragon screeching. Behind the dragon comes Thorn, his cloak flapping as he rides the thundercloud, his three-headed hound growling at his heels. He calls to me and I feel drawn, seduced . . . but I can't give in to him.

"They're mine!" the dragon shrieks. "Stay away, Thorn!"

Suns and moons crash into each other above our heads as we race upriver and our gaze windows in on a hundred disparate universes. Thorn has plucked a burning sword from the air and hurls it into the dragon's mouth. She bucks and we go under a wave, we go crashing through a wall of water.

"Hold on," I say to Josh. I grip his hand. My nails dig into his wrist. Instinctively I understand what I have to do now. I'm still holding the marble aloft and my fist is sparking and flaming like a catherine wheel. I've got to thrust out into the space between worlds, pulling the river along with me, forcing a new gateway open.

I whisper a word that cannot be spoken, a word that has come to me suddenly, as in a dream. It is the True Name of a thing that has never, until this moment, existed.

Then I swallow the marble again.

Katastrofa shrieks—a sound of timeless despair.

There's a sudden disjunction. I feel inside me all the pathways that have ever been, that might have been, that never were. I can hear the beating of great wings and smell the fetor of Thorn's breath and feel the wind of Katastrofa's passing all at once . . . but I no longer see them. There's nothing. The world has gone black. A tiny moment of stillness now. All I am conscious of is Joshua's wrist. Warm blood trickling against my fingers.

"Listen," I say, "listen."

Out of the silence comes the sound of water.

Then light.

Joshua Etchison

I'm not really sure how it happened. I wasn't conscious a lot of the time. Theo had rescued me and we were fleeing somewhere. We were trying to find the old king who was going to restore me to life except life was such a radical concept by then that I wasn't sure I wanted it. There were two things pulling at me. There was Theo and whenever he touched me or even looked at me I could sense the past inside, animating my corpse . . . making me move of my own free will . . . and then there was

Katastrofa who was jerking my corpse up and down on a
string. You'd think I would want to be free but there were
advantages to being a puppet too. I mean when Katastrofa
touched me I wanted to be dead forever, I wanted to be
led around on her leash, I wanted to like melt right into
her as though she were mother earth folding me up
between her breasts soft as warm sod ready for ploughing.

I was ready to run back to her when Theo dredged up
one of our shared memories and got me all confused. We
were in our light-raft and then we were in a chest in our
grandma's attic and then we were like on a big pirate ship
and being menaced by a monster or maybe like Moby-
Dick . . . and when the monster called out to me it was
her voice. And then Theo did something and we were
sucked back into the whirlwind.

We emerged out of darkness into a place awash with
light, soft, like an overexposed photograph. We hit the
ground running but we weren't so much running as kind
of floating along. I guess the world we had reached must
have had a lower gravity or something.

"Stop, Theo, stop," I said.

We kind of slowly braked ourselves. Skidded against a
charred tree stump.

"Where are we?" I said.

"I don't know. Do you feel . . . do you hear her calling
you?"

"Not at the moment." Maybe I did feel something—
but it was only a faint echo of the force that had yanked
me out my universe—and I felt less dead somehow.

"We don't have much time," Theo said. "I used my
truthsaying to blast open a new channel. But now that it's
open they can follow us. It'll slow them down but they'll
be able to pick up the trail."

"What place is this?" I asked him.

"I don't know what it's called," he said. He was
breathing hard. The air was different too—it smelled of
fresh flowers and pollution.

We heard something in the distance. Explosions. Very far away. We stood next to the stream we'd emerged from. The landscape was smoky. Trees with gnarled arms swayed back and forth though there was no wind, and the creak of their branches made a kind of music, the kind you always hear in those African jungle movies on those xylophone things. There were three round things in the sky but I couldn't tell if they were faint suns or brilliant moons. They seemed to give no heat. The trees cast shadows within shadows, fringed with purple and indigo. The air was soggy. We walked on. The forest thinned and there was an open area. The grass was all gray. Here and there was a charred shrub or cactus. There was a burning smell that made us want to stop breathing.

Theo screamed and pointed. There was a naked man impaled on a cactus. He'd been dead a few days I guessed. Not as long as me. But he was in worse shape. Since I'd been with Theo I'd felt my body regenerating a little. I'd had to start biting my fingernails again. There were more bodies scattered about. Some were eviscerated. Others had burned to death.

"Jesus," Theo said, "I hate death, I hate the idea of dying."

"What about me?" I said.

He didn't say anything. He just went right on walking. He wasn't looking at the dead people anymore. He was walking fast, maybe so I wouldn't see him cry. I could barely keep up even though I wasn't falling apart anymore. But I could see where he was going. There was a city in the distance, a mass of spires and emerald towers nestled beneath a snowcapped volcano.

At last we reached a highway.

It was full of people and they were all making toward the city. They had carts drawn by weird beasts of burden. They were in rags mostly. They had banners and placards. I couldn't read them. It looked like Russian or maybe Greek. Many of them were carrying babies in their arms.

There were thousands of them. Some had dead people
with them, stacked in wheelbarrows, carried on stretchers.
A lot of them were maimed. We couldn't see any end to
the procession. The road snaked from the city on the horizon way across the plain until it vanished into another
forest.

They didn't say anything as they walked but there was
a kind of murmuring chant. Now and then there were like
these high priest types in flowing robes that were swinging
these incense burners. That was how the smell of flowers
came to be mingling with the stench of spilled gasoline
and stale vomit. I had a hard time keeping up with Theo.

"I guess they're refugees."

"Who are they? Where are they going?" I said.

"We did this," Theo said. "We're the assholes who—"

Then I understood. It was the game that was causing
this. We played at tossing video images through a simulated universe but somewhere it was all really happening.
The children of Strang were all at war and burning up star
systems and making people die. The games we played
were real.

"Let's join them," Theo said.

"How can we face them?—"

"We're refugees, too," he said.

He led me by the hand. We kind of blended in with the
group. The priests were pounding drums and blowing on
conchs. There was mud on their faces. They trudged forward in a weary, steady rhythm. Now and then a car
moved slowly through them packed with people, with kids
riding on the hood, their horns honking out a lugubrious
melody. In this world the cars looked sort of like '57
Chevys except for the psychedelic body paint.

We didn't know what language people'd be speaking
here but it seemed like English more or less although
sometimes the way their mouths moved didn't seem to
match the sounds that were coming out. I guess they
weren't really speaking English at all—Theo was kind of

"dubbing" it with his mind. I wondered if the picture was "dubbed" too . . . whether the half-familiar images in this world had just been put there to give me a point of reference.

Like that city up ahead—looking like a cross between the Emerald City and a fortress from a samurai movie—why did it seem like I'd seen it before? In a dream maybe. Or perhaps I had somehow eavesdropped on Theo's dreams.

We were walking beside an old couple. He had his arm in a sling and she had burn marks all over her face. They were walking with canes, easy to catch up to. I said to the woman, "What are you running from?"

She said, "There's a war. And a dragon that's burning down the villages."

"Hurry up," Theo said. He tugged me onward. "We have to get inside the city. Katastrofa has found the new course in the River. Fucking Jesus, run, Josh!" He yanked me ahead by the elbow. We overtook the old couple.

Sprinted past women who were singing a whining song and making their tongues dart in and out—*lulululululu*—while slapping their breasts with an open palm and tearing out their hair.

"Look," said Theo, "there's a pickup truck that's moving faster."

I saw it. Weaving in and out. A group of men pounding on drums sat on the back and there was something—a statue maybe—covered with kind of a Navajo blanket. A couple of kids were holding the corners of the blanket tight so it wouldn't flap. There were other kids with warpaint sitting with their legs dangling from the back. It looked like they were flicking spitwads down at the pedestrians.

"I'm too fucking tired to go on, little brother," I said. I could feel her, far away, could feel her stirring in my loins. I think she was making my dick tingle a little. I could feel the life oozing from me and I didn't even mind.

"She's here," he whispered. He ran up to the pickup truck. "Hey," he shouted to the kids, "my brother's tired and like he needs a ride."

"Come on up!" said one of them. A spitwad sailed past my ear. A second kid, with a mohawk a foot high, cackled. "If you can catch up!" He slammed the side of the pickup. "Giddyup!" It wheezed and started to move a little faster.

"We can make it!" Theo said. He came back to me and started to pull me forward. We ran. We elbowed people out of the way.

"Whoa!" the kid screamed and the truck halted momentarily. A dozen pairs of arms reached out to us. They pulled us aboard. I scraped my skin. It hurt, so I knew there was still some life left in me.

We slumped with a thud onto the back of the truck. I looked up and saw the covered-up statue shaking.

"Shit—it's the Mother—get her!" one of the kids bawled out. All at once they dived. Too late. The blanket slid off and I saw the statue's face.

"Jesus," Theo said, "it's Mom."

Silence. I got up and so did Theo. Everyone on the truck was flat on their face. I looked around. The procession was jerking to a halt. I could hear people whispering: *The Mother, the Mother.*

The statue had our Mom's face. It was made of marble. Except for the eyes, which seemed to be alive. She was in there somewhere.

Slowly . . . agonizingly slowly . . . the statue began to topple. The people on the truck were too petrified to do anything. Only Theo could act.

He stepped forward. Held out his hand. Propped up the statue and pushed it back into a precarious upright position.

The statue smiled.

"Y-you touched the Mother," said one of the kids. I

guess curiosity had gotten the better of him and he'd
sneaked a peek. "And you didn't—shrivel up and die."

They scrambled up and threw the blanket over her
again.

"She smiled," said one of the drum-toting dudes.

Somebody whispered "Truthsayer." Then I heard the
word ripple through the crowd . . . could see the reaction
work its way down the highway like a mouse down a
snake's gullet.

"It's gonna be hard to stay anonymous around here,
Theo," I said.

"Shh! Listen!"

Other noises were working their way up the highway
toward us. Screams. Explosions. Someone was attacking.
People started pointing at the sky. I looked up and saw
them. Metalskinned vultures. Swooping down with the
three suns at their back. Lines of liquid fire were spurting
over the landscape. The pickup revved up. People began
stampeding toward the city, trampling over each other.
Babies were screaming. The boys on the pickup started to
stamp their feet and chant and clap their hands while the
older men banged their drums and danced.

The vultures made another pass. People sizzled and
charred. A banner collapsed on a troop of drummers. The
priests began to whirl and shriek and the women's ingula-
tion went up a couple of octaves. Why were they strafing
us? And what was our Mom doing here, frozen into a
marble Madonna?

The pickup was moving faster. We ran over something
squishy. "It's not human," Theo said, but I don't think
he was convinced. There were hundreds of vultures now
and the sky had gone black.

Then, bursting out from behind the wall of deathbirds,
came Katastrofa. She was a dragon all in crystal, writhing
against the vultures and knocking them out of the sky.
People screamed. They left the highway and moved in a
mass across the landscape toward the city. Cars exploded.

Body parts rained down on us and still the kids did their ceremonial dance and the men drummed. People were really dying and I had done it—I had caused it to happen by diving into the Nintendo of death.

"She's only after you," Theo said. "She wouldn't have come herself otherwise."

"I—"

"Come on."

I could feel Katastrofa now. I wanted to die again. I didn't want to run from her. I wanted to wrap myself in dragonflesh and forget how many people I had killed.

He grabbed hold of me. Pushed me forward until we were crouching at the feet of the statue. "Quick," he said, "under the blanket."

We crawled inside. We huddled under the blanket, clinging to Mom's image. There was a familiar smell under the blanket—the smell of our mother dying. We drew the past around us and tried to ignore the sounds that burst over us, the screams of the dying and the roar of the angry dragon. The pickup lurched and bounced and skidded. We weren't driving on the highway. We could hear the kids' bare feet tramping on metal. One of them was crying instead of chanting. Maybe he was hurt.

I held on to the statue and tried to shut out Katastrofa.

chapter twenty-one

========================

The King is Mad

Serena Somers

Night fell and the city shifted into high gear. Me and Mr. E., we stayed in the chapel where they were worshiping Mrs. E. for a while. We knew the city was navigating through Theo's River because there was this humming and because, if you looked out over the balcony of the palace, there were streaks in the sky where the stars should be. Mr. E. smiled when he saw it and quoted a Japanese haiku by some dude named Basho:

" 'Over the sea, a tempest!
Over the Island of Sado, flung out—
The river of stars.' "

I guess it must have been profound because he was like weeping and all. Poets get that way I guess, it's their job to like launch into this heightened emotion thing. He was pacing up and down and murmuring to himself and you could tell that there was something inside him about ready to burst, a new poem. I think maybe he saw himself as the island with the tempest raging around him and the stars all swirling in the night sky. Mr. E. can be beautiful sometimes, when he doesn't get too pretentious.

I wasn't feeling pretentious. No, I had like this gnawing emptiness inside me. I get this way when the old eating disorders kick in. I think it was because I knew that Joshua wasn't really alive anymore. I'd overheard them talking. It was always Theo Truthsayer this, Theo Truthsayer that . . . and Josh wasn't really in this cosmic equation of theirs, he was just one of the little people like me and maybe Mr. E., crushed between the millstones of destiny.

All I wanted to do was eat. That's how I found myself slipping out of the palace, leaving Mr. E. to his Byronic posturings, wandering down a dark alley in an alien city that just happened to be hurtling from dimension to dimension at the speed of thought.

Phil Etchison

We were moving closer and closer to our moment of truth. I was in the control room of the flying city. It was fascinating to watch Corvus at work. Ash I saw less of; he had withdrawn to some private room. We were getting closer to Josh and Theo; but we were also getting closer to Ash's father, and that put him into a state of melancholy from which neither food nor conversation could retrieve him.

But Corvus had become positively loquacious.

In the observatory at the very summit of the flying city—which was as unlike Jonathan Swift's Laputa as could be imagined—we watched the universes rush by. Although the city was enclosed within a sphere of force, which was able to contain an artificial environment and project a simulated sky overhead, Corvus showed me that we were actually engulfed by the River itself, and that we were racing against the stream, toward its source. We sat in a domelike structure from which Corvus could send messages to his control room. On the screens that surrounded us I saw only water—water of many colors, water that dashed against the portals of the city, water that frothed, seethed, bubbled.

In the center of the chamber was what Corvus referred to as a map—a continually shifting hologram of a single strand of light, folded over and over on itself, continually writhing and changing direction and thickness. At Corvus's command the view would zoom or telescope, so that now and then we could see little blips moving up and down the light thread, and Corvus would say: "There they are! Let me get a fix on them!"

In a little niche on one wall was another statue of Mary. This one was only about a foot tall, but the eyes were the same—unmistakably alive. I asked Corvus about it.

"They are all fragments of the same Mother," he said, "all of them equal, all of them containing her whole essence, although the one you have restored to the Cathedral is, of course, the *original*."

"Let me get this right—my wife is worshiped here as a goddess of some kind?"

"No, she *is* a goddess of some kind . . . *the* goddess. And you, while not a god as such, Phil, you have a certain status in the universe, since you're the Truthmaker—the father of Theo."

I watched the patterns change in the map; I watched the waters surge against the viewscreens; now and then the city surfaced, and we were momentarily touched by the light of alien suns and moons; I listened to Corvus discourse learnedly about the place of the *nadle* in Navajo society. "I play the ambiguous shaman in countless universes," he said, "but only in this one, the universe of my birth, am I aware of all my secret selves. . . . Sometimes, as a shaman, I have an inkling of them . . . some unborn memory stirs. . . ."

I wanted to know the rules by which these parallel worlds operated. Surely there were paradoxes to be encountered. I recounted the unnerving incident in which I had found myself speaking to myself on Milt Stone's cellular police phone.

"Each one is a continuum," said Corvus, "across a number of dimensions. Sometimes one changes little from world to world; sometimes the changes come in discrete, disjunctive quanta. We are all Heisenbergian to one degree or another. If philosophers were cats, they'd think of us as Schrödinger's catnip. Why, even the map of the River resembles nothing so much as a ball of yarn sometimes, the very ball that Theseus used to scry his way to the monster at the heart of the labyrinth."

"Your conversation works on so many levels," I said, "that I can't decide whether you're brilliant or you're mad. . . ."

"The shaman as paranoid schizophrenic . . . surely you've heard that thesis before," said Corvus. Flapping his wings, he began to sing.

Serena Somers

Okay. I had to find food, but I doubted whether there was going to be a McDonald's in the area. We were in sci-fi land here, so I imagined there'd be one of those dingy taverns full of geeky aliens guzzling smoking blue drinks and robots with enormous breasts. But I didn't see anything. Where the palace was, the highest level of the city, was mostly monumental buildings; the big square I'd seen from the pavilion was a long way down, and could only be reached by winding pathways with steep steps.

Finally I found a street vendor who was selling something that looked like barbecued chicken livers on skewers. I didn't have any money but when I told her I was from the palace she let me have all I wanted. I bolted down a couple of the sticks and washed it down with like this fermented grape Kool-Aid stuff.

I walked downhill a little more and then I saw—a phone booth. Yeah, they had phones here and somewhere in this town, maybe, there was a phone with my number. I remembered how Mr. E. had been able to call places on the police car phone back in the last universe. What'll happen if I call home? I did. Collect. Yeah, our calling card number worked here.

I heard myself answer. Maybe I wasn't so far away from the real world. Maybe we were separated from each other by the mere width of a single electron.

"Is Mom home?" I asked myself.

"Are you still at the mall?" said the other Serena. Who did she think I was?

"Yeah, the mall," I said. Back home, that's where my Mom still thought I was. "Like, aren't you surprised to hear from me?"

"Why should I be?" I guess in this universe Serena was a girl who talked to herself a lot. I wondered if she was fat. Maybe she was anorexic in this universe—that'd be cool.

"What'd you have for dinner?" I said. "I'm starved. I haven't had anything to eat in about the last six universes."

"Oh come on, Serena, you know I don't eat." Bingo!

"Where I come from," I said, "I always eat. But lately, with the Walter Hudson diet—"

"You really can be full of bullshit. All this nonsense you start spouting sometimes." She chuckled. "Thank God this is only a dream," she said wistfully.

"Thank God," I said. Then I suddenly thought of something. "Hey, Serena," I said, "you think we could like . . . meet somewhere? I mean, if you're only dreaming, I guess it won't matter if Mom catches you sneaking out of the house, right?"

"Sure. Be right over."

"But you don't know where I—"

And then she was there. Popped into existence right next to the phone booth. I stared at her. And at the phone. Funny how I hadn't noticed the extra buttons it had—the % and the & and the @ beneath where the * 0 # is on a regular stateside phone. We *were* in sci-fi territory after all. Jeez!

"Serena!"

"Serena!"

Hey, wait a minute, I thought. "Isn't it supposed to drive you crazy if you meet yourself face-to-face in an alternate universe? Anyone who's seen *Back to the Future* knows that!"

"Alternate universe? What are you talking about? Besides, you're not me, you're *fat*. And you're here because I always wanted to have a twin and I was lonely and I started to hear you talking to me in the middle of the night somehow, like tonight. I prayed for one who'd be fat because I wanted someone just like me but who wouldn't, like, eclipse me on Mother's Parade."

"I'm not fat—" It was useless. Why had I tried to kid myself? Pretending I'd been dieting. I was the same as I always was. The difference was that I knew it was okay to be myself. And yeah, I wasn't sluglike anymore if that was what one meant by fat. But it was half cholesterol, half attitude. "You could learn a thing or two from me," I said. "Before I saw you I thought it'd be cool if you were an anorexic, but now I know better. You hate yourself, just the way I used to."

"You bitch! Get out of my life! Who needs fantasies anyway—I should have outgrown them a long time back. Now if you'll excuse me, I think I'll get back to dreamland."

She punched a few buttons on her phone and disappeared. I looked at the phone for a moment, wondering which one the beam-me-up button was. It stood to reason that I wouldn't get along with myself.

I guess I'd better get back, I told myself, and started

trudging up the hill. I stopped at the sidewalk vendor for a few more skewers first.

Phil Etchison

After a while things became less ludic in the observation chamber. The city was having a hard time negotiating the current. The map was changing faster than we could follow it.

"It's the boy," Corvus said. "He's making it up as he goes along!"

"My son?" I said, still getting used to the idea I *had* sons.

Serena popped into the chamber out of thin air. "I see you've figured out how to use the phone," said Corvus.

"I went outside—Mr. E., I met myself—it was awesome, it was horrible at the same time!"

"We were just discussing that possiblity," Corvus said, turning his attention quickly back to a Frankensteinian control panel with flashing lights, bubbling retorts, Tesla coils, twittering electronic noises, and keyboards full of hieroglyphs. "Oh . . . the boy is really something, let me tell you . . . blasted a new path, he has."

A puff of blue smoke and a burst of static on the console.

"Brace yourselves!" Corvus shouted.

I clung to the nearest chair. On the viewscreens we could see a lightning montage of a city in panic—earthquakes, traffic jams, swaying pylons, people running in the streets. I could see Serena sliding down the floor.

"Another jolt!" said Corvus. I squeezed my eyes tight shut . . . and then it was over. We were stable again. "Screens on the River," Corvus said softly.

Serena and I looked around. The River ran black here, battering against the shields of the city. On each of the screens there formed the image of an old man, haloed in a diffuse blue light, white-maned, white-bearded, with a scepter in his hand.

"It's the king," said Corvus. "He's blocking the new fork in the River."

The image became more focused. His robes billowed in the wind. His eyes burned. What I saw in his eyes was arrogance, power, and a terrible desolation. He stood, his feet skimming the water, his arms in the air, in the kind of pose one always associates with King Lear. The tempest raged about him. It seemed to emanate from him. He was at its center.

"The king is mad," said Corvus.

"How are we going to get past him?" Serena said.

"I don't know."

Images of King Strang on every side. Closeup of his eyes. He was a king from an antique tragedy, going through the motions of pity and terror, and yet there was also in him a quality of soullessness; the carbuncle on his scepter seemed to have more life than was in his eyes. It glittered and showered the air with sparks, and every spark was human. I had read enough of Theo's dream book to know that the sparks were the lives that the scepter had stolen—that the gem in the scepter was the visible metaphor of the corruption of absolute power.

"There is only one person who has remained loyal to him," Corvus said, and once again I recognized the archetypal matrix around which our adventures were woven, "and that is Ash; and King Strang will not see him. But Ash could move the king to compassion, away from the darkness. If only the king would—"

I said, "How far are we from Theo and from Joshua?"

"They're very close. The city can feel them." He indicated the map with its fibrillating strands of light. "Thorn and Katastrofa are also there. Everyone is converging on a single world, a single city. . . ."

"Which city?"

"This one," said Corvus. "For, you see, our flying

city is only the top half of the great city of Caliosper; the rest of the city is anchored to the planet Sharán, which was once the third capital of the empire, and the home of my prince and my commander, Ash.''

"But," said Ash, emerging out of the empty air so that it seemed he had been with us all along, "I have been banished from the world. It is my punishment for telling my father things he did not want to hear."

"Surely there is someone who can talk the king into listening to us," I said. And even as I spoke, I felt myself being sucked into their world, their mythos.

"Couldn't you?" said Ash.

But it was Serena who answered him while I hesitated. "Come on, I'll go," she said. "Me and Corvus'll go and see the mad king. Something has to be done."

"Yes," I said. "If he could just lower his guard for a few minutes, we could sneak into the city past him and his henchmen—" Amazingly, the plan sounded sensible even to me. Which showed how deeply this universe with its fluctuating realities had seeped into my consciousness. Perhaps I was starting to be a real poet after all. Realities are infinite, I told myself, but there is only one truth.

It wasn't fair! I told myself. I was a father who desperately wanted to see his children—even though my memories of them were confused—and the king who thwarted me was a madman who never wanted to see his children again. That was, I realized, the very essence of his madness; that he had cut himself off from a part of himself, wilfully refusing to be healed. It was the essence of my madness too. I was sure that I was mad at least some of the time.

I wanted to see the king, to come face-to-face with my own dark secret self, to face my fear of becoming whole.

"Yes, Serena," I said, "we'll all go."

"I cannot," said Ash. "This reality is foreordained and cannot change."

We left Caliosper in a shuttlecraft shaped like a golden

swan. Presently we came to the fork in the River. A wall of water climbed halfway up the sky. Beyond the wall, I knew, were my sons. On an island in the center of the interchange stood the old king, much as we had seen him in the viewscreens of the observation deck.

Serena Somers

We touched down on the island and there were these lizard soldiers who took us into custody and took us to the king. Me and Corvus and Mr. E., who when he saw the king went white, as though he had seen his own ghost. And I knew what that was like, since I'd just done the same thing in a back alley in Caliosper.

We parked the swan just inside the eye of the storm. The whole island was the center of a whirlwind but around the king the air was perfectly still and stifling as a closet. We knelt down in the presence of the king but it was like he didn't even see us.

King Strang stood there staring at something beyond the tempest. I couldn't take my eyes off his scepter. I was scared and awed at the same time. The king had Ash's eyes, the eyes that had haunted me since I was a little girl. But his face was half eaten away by rot. It was like he was the kingdom and the kingdom was him, and whatever happened to the cosmos could also be seen on his face. It was being consumed by death. This was the person who was preventing us from reaching Josh, but I couldn't feel anything but pity for him.

At last Corvus said softly, "Your Majesty."

The king didn't look at him. He tilted his head slightly and said, "Corvus?"

"Yes. I am your old retainer, the one who followed your son into exile."

"Get out," the king said.

"Thorn and Katastrofa are burning down the universe," Corvus said. "Right now they're on the other side of that wall of water. . . . The world they are fighting over is Sharán. You used to love that place. You called it the treasure of your old age. You used to walk through its silent forests. They are desolate now. You willed the planet to your favorite son, but now you have dispossessed him.''

"Who are you?" said the king. "Why are you telling me these terrible, terrible things?"

"I am, O King, your servant," said Corvus. "And this is the father of the Truthsayer. And this is the woman who loves the Truthsayer's brother.''

I didn't know what to say so I kind of curtsied, like in an old movie. I looked from Corvus to Mr. E. The medicine man-astrogator was speaking in I guess a ceremonial way, sometimes flapping his wings to point up his words, and hopping back and forth in a semicircle. It reminded me of the minuet from Mrs. Mueller's ballet class, which I stopped taking when I started to bloat.

Mr. E. started babbling. "Jesus," he said, "a complex, recursive, solipsistic metaphor—the endlessly replicating self—''

What was he talking about? Mr. E. always withdrew into a fog of philosophy when he couldn't cope. I'd seen it before.

"Corvus? Is it really you? Have you come back to me, abandoning my faithless son?" King Strang spoke very softly, but his words had an echoey quality, as though you were in a cathedral.

"I haven't abandoned him, King; I haven't abandoned you. He is the only hope for conciliation between your children. You have to let us through.''

"I don't care about the universe anymore," said the king. "I don't care about conciliation. Can't you see that I'm angry, that I'm disintegrating?"

"But you must remember how it used to be . . . before you plucked the scepter from the source of the river. . . .''

"What I have spoken I have spoken," said the king.

"It cannot be unspoken. To unspeak the words of the king would undo the fabric of the universe."

I just couldn't help myself anymore. "What bullshit," I blurted out.

Suddenly everyone was staring at me. The wind was dropping. I could see chinks in the wall of water. The king's face darkened. But I didn't care anymore. The silence was appalling and I had to fill it. "Ash is like the only one who's ever loved you. If you can't understand that, you shouldn't be standing around hurling the whirl-wind at people—who do you think you are? If you can't even do the right thing anymore, you're not even a real king! Mr. E. and me, we came a long way to save the people we care about. I don't know why you're trying to stop us but I'm not going to let you stand in my way, you, you, you mega-dweeb!"

It was an intense moment. Mr. E. and the king were facing each other off, having a staring contest. The lizard soldiers were so shocked they were actually tripping over each other.

"I—" said the king. His soldiers leaned forward to listen.

At that moment the wall of water kind of shimmered and started to fade.

"Command—" said the king. He gritted his teeth. His scepter began to sparkle, and I knew that it meant he was thinking about killing people.

"Quick!" said Corvus. "Into the swan!"

Something snapped. We sprinted into the swan and Cor-vus aimed it right at the disintegrating wall of water.

"Death!" the king screamed.

The spears started flying.

I don't think that Strang could control the tempest and order his lizards around at the same time. At that moment the storm fizzled out and the city of Caliosper rose up behind us out of the mist-covered water. We streaked up into the sky and swan-dove at the wall of water with the city on our back. I shrieked. We hit the wall of water with a thundering slap and then we were somewhere else altogether.

chapter twenty-two

Caliosper

Joshua Etchison

So my brother and I didn't sneak into the city after all. We were brought through the city gates in triumph. We stood on the back of the pickup truck on the shoulders of shamans and were drummed and chanted and gonged and fluted all the way in. They were all chanting "Truthsayer, Truthsayer," and the more they chanted the more I felt that I was finally leaving death behind.

Of course, you never really leave death behind. I'd learned that since crossing over into this other world. I'd learned that death is always with you, that it's as much a part of you as your shadow, lengthening as the sun begins to set. Even now I knew that Katastrofa was outside the city and moving in fast.

The walls of the city were so high that they muffled the shrieks of the dying outside. The metal vultures dashed themselves to pieces against titanium bricks or against the forceshield that extended above the walls high into the stratosphere of the planet. I learned these things from picking up bits of people's conversations as the procession moved uphill along steep narrow streets and the mood became less fearful and more festive.

It seemed Theo was the only who wasn't getting a high off the sense of rejoicing. He stood beside me—well, we were both standing on this kind of platform that rested on the shamans' shoulders—and stared off into space the way he does when he's in his private universe. (Of course we were *all* in his private universe in a way, but I guess he had found a private universe within this private universe . . . the way he'd found this planet inside a river inside a marble.) Looking at him made me afraid. I said, "C'mon, little brother. Look at all this fucking spectacle, dude!" Dancing girls were just running out of the houses and thrashing and writhing and stripping right there on the street. Trumpeters were playing wild riffs as they skateboarded up the pavement.

"Something's going to happen," Theo said. "It's Mom and Dad . . . they're coming to rescue us. But . . . but . . ."

I thought of the shadow death. Suddenly I could feel Katastrofa outside the walls, I could feel her tugging at me. I remembered the way she smelled—of musk and lizard and a grown woman's thighs. God I started shaking then, and just like that I couldn't hear the music, couldn't hear the cheering of the crowd.

Theo Etchison

We're at a high point. I've almost managed to bring Joshua back into the real world. The walls are blocking out the dragon woman. And also the people. I can feel them, thousands and thousands of consciousnesses, flitting like fireflies through the darkness of the inanimate. They've set up a wall that blocks off Katastrofa's influence even more effectively than the city does.

But I'm really scared now.

Scared because I can feel Mom and Dad coming toward us, and Thorn, and Ash, and Katastrofa, and even Strang, yanking at their frayed puppetstrings.

The thing is, Joshua has started to breathe again. When I first saw him in this country, he didn't breathe at all. When he spoke those few words to me he would suck in the air and kind of bend it past his vocal cords and back out again but you couldn't really call that breathing. That's the thing about Joshua that I've been least willing to see, but now that he has started to take slow gasping breaths now and then, I understand what it was about him that made me *know* he was dead—not the dripping wounds, not the pallor, not the maggots crawling out of the gashes in his arms—it was the breathing. Now he's halfway between death and life and it makes me even more afraid of him.

Even though there doesn't seem to be anything to fear for now. There's music in the streets and dancing girls and laughter. The pickup strains and groans its way uphill and Joshua's even smiling a little. Jesus I'm scared. Even the smile scares me.

Suddenly there's like a loud blast from a dozen trumpets and the music stops. Everyone stops in midstream. They turn their faces skyward. A shout goes up: "The citadel! The citadel!" I follow the line of their gaze . . . up the hillside where the streets converge upon a plateau where it seems the rock has been sheared flat . . . upward to the sky where two suns blaze while a third is in eclipse . . . and I see another city descending on this city, a city like a cluster of lights, like a gemstone with a thousand facets, and I see that the mesa is designed to nestle the citadel, that the diamond in the sky is made to fit the greater city like the jewel in the scepter of King Strang.

Joyful chaos in the streets! Children are scrambling over the roofs of cars, the drumbeats are coming thick and fast and rhythmless no . . . oh Jesus, I'm thinking, it's awesome, it's intense, it makes me tremble. . . . We're racing up the mountain now, cutting through kidney-shaped parking lots and zipping through tunnels painted with garish abstracts. . . . I know who's in the citadel. We're getting closer and closer to the moment when things will all come together, the Rome all roads lead to. I'm scared and elated and . . . I turn to look at Joshua. He's still smiling. He can't see the way I see.

Oh what a citadel it is. I mean like it's Xanadu and Oz and the Forbidden City of Peking all rolled into one. A cathedral rises out of a faery mist, and on its topmost spire is perched an image of my mother with outstretched arms and wings, and out of the cathedral comes a strange celestial music, like windchimes, whale songs, and the roaring sea all blended into one massive surfer wave of sound. Beside the cathedral there's this palace with a parapet that soars across the town square. That's where we're headed now, me and my brother and a million other people, oozing up the side of the mountain.

Then I see them standing up there at the edge of the veranda. I see Dad and I see Serena Somers—I think it's her, although she seems to have fleshed out a little bit once more from the last time I saw her—and next to them I see someone I recognize only from my dreams, Ash, the third child of the old king. Next to him is this bird-man. I think he's like the exalted grand vizier or chief minister of Ash's kingdom. They're all tiny figures, up there, waving and nodding their heads.

I know that Ash isn't supposed to be here; that he's been dispossessed and driven away, with only the immediate world of the floating citadel to call his own. But you couldn't tell that from the way the people are reacting. They've stopped yelling out my name now and they're calling for their prince. They just keep cramming into the town square and I can see banners being erected and lasers zapping patterns into the sky. They've started a rhythmic chant of Ashhhhhh, Ashhhhhh, and every time they say

the *shhhhh* of Ashhhhhh it sets up a whooshing in the air
as if a tornado was brewing.

Josh is shouting it too. Good, I'm thinking, it'll stop
him from feeling the deathspell of the dragon woman. And
pretty soon I'm screaming out Ash's name too, screaming
my throat raw.

The crowd parts to let the pickup through. A crystal
staircase unfurls from the parapet. The steps are as wide
as one whole side of the square and they come down to
just where the pickup is parked. They're made of some
kind of forcefield material because you can see right
through them, they're like a rainbow-fringed hologram-
looking mirage just hanging in the air.

The shamans who've been carrying us on their shoulders
let us down. The statue of the One Mother is hefted onto
a litter. The Navajo blanket is removed and we see her
dazzling eyes, shining with the light of all the world's
suns. A gasp goes up from the crowd. There is a moment's
silence before the hubbub starts again.

The head shaman calls to us. We board the litter.
Twenty men raise us up as we stand on either side of the
statue. Twenty boys and girls swinging incense burners
walk ahead of us up the steps, and chanting priests walk
behind us with their eyes downcast, holding their palms
in front of their faces.

So there we are being carried up the crystal steps amid
a crowd gone crazy with weird music blasting us from
every side and it's a freaky feeling because I want it to
go on and on, my heart's pumping like mad and I'm on
top of the world, the local god or something like in those
movies where this majorly smart white hunter dude stum-
bles into a lost civilization somewhere in Africa and they
mistake him for the Mega-Juju. It's fantasy and it's my
own and I remind myself that it's just a metaphor like
everything else in this country on the other side of death,
but you know how caught up I can be in my own fantasy,
and how other people can be caught up in it too, and it

just replicates itself over and over like the shouts of the crowd that echo from the spires and towers and parapets of Caliosper. Jesus fucking Christ. That's who they think I am. Kind of.

The drums get faster now. The litterbearers are huffing and puffing their way to the top. We are being carried up the sky. The crowd sounds distant now, one mass of indistinguishable sounds.

Finally we're on the terrace. The light is so brilliant that I can't help crying. They let us down slowly. Someone bangs on a big old gong and the incense-swingers start swinging insanely, so that the smoke blocks out some of the suns' light and engulfs us in a fragrant haze.

Joshua looks afraid suddenly. I touch him on the shoulder. He has seen Serena Somers. Dad has seen me.

He says, "I seem to know you now. It's like taking off a pair of dark glasses. Theo. Theo."

And embraces me. I start to cry. But he doesn't embrace Josh, who has the stink of death still on him and whose skin is still blue. And yes . . . I think maybe he's stopped breathing again. Sometimes like in a low budget horror movie you see the corpse lying there and you think it's some actor desperately trying not to move, not to breathe, until they cut away. . . . It seems like this for Joshua only it's life he's imitating . . . waiting for my Dad to look away so he can be dead again.

Dad says softly, just for me, " 'Who knows if in the land of the dead they think that *we* are dead and that it is they who are living?' " It's a quote from Euripides or one of those ancient Greek dudes; my Dad's brain is like a giant CD-ROM, and when he's at a loss for words he has the whole of Western literature stored in neat little packets of gray matter, stacks upon stacks. I love him for it though. I love him fiercely even though he only half knows me.

"Dad," I say, "it *is* Joshua. That's what they've done to him for not being me. Dad, there's still life in him, I can feel it, and you know I can't help feeling what's true, it's the way you made me."

"We're going to take you back," my Dad says. "We're going to be together, you and Joshua and Mary and me, all together, like this never happened, I swear it." He hugs me again and he is crying too.

Joshua Etchison

Serena Somers. Sluglike Serena. She stood there like a butterfly just popped from her chrysalis, and she kissed me, even with the skin peeling from my blue-gray face. She had come a long way to find me. A long way from the safe world of Twinkies and soap opera death scenes. I kissed her back and life flooded me. . . . It was like getting a blood transfusion . . . or like a dead man, a vampire, drinking the warm blood of a living person and raging because what he feels is only a shadow of what he remembers.

Then there was Dad. But he wasn't sure about me. He was confused. He didn't have a single strand of yarn to cling to like Serena had. Serena loved me, had always loved me. It was an obsessive thing, a thing only teenagers can know, because when you're Dad's age you're past the idea that there's only one thing in the whole universe that matters. Serena's singlemindedness had been so overpowering that she was able to cling to her memory of me even while the universe changed around her, even while it tried to obliterate my existence and wipe out the paradoxes of our transdimensional journey.

I could feel that intensity. It wasn't comforting, not like the embrace of Katastrofa which made me forget everything because I knew I was dead and death was the end the solution orgasm without end amen. No she was like my brother—even more so because she found the part of me that refused to know that it was dead and wanted her bad even though it was true what I'd told Theo, we'd never really done it but we'd come pretty close sometimes, especially that one night at *Friday the Thirteenth Part Umpteenth* when Theo was snoring in the front seat covered in popcorn.

"Kiss me back, Josh," Serena said. "I didn't come all this way to star in *I Walked with a Zombie*." I looked over to where Theo and Dad were, they were all crying and hugging each other but I thought, I'm too old for that now and too young to be like Dad.

Philip Etchison

—and I saw my two sons and knew them for what they were, and knew that we were participants in a timeless drama on a stage free from the constraints of day-to-day logic; another logic ruled here—the logic of myth, the semiotics of dreaming, the labyrinthine symbolism of Messrs. Jung, Frazer, and Campbell. We had our masks to wear and our selves were subordinate to our mythic roles.

But under the masks we were also ourselves, worrying about the mortgage and the IRS. I remembered it all now. My wife falling ill. My two sons: Joshua with all his friends, Theo the inward-looking one. I remembered, too, how the world had shifted back and forth. The peyote juice had annulled the drugs that Cornelius Huang had given me. It was one of those *Alice in Wonderland* situations with all the bottles marked "Drink Me" that turned you into someone else and the mushroom antidote that the caterpillar prescribed. I was myself now. The son who had always seemed devoid of feeling to me was bursting with emotions; the son who had been full of vitality had become one of the living dead.

And of course, my wife was a self-replicating statue of whom each part was the whole.

"All right," I said. "I am nothing if not the head of this family. I came here to fetch you all and I'll do it even if the world comes to an end. Goddamn it, let's get out of here, let's pile into the stationwagon and get back on Route 10.''

"Easier said than done, Mr. E.," said Serena.

I could hear the beating of mighty wings. I could feel the heat in the air and knew that it was the breath of a distant dragon. Some of the incense wavers had dropped their censers. The priests were no longer chanting. Something had come over them.

Prince Ash looked at the four of us and the statue. He had not said a word during the reunion scene, but had stood afar off, fearful, perhaps, of intruding. Perhaps, not being a human being, he didn't even really understand the way we humans love each other, which is a beautiful and terrible thing and not easily comprehended by aliens.

He gazed at me now, saddened, I think; he said, "Our problems are not your problems. Your Earth is only at the periphery of all this. Perhaps, as a consequence of the power struggles that are going on in our kingdoms, it will even cease to exist, but it will be as though it had never existed, so you would not be there to suffer the loss of its never having been. We had no right to pluck Theo Truthsayer from the world. He should have gone on living there, shedding his own kind of light on his own community of humans. I have no right to keep you here."

He waved his hand. The family stationwagon rolled onto the pavilion, somewhat in the manner of *The Price is Right* or one of those other game shows. With the crowd cheering in the distance, there was a distinct ambience of television.

"I didn't bring you here, Theo," said Ash, "but I am glad you came. You gave us hope. For a brief while at least."

I looked at Theo.

"I know the way home, Dad," he said. "Or if I don't, I can blast our way home, I can cut a new canyon for the River to follow."

He pulled a marble out of his pocket. He held it in his fist, held it to his forehead. We waited, the five of us: a dilapidated poet, a teenage zombie, a boy messiah, a girl with an eating disorder, and a statue.

We waited.

"I don't think we can leave yet," Theo said at last.

"Why not, son?"

"Listen!"

The beating of mighty wings. Fire in the sky. Dragon's breath. The crowd in the square in panic now. I couldn't read Ash's expression; he had hidden his sorrow behind a mask of civility.

"What is it, son?" I said. "Is it the end of the world?"

"Maybe," Theo said.

A fireball struck the stationwagon. It exploded. Serena began screaming. Joshua looked at the sky. His eyes were full of terror and of lust.

And Mary's eyes too had changed. The statue of the One Mother was weeping.

chapter twenty-three

Losing Our Marbles

Phil Etchison

To say then that all hell had broken loose would be to succumb to cliché and belabor the obvious. Hell was the most obvious image that came to mind at first. Fire ripping down from the sky, fire threading its way up the streets toward the citadel, fire crackling along the walls of Caliosper. There was also something of the quality of the climaxes of the *Alice* books—playing cards with truculent expressions flying in our faces, roast legs of lamb and suet puddings stalking around in a rage, lizards and flowers running in circles. There was also, at first, the feeling that we—my family, the prince, Corvus—were enclosed in an inviolate faery circle that the fire could not touch. As I watched the conflagration spread, I couldn't quite grasp that it was really happening. I was still seeing it all as metaphor, as bits and pieces of someone's—perhaps Theo's—dream. The extravagance and extremity of these visions suggested the febrile fecundity of a child's imagination. Truthsaying and mythmaking are, in essence, the same thing.

That's why, as I watched more and more truckloads of refugees cram into the town square, as I observed, in the distance, beyond the city walls, forests flare up, villages explode, exaltations of metallic vultures smashing themselves to bits as they tore at each other amid clouds of flame, I felt no panic. I had begun this adventure as a poet without a soul, but now I had something I had never had before—I had faith in the power of my son's imagination, which was fueled by his love for me, for Mary, for his brother. Theo's imagination was born from love and sustained by grace. We had recognized each other, embraced, forgiven; in understanding him, I was also coming to grips with a kind of theology. Epiphanies blossomed into new epiphanies. I was drunk on epiphanies.

Therefore—as the palace began to shake—as gargoyles tumbled from the cathedral's topmost spires—as clefts opened up in the floor of the pavilion and sulphurous fumes began to pour from them—I was untouched by any sense of alarm.

Corvus was relaying orders to some of his helpers.

"If we get as many people as possible into the citadel," Ash was saying, "maybe we can save them—make it to the River before the world blows—" I saw the desperation on his face and felt for him a sublime compassion.

Calmly I walked up to the family stationwagon, which was still smoking from the exploded fireball. It no longer had a roof, and one of the tires was flat, and the trunk seemed to be on fire.

"Kids," I said, "let's get in the car. Enough bullshit now."

Serena Somers

So like, there we were: Mr. E. charging toward the car, Joshua wresting himself from my arms and shambling distractedly around the parapet, Theo waving the marble at the sky, the marble that was sizzling with lines of laser light . . . and we were under attack.

So maybe this planet was going to blow up or something, but I really only cared about what happened to the people I loved. And Joshua was going berserk now— deader than ever—I thought he was going to lose more pieces of himself.

Fire was in the sky. I ran after him and shouted, "The car's that way, Josh! Mr. E.'s planning to leave now!"

When I caught up he twisted free again, saying over and over, "It's no use, Serena, everything's changed, I can never come back . . . I drank the water, I ate the food, I fucked the girl—I belong here now."

"Fat lot of good it was saving myself for you," I said. "Look! In the sky!"

The fire parted. There came a dragon with black leathern wings and scales like polished copper and eyes like suns. The dragon—

Joshua Etchison

—came toward me. The dragon had been calling me all along. My penis strained against my underpants. I remembered the water from the cooler flooding the office in the police station and the face of the woman detective and her voice and her soft hands that gripped so hard, like lizard claws, and her eyes burning—

Phil Etchison

I was trying to get the car door open. When I saw the dragon I suddenly didn't feel so detached anymore. The door was jammed or something, maybe from the explosion. I tried the handle again and again.

Theo Etchison

I am holding the marble high in the air. Thousands of true names whir through my mind. I'm holding up the marble and trying to see into it with my inner vision—

Everything's on fire. They're going to blast away the world, they're going to rip the fabric of the universe to shreds so they can pull me out and use me. The flames are everywhere but instead of fire I think of water. . . . I think of the River. . . . I think of the source. . . . I think of the stream that once flowed through all things and now has been bent and twisted and dammed up so many times that it's forgotten its true course. . . . I think of water, cool, healing, life-giving water . . . water . . . the fountain . . . the source . . . the spring . . . the beginning and the end . . . water . . . water water. . . .

The dragon wheels overhead. She screams and the towers begin to topple. Then from the oppoiste side of the sky comes the ship of Thorn . . . the ship at the head of a fleet of ships, bursting through the clouds and the flames. . . . There's Thorn, there's Cornelius blowing on his conch, the blasts of trumpet music harsh against the dragon's screeching. . . .

Philip Etchison

I couldn't get the door to open. I stood openmouthed on the parapet watching the dragon and its attendant vultures and the fleet of ships with death's head prows. . . . I saw the dragon with a ship in her talons, tearing it apart, saw the ship's crew spiraling toward the ground, each with a trail of smoke and flame. . . .

Serena Somers

I saw Joshua and like he couldn't take his eyes off that dragon and he had gone all cold and his eyes had gone dead and I shook him and all I did was gouge the flesh from his shoulders and—

And then there were two colossal shapes in the sky, one like a dragon and the other like a bat and they were clawing and shrieking and it was like something out of *King Kong*, the pterodactyls rushing at one another ripping out flesh with their beaks—

"Ash!" I turned to look for him. But he wasn't there anymore. He had deserted me.

Phil Etchison

Two monsters battling in the sky. They were locked together, plummeting now, unable to stay aloft anymore . . . and they were transforming—the bat-thing into a tall man with a dark cloak that trailed up into the fiery mist, the dragon into a woman with blazing red hair—and still they fought. . . . I knew then they must be siblings . . . only siblings fight that way.

But where was Ash, the third sibling? I saw him now, standing on a hovering platform with Corvus by his side, flitting above the crowd, trying to allay the panic. The throng jammed the square, people piled on people, screams upon screams. They must have been suffocating. I kept banging on the door. At last it came open.

"Get in!" I shouted. "Serena! Joshua! Theo—"

The man and the woman were still falling out of the sky. The man radiated an utter darkness, the woman an overpowering sensuality. My son Joshua was staring at the woman and turning more and more corpselike.

"Get in the car!" I shouted. I slid into the driver's seat. Screamed through the open window at the three kids. Joshua seemed not to hear me.

Theo said, "I have to find the way," and slipped even further into his somnambulistic state.

Only Serena heard me. "He won't come, Mr. E.!" she said. "He's totally under her spell."

I started the car, gunned the engine. A lightning bolt struck the car. I was shaking. But I had to control myself. I was still their father. I had to be strong.

"Get Theo!" Serena screamed.

I saw Theo bolt. The man in black was gaining on him. I had to do something. I released the brake and sputtered forward. They ran into the palace and I crashed through a window in pursuit of them.

Theo Etchison

Thorn is coming down toward me out of the sky! I clutch the marble tight. That's what he's after, I know it. I run from the veranda, run into the great hall of the palace. People are scurrying around inside. They all seem lost. A child is sitting in a corner drooling and playing with a yo-yo.

I run. Down corridors, down caverns, down, down, down. . . . I think I'm running down to the heart of hell . . . and he's following me. Never more than a few steps behind. The dog growls, yelps, snaps at my heels. There's nowhere to run, but still I run.

I run.

The flames are gaining on me, hissing down the corridors of the palace that is also a starship and a cavern and a maze and the inside of my mind. I run through a knot garden, where the paths transform into new shapes even while I'm running, where the hedges touch the sun and stone sileni stare and grimace. . . . Thorn is right behind me. I can hear the yapping of the three-headed dog. I don't know where to go. There are doors and doors behind doors. I open one randomly and see an old woman wrapped in a Navajo blanket look up at me with sunken eyes and I know it's Mom a long way in the future in some other future dying and I slam the door and try another and

another and there are mirrors behind mirrors and doors
behind doors and—

Somehow I'm on the street now. People are jostling
me. I can smell Thorn and the dog at his heels. Thorn
tackles me. The marble slips from my fist and rolls away
. . . somewhere . . . where? There are people everywhere,
running into each other, trampling over each other, wailing
. . . people on fire, people tearing their hair and their
clothes, people packed into sobbing heaps, people walking
in circles—

"The marble!" Thorn says.

There's no sign of it. It's somewhere under all those
people. I feel it, because the thread that connects me to it
is not the kind of thread you can cut; I am made of what
the marble is; I can't help being the truthsayer.

But Thorn can't feel what I feel. He lets out a cry of
despair that seems even to outthunder the clamoring sky.

He doesn't let go of me. He holds me tight. Pins me
to the ground. His fingernails dig into my back and he's
foaming at the mouth and his fangs glint in the light of
the burning sky.

"Let me go," I say. "I can't belong to you. A truthsayer is just a truthsayer. A truthsayer can't be bent. You
have to understand that, Thorn."

His grip loosens a little. In the pandemonium the two
of us seem enclosed in a private bubble of silence.

"But I showed you my innermost torment!" he says.
"I showed you the harvester of tears. Theo, Theo, do you
think I enjoy being the Prince of Darkness? Together we
could have conquered the terrible destiny that corrupted
my father. I cared for you, Theo. Perhaps I even loved
you."

"Perhaps you did," I say. But still he won't let go of
me. "But you're never going to own me, and until you
understand that you'll never be ruler of yourself, let alone
your father's kingdom."

"I need you," he says at last. "You're right, it's

because I can't own you that I'm obsessed with possessing you . . . but the kingdom's mine by right, I am the oldest. . . . You know that my father shouldn't have divided it up . . . he sowed the seeds of chaos and I can't reap alone. . . .''

I know he'll say anything to make me stay with him. And I know that, in his own way, he does love me. I know that this pleading is the most difficult thing he has ever done. He weeps. His tears are tears of blood. We look into each other's eyes for a long moment and I start to feel as though it's my duty to heal the universe . . . that there's a kernel of truth in what he says.

But at that moment the bubble of silence bursts and the hubbub breaks out all around us again.

"Help!" I scream at the top of my voice. "Help!"

A battered stationwagon screeches to a halt alongside us. Dad! Somehow Thorn seems to lose all his strength. I twist free of him. Dad gets out of the car. I run to him.

"Stay the fuck away from my kid," Dad says. Very softly. I almost have to read his lips.

Thorn stands there, his cloak flying. He seems very frail suddenly. Behind him is his ship, plowing through the mass of people as though they were the sea, lopping off heads and arms and churning up blood as it comes to a stop behind the vampire prince.

"Let's go get the others," Dad says. I climb into the front seat next to him. He starts the car again. The crowd parts. "Do you know where we're going?"

"I think so."

"All right then, you steer. Scrunch up real close to me. Remember when you were seven years old and we used to do this?" I know what he's thinking. I'm too big to get into his lap but I kind of lean over and put both hands on the steering wheel.

"You trust me, Dad?" I say.

"Yup."

"Prove it."

He closes his eyes and slams his foot down on the accelerator.

chapter twenty-four

Trust Me

Theo Etchison

I concentrate. I don't want anyone to die. I can't just steer the car through people the way Thorn's ship moves, killing as it rives the human sea. I think: Part the sea. Like the Red Sea in that old movie, the one with the Egyptians in their cool chariots. I concentrate hard. The crowd begins to shift to either side of us. It's good because my Dad is flooring all the way.

His eyes are still closed. That was the game we used to play when I was little sitting on his lap and sliding with agonizing slowness from the gate to the driveway to the open garage. The name of the game was "trust me." One time I missed the fencepost by like a quarter of an inch, but Dad never said a word about it to me even though I guess it was like questionable if insurance would have covered it if I'd let him get it dented. I was seven years old. Dad never let me play "trust me" again until this moment.

How could Dad have known that of all the times we ever spent together—reading poetry—going to ball games and movies—fishing—sitting by the fire, him talking a mile a minute about some philosophy thing I couldn't understand, me crouching against the warmth and drinking in the awesome words, smooth words, words with shiny edges, words that hovered on the brink of understandability—of all the moments he and I were father and son, the times we played the "trust me" game were the times I truly loved him?

Because he's chosen to play the game now, while the world is collapsing around us, because of this, I know that the choice I've made is a true choice. Because of this I know I must go home with him, I must dream the true path that will take us to the true world. . . . I can't stay here with Thorn and become the instrument of his greed.

Because I've made this choice Thorn is enraged. He's called down his whole fleet out of the sky and they're slaughtering everyone they can. We're being pelted with body parts as explosions rock the town square. I turn on the windshield wipers and squirt the cleaning stuff on it so's the blood won't stay.

I steer into the path the crowd has made for me and now and then I feel a crunch of bone as we run over someone who I hope is dead already. My Dad doesn't know where we're going. He still hasn't opened his eyes.

"Trust me," I whisper, very very softly.

We lurch through the square. I spin the wheel like crazy. The ships of Thorn are chasing after me. I see the cathedral. There's a ramp leading up to the great open gates, guarded on either side by thirty-foot-tall stone demons. "Step on it Dad," I say. "Open your eyes—"

I dodge the nearest ship. It crashes into the steps. People are scurrying out of the way as I turn the car up the ramp. My Dad still hasn't opened his eyes. "I trust you," he says. Now I start to think maybe he's right not to look, because I'm linking up with the marble which is rolling around somewhere in the plaza. As I link up, reality begins to shift, and we're in more than one place at the same time—the cathedral ramp, the men's room of the Chinese restaurant in Arizona, the madhouse where they've been keeping Mom—all these places are here and now as I start to search for the way home.

The gates swing open like the swinging doors to the toilet like the tollgate on the airport access highway like the gate between worlds—

"Don't look!" I cry out. Because I've seen the ships of Thornstone Slaught as they slam into the sides of the cathedral, seen the gargoyles tumble and the mermaids gasping for sea water, seen Thorn's minions crush themselves between the prow and the limestone facing. . . . "Don't look, Dad!" I say, and he doesn't look. He's just sitting with both feet jamming down the gas. I think maybe he's asleep, dreaming. As we all are, all the time, reality or no.

Joshua Etchison

Serena was trying to push me toward the station wagon but suddenly it had zoomed off after Theo. She was shaking me and trying to put life back into me, but I didn't want life anymore because I could see Katastrofa coming down from the sky.

She was changing as she descended. Claws retracting. Her body collapsing in on itself. She danced on a cloud of fire. Her eyes flashed. She was becoming a woman.

The bat-thing was transformed too but I could see that it was after Theo, not me. I smelled Katastrofa's breath on the wind and it was like the burning world wasn't there almost—almost, it had backed off, the sounds of the desperate dying were faint, almost like surf beating against some seashore far away, and the fire in the sky seemed cool. That was because I was beginning to die again and to die means not to feel to sleep without dreaming to dissolve out of the matrix of the world; but dying for me was to be able to feel only one thing, Katastrofa and her embrace of darkness.

"Don't look at her," Serena said. She was tugging at my arm. "She wants to drive you out of your body, she wants to make you into a shell and fill you with herself—" And she pushed me away from the parapet, through the great French doors with their billowing drapes that had caught the fire from the sky and she pulled me into the great hall of the palace, pulling with all her might because I was dead weight, not helping her at all.

She dragged me across the hallway. A chandelier crashed onto the mirror-marble. A throne crumbled and crushed a fleeing man. I couldn't feel the palace shaking or the rubble smashing into my face or the dust I was breathing in. I was dead. I went whatever way I was pushed. We reached a staircase and I tumbled down it with Serena leaping after me two and three steps at a time. After a while we seemed to be in a cavern. Or a well. We were still running. Katastrofa was behind us. Gaining. I could feel her in my mind, the slimmest sliver of heat and arousal, the only sensation I could feel at all.

We were running across bare desert now. Mesas reared up against the horizon. The scorching sand was like snow to my feet, numbing. I saw Serena sweating, crying out because of the pain, and still she was dragging me, pushing, pulling, shoving me away from Katastrofa. Sometimes Katastrofa seemed to be a woman and sometimes she was like a dragon and filled the whole sky with her eyes as twin suns beating down on an alien landscape.

"Oh Jesus, I can't go on, I can't, I can't," Serena said at last. Her hands, slick with sweat, slipped from my arms. She sank down on the sand. I crumpled down beside her. There was no shade. The eyes of the sky shrank into the eyes of the dragon. Katastrofa stood above us. Her shadow fell on me, wavering, dancing.

"Give him to me now," Katastrofa said to Serena. And

she knelt down and touched me . . . and I felt the woman-
warmth flooding me. . . . I felt myself getting sucked
in. . . . She licked her lips. . . . Her saliva dripped onto
my side and where it struck my skin it burned me and it
was all I could feel even in the streaming sunlight. . . .
"Death," she said, "death, death, death . . . you have
been consecrated to death . . . you don't want to go back
. . . you want to stay in the safe dark cold numb stillness
where only one mind can touch yours. . . . oh, Joshua,
Joshua, listen to me, listen to me because I'm the only
one who has really loved you, I'm the one who will make
you king of the infinite gray spaces, king of the dark
kingdom, king of the dead."

And she flung her arms wide and blocked out the sun.
And she bent down to kiss me and I knew that there was
nothing I could do except return to darkness. . . . It's only
when she'd blocked out the light completely that I felt
warmth at last, the warmth I'd always craved, the warmth
of womb and woman.

Serena Somers

I knew I was losing him. He was lying on the sand like
a sacrificial victim and she was swooping down on him
like a scavenger bird. There was only one thing left for
me to do. I threw myself between them.

"Get away from him, bitch!" I yelled at her.

She raked at my eyes. Her fingernails were pushing into
claws. She couldn't stay human that long because she
wasn't really human at all. I punched her in the face as
hard as I could. She recoiled. I guess nobody had ever
fought back before because she seemed like majorly
surprised.

"I knew him long before you did," I said. I was sur-
prising myself. I mean, when I was facing the mad king,
I'd been so much at a loss for words that I'd ended up
calling him a *mega-dweeb*, which must have made me

sound pretty stupid, I mean, you summon up the courage
to sass the king of the universe or whatever he was and
then you find that you're stuck with the vocabulary of an
eighth-grade Valley girl. I didn't think I'd ever live that
down, but I was angrier now than I ever was then, because
I knew now for a fact that this rotting corpse flailing away
in the desert sand was the man I loved.

How many times had I eaten an extra pound of M & Ms
just because I thought Joshua wasn't going to speak to me
anymore? How many times had I sat beside him at the
drive-in, talking too much because I wanted him to touch
me so so bad but I was afraid so I would flinch away even
before his hand started to inch across the frayed green
vinyl? Too late to regret it. I had to fight to keep my man.

Katastrofa . . . the scales kept rising up to the surface
of her skin . . . her cheeks undulated and I could tell that
she was barely keeping her shape. "What can you give
him?" she said derisively. "I was the one who embraced
him when you wouldn't. I have power. I am a queen and
you're nobody at all. I can give him the world. Many
worlds. Maybe he's not the great one, the Truthsayer—
but he's got the talent and he can win the kingdom back
for me, he can glue back the pieces of the shattered
empire. What can *you* do for him? You're a fat little slug
who never even let him fuck you."

"I'm not a slug anymore," I said. "And as for not
fucking, I'm going to fix that right now, right here."

Slowly I started to wriggle out of my clothes.

"You can give him the world," I said. "I can't argue
with you there. But I can give him my chastity. To heal
him, I can sacrifice a virgin—me. That's more than you
can do, because you've never loved the way I've loved,
in secret, hiding myself inside my walls of lard."

I could tell that what I was saying hit home. She started
to back away. And then she began to howl. Not like a
human being at all, but like a wolf in the forest on a
freezing winter night.

I knelt down beside Joshua and I kissed him. I kissed the scars on his cheeks that crawled with maggots. The scars began to knit together. The gray started to leave his face. I kissed his mouth and felt the lips turn warm. And I started to remember those summers when I had lain awake half the humid night thinking about him not daring to call him because I was afraid he wouldn't answer, stuffing the warm sticky chocolate bars from under my pillow into my mouth so I wouldn't have to think about him. . . . There was no chocolate here. Only his parched lips.

I devoured his lips. I breathed the moisture back into them. I shielded him from the dragon's breath with my body. I wrapped my legs around his thighs and felt him become aroused and wasn't scared anymore. And all the while Katastrofa screeched and beat her wings and stirred up the sand to sting my eyes and irritate my tissues but I wouldn't let her hurt me. I thought of water, cool spring water . . . I dreamed my most private dreams . . . at last I kindled fire in Joshua and he began to move, slowly at first, and to breathe in piping arrhythmic breaths, and then I felt his hands clench my buttocks, my thighs, smelled sweat as it burst out from newly opened pores. . . . I teased his penis free from whatever it was he was wearing, some futuristic-looking tunic kind of thing, I held it between my palms like a votive candle and then I kissed it again and again, watching it grow hard, watching with wonder because it was something I'd only ever imagined before. Then I let him plunge it slowly into me and at first it didn't feel that good because maybe I wasn't moist down there, it wasn't simple to get moist the way it was when I used to do it alone in the dark, but suddenly there came a moment when it all seemed to fit perfectly together and I hugged him hard to me and his eyes were right over my eyes and there was so much joy in them that I knew he was coming back to me out of the dark country and that the dragon couldn't hold him after all. . . .

And with a terrible cry, Katastrofa spread her wings wide and soared up toward the sun, and . . .

The desert dissolved. We seemed to be in another place altogether . . . a cathedral with brilliant abstract stained glass windows. . . . We were making love on the altar of the one Mother . . . the shrine was the *kiva* and the stained glass was the sand painting and we were thrusting hard now, our two rhythms melding into one into the heartbeat of the world and the drumbeats of the shamans as they danced and our breaths were the sacred incense rising up to smell fragrant in the nostrils of the Gods and we clung closer and closer now laughing and warm in the glow from the fire and the magic potion of life and death. . . .

Phil Etchison

We pulled up beside the altar. The image of Mary stood watch over them. Incense burned in a brazier next to them and smoke filled the cathedral so we could not see the ceiling. Here and there shafts of light pierced the gloom, light in the vivid colors of the stained glass windows. The cries of the dying could be heard, and the explosions in the burning city, but in this cathedral the sounds were muted, cushioned with stone upon stone.

Ash was seated on a throne at the Mother's feet, and Corvus beside him. Corvus was manipulating some kind of hand controller; Ash was deep in contemplation. He had isolated himself somehow; though he was close to us, he had surrounded himself with a circle of impenetrable loneliness.

Theo got out of the car first. I followed. He began to walk up the steps toward the statue of the One Mother. He was communicating with her somehow, I think, although she did not show any signs of change, except for the one tear that glistened on her left cheek and her lips, half-parted, as though on the verge of speech.

Joshua and Serena climbed down from the altar.

"He's on his way back," Serena said. "I showed that dragon woman what it's like to be young and human and in love." And she led Josh to the stationwagon and they sat down in the back seat, and they started to kiss; and I was so reminded of me and Mary and the first time we kissed because in that kiss came the potentiality of Joshua and Theo and all these worlds we had traversed. . . .

"Let's go, Theo," I said.

He stood in front of the image.

"Theo," I said.

"Not without her," Theo said.

Only then, it seemed, did Ash dissolve the circle of silence around himself. He got up from his throne and faced us. He seemed frail and lost. He said, "Don't take the Mother. . . . We will all be lost without her. . . ."

I followed Theo up the steps. He put his hand to Mary's lips. The marble fell into his hand. Light wove spiral patterns around them both. I heard celestial music above the distant screams.

Theo said to Ash, "My friend . . . the doom of the world was spoken when Joshua and I played for possession of it as puppets of your brother and sister. What we're seeing now is only the doom fulfilling itself. There's nothing I can do. That's the truth, Prince Ash, my friend."

Ash said, "I know you're right, Theo."

Theo said, "Fold up the city and everyone in it. When I open the gate, perhaps you can take a lot of the people with you—perhaps you can save some of them—but you know that your father will be on the other side waiting to slam the gate shut forever. I can't change that."

He lifted the marble to his lips. Placed it on his tongue and then, closing his eyes in a kind of private ecstasy, swallowed it like a communion wafer.

For a few seconds the strands of light danced around him, weaving, gyring, circling, zagging. Then they joined into one funnel of dazzling brilliance and Theo swallowed all the light into himself. He began to glow all over. He

was the brightest thing in the cathedral. Gravely he said
to me—with every word the light from within him flashed
all over the cathedral, driving away the shadows from its
darkest interstices—he said, "Dad, Joshua, Serena, Ash,
Corvus. You all have to trust me now. I don't know if I
can get us home, I don't know if I can even trust myself.
Only Mom knows. Only the dying and the mad can see
to the heart of things."

His brightness forced me to shut my eyes tight. I could
feel hot tears. I did not know if they were from the brilliance or from the intensity of love that I felt for him and
from him, or from my knowledge that I had, in my middle
age, finally put myself back on the path that leads to
illumination and redemption.

Reality wavered. For a moment Corvus became the
sacred *nadle* and the police detective and other figures I
didn't recognize from other universes. The cathedral's
vague loftiness transmuted into the tarp-topped kiva and
its dancing firelight.

Mary wept. And Theo, a shining figure, stood under
the effigy, and the tears rained down and became a torrent,
and the water ran down the steps. . . . I stood ankledeep
in water. . . . The floor was thick with foam and I could
hear the roar of the River. . . .

Mary softened. Still weeping the river from her eyes,
she descended the steps with her hands upraised in
benediction.

"Hi, Mom," Theo said, and kissed her on the cheek.

The cathedral . . . the world . . . rumbled. "Hurry
up," I said. The screams were closer now, more real. I
could hear the columns of the palace snapping one by one,
the rubble tumbling as the roof crumpled. "Into the car!"

Mary started running now. In three or four steps she
had become all human. I opened the door and threw a
Navajo blanket over her. She sank down in the seat. Water
was gushing down from smashed stained glass windows,
erupting from cracks in the walls. "Follow me!" Theo

shouted. I got in and started to drive. Water engulfed us but Theo ran ahead, a smear of dazzling light against the wall of darkness. I floored it. I could feel us moving but I didn't know where. I knew I just had to keep my son in sight.

We breached the water. We were skimming the surface of the River. How were we managing to drive on the water? I didn't stop to think, although I noticed that we had somehow acquired those extra gears that we had seen on Milt Stone's police vehicle.

Something streaking overhead—a bird, a plane—Theo landed on the hood, climbed over the roof and in through the back window. Then he sat down beside me. He was a small, wet boy, and the glow was fast fading, but only because it had become a part of him, inside him always. "Which way do I go?" I said.

"It doesn't matter, Dad," he said. "As long as you never lose me again."

The stationwagon rose into the air. Beneath us, I saw the spires of the cathedral jutting from the water. Then, abruptly, the city seemed to fold up on itself and vanished beneath the water. . . . In a second I saw Milt Stone's police car soaring up above the water.

Serena said, from the back, "Neat! We're flying!"

"We're not flying . . . we're not even really moving," Theo said. "The universes are moving and we're staying still."

And then, rising out of the water, came Strang. A giant Strang, a thousand feet of Strang, breasting the current like a classical Neptune, wielding the scepter. He was scooping up the water, making it play tricks, sculpting it into the image of a gate.

I looked into Strang's eyes and saw my own eyes stare back at me. I saw my own past failure. I had called myself a poet but I had not listened to the truth. Strang had wrested his power from the source of all power, but he had refused to hear the truth about the nature of his power.

We were each other's shadow. I could not conquer the
mysterious lord of some extradimensional empire, but I
could conquer myself. If I had the will for it, and the
heart.

"Ram it, Dad!" Theo said.

Behind us, the police car's siren came on.

Strang smiled at me. I knew that he recognized me too.
But he was not yet ready to accept himself. We are all
fools; one day we will all die. I wanted to tell him that.
I wanted to embrace him.

I rammed the gate. We could see nothing but water on
every side. Then we burst through—

The gate sluiced shut behind us—the Red Sea closed
up—the way between the worlds was lost to oblivion—

A starfield, perhaps a computer simulacrum, where suns
and planets whizzed past and nebulas swam through emptiness and here and there shadowy entities, thinner than
vacuum, flitted past playing at being gods—

An arena where lordlings watched games of life and
death and languidly placed bets on the fate of worlds—

An ocean of tears—

We fell from the sky onto the tabletop rock that was
already beginning to crumble—

A stone room where a hanged shaman is tearing away
the rope that hangs down from the sky and is leaping down
onto the sandpainting singing a wild song and asperging us
with peyote tea—

We saw our own lifeless bodies frozen in a weird
anthropology tableau around the fire, pierced with arrows,
leaning against the standing stones, and as the drumbeats
pounded we slipped back into them—

And fell with the shards of rock that dissolved into
desert sand, and then—

An ocean of sand—

We were racing down Route 10. They were giving us
a police escort toward the border, toward Mexico and the
laetrile clinic, and—

Theo Etchison

—and the airconditioner is sputtering dust into the old stationwagon as we rattle southward alongside the shimmering sand, and my father's eyes are hypnotized by the road, and my brother Josh and his girlfriend are in each other's arms where they've been, sucking face, since Phoenix if not Albuquerque, and there's a smell in the air like stale orange juice, the smell of my mother dying.

epilogue

oceanus, the river that surrounds the cosmos

Καινούριους τόπους δὲν Θὰ βρῆς,
δὲν Θὰ βρῆζ ἄλλες Θάλασσες.

You will not find new places;
You will not find other oceans.

—CAVAFY

TO MYSELF

I have come back from the river's edge; sometimes
I wish I had never gone, sometimes
I know I cannot stem the stream of time, however hard
I long for the river to run backward to the mountains,
Blue as the sky, as grief, as delusion.

They have stopped playing by the river's edge; but sometimes
Long past sunset, I still hear them in the wind that shakes
The cottonwoods. I cannot bear to listen.
In my heart I know sometimes
That the river has reversed its course; I know sometimes
That the river will not turn back till its watery end,
Black as the sky, as grief, as disillusion.

I will not follow them back from the river's edge; sometimes
I do not think they are coming home. Sometimes, not daring
    to look,
I say when I open my eyes they will be long gone, not gone;
That the river will run upstream, downstream.
I have named them after the gods, hoping to become one
    myself.
Better not to look at all; for in the momentary closure,
The blink's breadth between two truths, two truths can both
    be true.
The tension between two truths is what I feel for them;
    sometimes
I know it to be love,
Red as the sky, as grief, as joy.

The River of No Return

Theo Etchison

We've been in Mexico a week now. The laetrile clinic is by the sea, in a small resort town that's crawling with Americans and has so many Burger Kings and McDonald's that you'd never know it was another country. They even have Taco Bell—can you imagine that?

Oh, but it is different though. Our hotel is by the beach and although it's hot there's always a breeze. It doesn't feel like an American hotel though it is really. We have like our own adobe cottage and there's a cliff nearby and steps down to the sea.

It's like nothing happened. Mom is still dying and I'm still having these dreams. I can't sleep. Joshua spends a lot of time alone now that Serena flew back to Virginia. Without Ash there to keep the illusion going she couldn't keep her Mom thinking she was still at the mall.

Josh goes down to the sea every day and stares at the sunset or the yachts or at nothing in particular. Every day he says less and less. He is waiting for something to happen.

I've made friends with a Mexican boy who hangs around outside our bungalow. The only English phrase he knows is ''teenage mutant ninja turtle'', and he repeats it over and over, kind of like a ritual incantation. We talk at each other in the evenings when it's cool. I tell him all about my adventures in the other kingdoms. I don't know what he's telling me about. His name is Jesus.

This particular evening, Mom has come back from a bunch of tests. We're sitting outside, by our little pool, in the place where the cliff-top overhangs the ocean. We've ordered Chinese food. Jesus and I eat our sweet and sour pork off the same plate. Only Mom isn't eating with us, because she has a special diet they make her stick to.

Mom has never talked about it. As far as outward appearances go, she acts like she believes we drove straight down from Alexandria and there never was a Chinese restaurant or a transdimensional empire linked by a river that flows through every place in the cosmos. She's dying, she's always been dying.

But I know that she knows everything. Because of what she was in the other world. I know that when she was standing in the cathedral and I was like praying to her almost, I know that she held one end of the marble just as I held the other end of the endless strand of light. I know that her tears are the source of the River. I know that her cancer is the same cancer that is eating away Strang's kingdom. I know that to heal her is to heal the other world.

I know the journey has only just begun.

Dad has started a new poem. It's different from what he wrote before. It's full of images from the other world. I know he remembers. He was always the one who remembered the least before, but now he has changed. It's because of that game of ''trust me'' that we played over the dying city.

The sun is setting. The wind stirs. My Mom is getting cold.

"Maybe I should be getting inside," she says.

"Yeah, Mom," I say. I got to get her blanket and I throw it around her shoulder. Jesus I love her I'm thinking and the wind is so strong it blows away the smell of stalking death and masks it with the moist salt tang of the Pacific. Dad takes her by the hand and the wind becomes stronger now.

Jesus mutters something and Dad says, "What do you mean, a hurricane? There's no hurricane." But the little kid just points at the sunset and at something whirling above the water far out to sea. Something is churning up the waves, something big and vaguely dragon-shaped.

I hear a distant horn call. Is it a conch? And the wind gets stronger now and it's wet like somone breathing down on you from the sky, maybe a fifty-foot woman.

"Don't look at it, Josh!" I say. Because I'm getting a sinking feeling. Once they'd just have brushed off what I said with the old crack about too much imagination but this time they don't—not after all we've been through.

But Josh looks, of course. He looks out to sea because he's always looked out to sea every day and every night we've been in this town. And suddenly I know he's been waiting for someone to appear, and that the person he's been waiting for has arrived.

Josh says, "I can't help myself, Theo. I'm still dead. We never captured my soul back from the scepter of the king, did we?"

He strides away from me. He stands at the edge of the cliff. I don't know what he sees exactly. Maybe it's Katastrofa rising from the foam cupping one breast and lifting the other arm in a gesture of summoning.

"Don't go after her, Josh!" I shout.

"I can't help it, little brother. . . . I don't belong here yet. . . . I don't—"

Dad's risen from his chair and standing beside us. And Mom is here too, shivering, while the wind rises. Yes. I can smell the incense in the wind. We are only a blink's breadth away from the other kingdom. I carry the way inside me always.

"You can't go back," I say. "Strang closed the gateway. The worlds will never intersect again." But I am protesting in vain because I know that there is always a way to the other country.

And before I can stop him, Josh takes the way out.

"Katastrofa!" he screams at the top of his lungs.

He leaps.

He is a blur. The wind brings to our ears a ghostly mariachi music. We don't hear Joshua thudding against the rocks below. We don't see him anymore. By the time he should have reached bottom he isn't there anymore.

Only the three of us are left. We all know where he has gone.

"We have to go back," I say. Very softly.

"Yes," my Dad says.

"There's so much to be done. We've got to stop the war. We've got to reconcile Ash with his father. We've got to find Josh's soul in the king's scepter and maybe take the scepter to the source of the River and lose it forever." I'm saying aloud what we all know, because I can't bear us not communicating, because that would be like the old days before we went through all these things together when we first knew that Mom was going to die and no one could say what they really felt. There is one thing I'm not saying though because I can hardly dare to hope it. I think Mom can be healed. If we can heal the madness in the other kingdom. Yeah.

The three of us hug each other very close. We haven't done that in a long time. The sun sets and in the darkness we can hear the horn of Cornelius Huang, a strident note across the gathering storm.

"Let's all get some sleep," Mom says. "We've got a long journey ahead of us."

Mom and Dad go inside the house. They leave me alone on the cliff overlooking the sea.

I look around for Jesus. He's not here either. He must have panicked when Joshua jumped into the sea. Oh, now I see him. He's running on the beach, playing tag with the wind. He's a tiny figure. Otherwise the beach is deserted. Everyone's down at the local club where all the Americans hang out, getting drunk and brooding about the imminent death of their loved ones; because, beautiful as this place is, it's one long pre-mortuary wake as we wait for laetrile and miracles.

I feel the wind on my face. I feel my brother's spirit in the wind's breath. I feel everyone who has crossed over. Oh fucking Jesus I feel so much I want to burst because I can't even name one of my feelings.

And I'm thinking: Jesus I'm young even though I think I've lived a dozen lifetimes and I've seen, touched, tasted the dark river that leads every place, the river that you're only supposed to cross one time, the river of dying and never coming back, and it's going to be easy for people to say I made it up and blame my imagination even though I always tell the truth, too much, too much; I'm young and I feel a quintillion years old with the tangled strands of the River inside me that stretch from the big bang birth of the universe to the cold death far in the far far future; it's only because I'm young that I can feel this old; because to grasp eternity is a gift of youth.

One day I won't be a Truthsayer anymore. Only then will I be able to say it was "just" a dream. For now, my dreams are the world.

Los Angeles, 1988–90

About the Author

Somtow Papinian Sucharitkul (S.P. Somtow) was born in 1952 in Bangkok, Thailand, and grew up in Europe. He was educated at Eton College and at Cambridge, where he obtained his B.A. and M.A., receiving honors in English and Music.

His first career was as a composer, and he has emerged as one of Southeast Asia's most outspoken and controversial musicians. He has had his compositions performed, televised and broadcast on four continents. His most recent compositions include the dazzling *Gongula 3* for Thai and Western instruments, commissioned for the opening of the Asian Composers Expo, and *Star Maker—An Anthology of Universes,* for large orchestra, four sopranos, and other soloists, recently premiered in Washington.

In 1977 he began writing fiction. He was first nominated for the John W. Campbell Award for best new writer in 1980, winning in 1981. Two of his short stories, "Aquila" and "Absent Thee from Felicity Awhile," have been nominated for the coveted Hugo Award, science fiction's equivalent of the Oscar. He has now published eighteen books, including the complex, galaxy-spanning *Inquestor* series and the satirical *Mallworld* and *The Aquiliad* as well as the serious, philosophical *Starship & Haiku* and *Fire from the Wine-Dark Sea,* a short story collection.

S.P. Somtow's career as a novelist has expanded far beyond the boundaries of science fiction. His horror novel, *Vampire Junction,* written under the name S.P. Somtow, was praised by Ed Bryant as "the most important horror novel of 1984," and the New York *Daily News* called it "the grimmest vampire fantasy ever set to paper . . . sure to become a cult classic." His second mainstream novel, *The Shattered Horse,* has been compared to Umberto Eco and was called, by noted author Gene Wolfe, "in the true sense, a work of genius." A young people's book, *Forgetting Places,* was honored by the "Books for Young Adults" program as an "outstanding book of the year."

His second horror novel, *Moon Dance,* is already being hailed as a landmark in the field and has been nominated for the American Horror Award. Critic A. J. Budrys has compared the work to Henry James and Nathaniel Hawthorne. It is a vast novel in which a pack of Eartern European werewolves settle in the Dakota Territory in the 1880s. Somtow spent six years researching the novel, himself traversing every inch of his characters' odyssey from Vienna, Austria, to California, and studying Native American languages. *Moon Dance* sold out before publication date and has gone back to press three times.

The horror film that S.P. Somtow wrote and directed, *The Laughing Dead,* has been called "a horror film for the 90s" by *Cinéfantastique* and "one of the best independent productions in a long while" by Michael Weldon of the *Psychotronic Review*. It has been released in Europe and will appear in the U.S. later this year.

Riverrun is the first volume of a trilogy. The second volume, *Armorica,* will soon be appearing from Avon books.

The Epic Adventure

THE OMARAN SAGA
by
ADRIAN COLE

"A remarkably fine fantasy...
Adrian Cole has a magic touch."
Roger Zelazny

BOOK ONE:
A PLACE AMONG THE FALLEN
70556-7/$3.95 US/$4.95 Can

BOOK TWO: THRONE OF FOOLS
75840-7/$3.95 US/$4.95 Can

BOOK THREE:
THE KING OF LIGHT AND SHADOWS
75841-5/$4.50 US/$5.50 Can

BOOK FOUR: THE GODS IN ANGER
75842-3/$4.50 US/$5.50 Can